$\mathcal{A}$ SEARCHING HEART

Books by Janette Oke

CANADIAN WEST

When Calls the Heart • *When Comes the Spring*
When Breaks the Dawn • *When Hope Springs New*
Beyond the Gathering Storm
When Tomorrow Comes

LOVE COMES SOFTLY

Love Comes Softly • *Love's Enduring Promise*
Love's Long Journey • *Love's Abiding Joy*
Love's Unending Legacy • *Love's Unfolding Dream*
Love Takes Wing • *Love Finds a Home*

PRAIRIE LEGACY

The Tender Years • *A Searching Heart*
A Quiet Strength • *Like Gold Refined*

SEASONS OF THE HEART

Once Upon a Summer • *The Winds of Autumn*
Winter Is Not Forever • *Spring's Gentle Promise*

SONG OF ACADIA*

The Meeting Place • *The Sacred Shore*
The Birthright • *The Distant Beacon*
The Beloved Land

WOMEN OF THE WEST

The Calling of Emily Evans • *Julia's Last Hope*
Roses for Mama • *A Woman Named Damaris*
They Called Her Mrs. Doc • *The Measure of a Heart*
A Bride for Donnigan • *Heart of the Wilderness*
Too Long a Stranger • *The Bluebird and the Sparrow*
A Gown of Spanish Lace • *Drums of Change*

www.janetteoke.com

*with T. Davis Bunn

JANETTE OKE

A SEARCHING HEART

{Prairie Legacy • 2}

BETHANYHOUSE

MINNEAPOLIS, MINNESOTA

A Searching Heart
Janette Oke
Copyright © 1998

Cover by Jennifer Parker
Photographer: Mike Habermann

Published by Bethany House Publishers
11400 Hampshire Avenue South
Bloomington, Minnesota 55438

Bethany House Publishers is a division of
Baker Publishing Group, Grand Rapids, Michigan.

Printed in the United States of America

ISBN 978-0-7642-0528-6

The Library of Congress has cataloged the original edition as follows:

Oke, Janette, 1935-
    A searching heart / by Janette Oke.
        p.   cm. — (A prairie legacy ; 2)
    ISBN 0–7642–2140-X
    ISBN 0–7642–2139–6 (pbk.)
    ISBN 0–7642–2142–6 (large print pbk.)
1. Young women—Fiction. I. Title. II. Series: Oke, Janette, 1935–
Prairie legacy ; 2.
    PR9199.3.O38   S43   1998
     813'.54—dc21

                                                    98–217080
                                                    CIP

JANETTE OKE was born in Champion, Alberta, to a Canadian prairie farmer and his wife, and she grew up in a large family full of laughter and love. She is a graduate of Mountain View Bible College in Alberta, where she met her husband, Edward, and they were married in May of 1957. After pastoring churches in Indiana and Canada, the Okes spent some years in Calgary, where Edward served in several positions on college faculties while Janette continued her writing. She has written over four dozen novels for adults and children, and her book sales total nearly thirty million copies.

The Okes have three sons and one daughter, all married, and are enjoying their dozen grandchildren. Edward and Janette are active in their local church and make their home near Didsbury, Alberta.

Visit Janette Oke's Web site at: *www.janetteoke.com*.

DEDICATION

With love and appreciation
to

Vern and Alta Mae (Oke) Hannah
Brent, Lorna, Jennifer, and Lindsey
Kevin, Corinne, Jordan, and Emily
Carolyn
Greg, Cheryl, Alexander, and Adam.

Thank you
for always making me feel
welcomed and loved
as part of the Oke family.

A Note From the Author

A number of years ago I took part in an autographing event at The Christian Light Bookstore in Nappanee, Indiana. I looked up to see a tall young man, not more than late-teens or early twenties, before me. Assuming he had been assigned to get an autograph for someone else—maybe his mother, or perhaps a girlfriend—I asked if he wanted me to personalize my signature with a name. "Just put Thomas," he responded, which caught me by surprise. Then he went on to say quietly, "I guess *Love Comes Softly* is rather special to me. I, too, lost my mother when I was three years old."

So over the years I have thought about Thomas—and prayed for him. I did not even know his last name, and I had no way of reaching out to him but through my prayers. And then I thought of trying to make contact with him again through one of my books. I did that on the dedication page of *The Tender Years*:

> To Thomas of Nappanee.
> I have no way of knowing if you will ever read this dedication or have the assurance that it was meant for you. The years have passed quickly and you now have reached manhood. Be assured that I often think of you and remember you in prayer.

You can imagine my thrill when I received a letter that began, "I'm Thomas of Nappanee. I don't know if I'm the one. . . ." But he was. His letter reintroduced me to a young Mennonite minister with a beautiful wife and five wonderful sons. In a way I feel that I've been reunited with family.

CHAPTER 1

Virginia stepped from the mercantile into bright sunshine and shifted the parcels she carried to divide the load evenly. It was silly, she knew, to be out already purchasing materials for baby things. *I'm rushing it. Papa will be giving another well-deserved lecture on impatience*, she reluctantly admitted. After all, her sister Clara had only just announced the evening before that she, Virginia, was to become an aunt. But even as Virginia chided herself, she smiled at her indulgence and shrugged. How could one just sit back and do nothing? It would be hard to wait.

Virginia let her gaze sweep up to enjoy the brightness of the late autumn day. Everything seemed to be right with the world. A few playful clouds floated aimlessly, not obscuring the sun but roaming the heavens on an unhurried mission of discovery. Birds in nearby trees twittered and called. Nest building was past. Even their parenting duties that had kept them busy providing food for searching, noisy bills was over for another year. Young fledglings had been taught to fly and to forage on their own. Soon they would be forced to test those skills on a first migration.

Fall flowers nodded colorful heads in the stirring air. It could not be called wind—for no wind blew. But still there was a shift of currents, just enough to make the flowers nod and the softly turning leaves whisper.

It was the kind of day that called for adventure. Virginia felt an unnamed longing to be involved—to go somewhere, discover something, be a part of the world about her in a new and more fascinating way. Perhaps Grandma Marty would have labelled her feelings "the restlessness of youth." Whatever it was, Virginia yearned for something different, more stimulating, than her day-to-day world. Then her eyes shifted to the parcels she carried. Surely here was all the excitement she needed. A new niece. Or nephew. What did it matter? This new family member, though yet unknown, was already loved and anticipated.

Though it seemed impossible now, she knew that the intervening months would pass quickly and Clara's new baby would be welcomed into the world—her world. Still, it would be hard to wait. So hard to keep the secret that Clara had asked them to keep for a few more months. But she would honor her promise. She would not even write of it in her letter to Jamison, though she half feared she might explode with the effort of silence, particularly with Jamison, whom she told everything.

———

"Oh, my," commented her mother as Virginia entered the kitchen door. "It looks like you've done some shopping."

Virginia had hoped no one would be around to observe her impulsive purchases. Not that she felt they were wrong, but because she felt just a bit silly. She nodded now at Belinda's comment, her face flushing slightly.

"Going to do some sewing?" her mother went on.

Virginia nodded.

"Something special coming up?"

Again Virginia nodded. It was special, though she was

certain her mother expected something quite different in the packages she carried.

"Can I see?"

They had always shared peeks at new purchases, so it was nothing out of the ordinary for Belinda to be interested in what the parcels contained. Usually Virginia could not have waited to pour the contents out on the kitchen table to display all her girlish choices and watch for her mother's delighted response. Now she was torn, reluctant to reveal her impatience for the new arrival, yet anxious to share her excitement. Excitement won, and with a new flush to her cheeks, Virginia reached for the first parcel, ripping aside the mercantile's wrapping to reveal the soft folds of baby flannel.

She watched as her mother reached out to gently caress the fabric, her eyes misting. That was all the encouragement Virginia needed. Eagerly she tore the wrappings from the other bundles. Out tumbled more materials for baby garments and softly colored yarns for knitting.

"I thought *I* was excited," laughed Belinda, casting a glance at her daughter, then returning to examine the baby items.

"Oh . . . !" Virginia fairly squealed. "How are we ever going to wait? It will seem forever."

Belinda laughed again. "Time will pass much more quickly for us than for Clara," she assured her. "You will be busy with school, and I have more than enough to fill my days. Yes—time will surely pass much more quickly for us."

"But—June? That's such a long time to wait."

"About the time you will be graduating."

Virginia stirred. "I had thought graduating would be the most exciting thing to happen," she said thoughtfully, "but now . . . I think Clara's baby . . ." She let the sentence go unfinished.

Belinda reached out and patted her hand. "Time will pass quickly," she promised again. Then she leaned back in her chair and added somewhat nonchalantly, "By the way, Danny picked up the mail when he was out."

Virginia gave a shriek and raced across the room to where a lone envelope lay on the small table by the door. Another letter from Jamison! Even excitement over baby garments suddenly paled in comparison.

———

" . . . but Jamison doesn't care much for the new football uniforms. The color—"

"Jamison, Jamison, Jamison," Danny exclaimed, clanking his dinner fork on the side of his plate. "All we've heard this whole meal is Jamison. Jamison threw two touchdowns. Jamison doesn't like his sociology teacher. Jamison is first quarterback. Jamison runs laps every day before classes. Jamison wears pink pajamas. Jamison—"

"He does not," Virginia cut in sharply, then flushed. "I've no idea what color he wears," she quickly amended, "but I certainly didn't say he wore pink."

"Well, you've told us everything else about him."

"Danny," their father, Drew, reprimanded softly.

"Well, I get tired of hearing about the guy," Danny insisted.

"I thought you liked Jamison" was Francine's comment with little-sister directness.

"I do. He's fine. Just great. But do we have to spend all the supper hour talking about him? I mean—how much can you say? So he's in college. So he's on the football team. So he doesn't like his sociology prof but likes his—"

"I think we all have picked up your message," said Drew, stopping Danny's flow of words.

"It's true," spoke the unusually mild Francine. "We hear more about Jamison than we do about Rodney."

"Perhaps it's because Jamison writes," replied Virginia, a bit miffed over the entire conversation.

"Rodney writes," Francine flung back in solid defense of her older brother.

"But he's not on the football team," said Danny with a shuffling of his body and a flip of his head. "And he doesn't run laps before classes. He studies instead."

"Danny," said his father again.

Danny's quick glance toward his father acknowledged the second warning. It would be wise for him to keep his silence.

Virginia sat quietly, her face flushed, and her breathing quickened as anger washed through her. It was so unfair of Danny to make accusations against Jamison. Of course Jamison studied. He was getting good grades. He did write much more frequently than Rodney, probably because he had a better reason. Perhaps Jamison's parents didn't hear from him as often, either. And of course Jamison kept her well informed of all of his college experiences—not just the football games. It was only natural that he share with her his triumphs as well as his feelings about his classes and the professors who taught them. And in a college the size of the one that Jamison attended, wasn't it normal that some teachers would be more admired than others?

One by one, Virginia mentally defended Jamison on all Danny's charges. And Jamison passed each test.

"I enjoy Virginia sharing the news from Jamison," Belinda informed the table of five. "I think it's nice that she includes her family."

"But—" began Danny, then dropped his eyes to his plate, wisely leaving the rest of the comment unsaid.

"I'm pleased he is doing so well," Drew picked up the conversation. "It's great for a small-town boy to make the team at a big city college like Webster. It's quite an honor to be first quarterback."

Danny seemed to pull back into his chair. His quick glance around the table told him that he may be the only one tired of hearing about Jamison's exploits.

"Speaking of our number one son," Drew continued, clearing the air by changing the topic, "what would you think of taking a little train ride to see Rodney this weekend?"

Every eye fastened on Drew, along with a collective holding of breath. Belinda was the first to speak. "Is it possible?"

Drew smiled. "I checked the train schedules—and yes, it is possible. It's about a four-hour trip. The train leaves late afternoon around five, so it should get us in to the city around nine."

Danny whooped.

"If we go Friday evening we can spend the night in a hotel, have most of Saturday with Rodney, and come back Saturday night," Drew finished.

Another whoop from Danny as Francine clapped her hands, her eyes shining.

"Is there—would it be possible to stay over for Sunday morning?" Belinda wondered. "I mean, I am . . . well . . . most interested in the church he has written about. I'd love to attend a service with him."

Drew nodded again. "If you like," he agreed. "I hadn't really considered missing our service here, but I'm sure, under the circumstances, that . . ."

Danny did not even try to contain himself.

"And who will look after all your boarders?" Virginia asked him a mite cockily, taking pleasure in getting back at Danny for his digs at Jamison.

Virginia was referring to Danny's menagerie of wild creatures he had rescued in one way or another and nursed back to health for release again into their natural habitat.

But Danny did not even flinch. "The jay is ready to go, and the pigeon is almost as good as new. It might even be ready by Friday. That will just leave the toad. I don't think he's ever going to be well enough to be on his own with his leg like it is. But Rett will look after him. He's always glad to."

Virginia felt a flash of impatience that Rett was such a ready and willing stand-in, but her attention was taken by her mother.

"I guess I'd better get busy and do some baking," she was saying, a smile on her face clearly indicating her delight in taking her oldest son some of his favorite things to eat.

"And I guess I'd better be making a telephone call to let him know our plans," said Drew.

"Can't we surprise him?" Francine asked, clasping her hands together in anticipation.

"Yeah. Let's surprise him," enthused Danny.

Silently Virginia agreed. It would be so much fun just to walk in and watch Rodney's eyes nearly pop.

"That would be fun, but I'm afraid it is too impractical," Virginia's very practical father said as he pushed back his chair. "What if he made other plans for the weekend? We'd be left sitting in our hotel room staring at the walls."

"I guess," Francine said reluctantly, disappointment in her voice.

"Besides," put in their mother as she also pushed back her chair. "Think of the fun it will be for him, looking forward to our coming."

And Virginia knew that her mother would enjoy thinking and planning—and baking—her way through the entire week that lay ahead. She could already see the new glint in her mother's eyes. She was looking forward to the trip herself—now if only Jamison attended the same college. . . .

———

The train ride that had Virginia and her siblings so excited turned out to be rather a bore. First, they were late getting started. The passengers were boarded—and then just sat. Virginia never did hear the reason for the delay, but it was so difficult to just sit there stiffly in the straight-backed seat and fidget with no clack of the wheels ticking the miles away.

Danny, the most impatient one of their group, grumbled and shifted and fretted and stirred. Virginia was sure he would have been up pacing the narrow aisle had their father not objected.

It was pitch black outside before the whistle finally announced that someone, somewhere, had decided it was indeed time to move. Virginia heaved a sigh of relief and pressed her shoulders back against the worn maroon plush. But now there was absolutely nothing to see once they had moved beyond the lights of the small town. Here and there a dim light flickered, indicating a farmhouse cuddled in the darkness. Virginia had looked forward to seeing the sights between their hometown and the university city where they would find Rodney. Now—nothing but the inky darkness. Inky darkness and monotonous, jerky train-car travel. Like Francine said, it felt as though the train had a bad case of hiccups.

And Danny still could not relax. His constant shifting irritated Virginia. She was inclined to reprimand him sharply, but she was sure she would get a stern glance from her father reminding her that she was not the parent.

Francine soon—in boredom, Virginia was sure—leaned her head against her mother's shoulder and drifted off to sleep. Virginia longed to join her. The miles would pass so much more quickly if only she could sleep them away. But there was no place for her to be comfortable enough to sleep.

Even the other passengers provided no distraction. Virginia could see the backs of a few heads. Doing nothing. Making no sound—except for the man three seats down and across the aisle who was soon snoring loudly. *If this is train travel*, thought Virginia glumly, *it certainly is nothing to get excited about.* She had looked forward to her first train trip with such anticipation, expecting it to be filled with drama and intrigue. But it was just a dimly lit, unassuming car, rattling its way noisily and rather clumsily through darkness, with stiff, silent figures for traveling companions. Virginia sighed, sure that there would be more excitement sitting in her school classroom watching the somber teacher chalk a late-morning assignment up on the blackboard.

She yawned and longed for sleep that would not come. She told herself that once they reached Rodney's university, things would quickly change for the better.

———

As expected, they were late arriving. Virginia knew her father had taken advantage of the delayed departure to phone Rodney about not trying to meet their train. The next morning he could join them at their hotel for a late breakfast. Anxious to see her older brother, Virginia was further frustrated at the call. But there was no use complaining. It didn't make sense for Rodney to wait around, she knew. Once they arrived in the city, she was hopeful at least some of the excitement would return.

But there was little to revive her when the huge, puffing locomotive pulled into the dark and dreary station. The wooden benches looked as worn and tired as the weary and stoical passengers following them from the train. The waiting room floors of dark parquet were horribly grimy, to Virginia's thinking. She shuddered as she avoided areas that seemed to be stained by some slovenly man's chewing tobacco.

The few people lingering about looked like loiterers with nothing better to occupy their time. Virginia could feel their eyes surveying her and each family member, making her feel dreadfully uncomfortable. She was glad to hear her father announce that he had procured a cab waiting just outside the door.

It did not take them long to gather their luggage that, to Virginia's thinking, contained more treats for Rodney than actual items for their short stay. With Drew in the lead, they exited the dismal station and climbed into an equally dismal city cab smelling of stale cigars and odors of past occupants. Virginia cringed again and fervently hoped her feet were not planted in someone's spewed-forth chewing tobacco.

Her father gave the instructions to the cab driver, and they lurched forward with a grinding of gears and blaring of horn. Virginia noted that the driver's hand was never far from the latter all of the way to the hotel, though he used it only intermittently.

The hotel her father had booked was touted as one of the best in the city, but Virginia was unimpressed. There were no voluptuous chandeliers reflecting dancing prism-rainbows over vast, thick carpets. The lighting was quite plain and rather dim, the carpets rich in color, but worn. There were no elegantly dressed gentlemen rushing about, bowing to newcomers and reaching out for luggage and asking how they might be of service. One man sat behind a desk and looked reprimandingly at them over the rim of small round spectacles.

"Simpson," he muttered just loud enough to be heard when their father announced his name. "Yes. You were to be in over three hours ago."

"The train was late," her father offered.

"Mmmm," the man murmured, looking up again over the glasses. His expression declared that late guests always had some excuse. The railroad seemed as good a scapegoat as any.

"Rooms 315 and 318," he finally said and slid some keys across the desk's worn surface, tracing the path of many previous keys.

Virginia heard her father politely thank the man, and then they moved as one little huddle of humanity toward the long stairway.

It was well after midnight and they all were weary. There was little conversation and certainly no shared exclamations over exciting discoveries in Rodney's city. Her father brought the little group to a halt when they reached room 315, opened the door, and reached inside to find a light. Hesitantly their mother followed. Virginia did not move, but from where she stood she could see two beds, their dark flowered spreads clashing with the equally colorful but worn floor covering.

"This must be your room," her father was saying. "It has the two beds."

Two beds? Virginia found herself wondering how three people were going to sleep on two beds. Then she knew. She was expected to share a bed with her sister. Inwardly she groaned. She would never get any sleep. Francine churned like a windmill in a gale. Arms and legs flung this way and that as she tossed and turned and sought new and better sleeping positions.

"We'll take this bed, Francine, and let Virginia have the one by the window," her mother was saying. She moved forward to deposit her heavy load of carefully packed and tenderly carried baked goods on a table.

Virginia felt a moment of guilt even as she felt relief. Her mother would have to put up with the windmill. "Francine can sleep with me," she heard herself saying. "I don't mind sharing a bed."

"I've a better idea," spoke up Francine, who had been teased and tormented over the years about her sleeping habits. "Why don't the two of you share a bed and let me have one to myself? Then we will all get some sleep."

Virginia looked with some astonishment at her twelve-year-old sister, then found herself laughing. She heard her mother's soft chuckle join her. Soon Francine was laughing, as well. It felt good. Virginia felt the tension and exasperation of the whole tiresome trip drain away and saw her mother's sagging shoulders lift a little. Perhaps a good laugh was what they all needed. They should have tried it earlier. The trip might not have been so difficult.

Virginia saw her mother reach out a hand to brush a stray curl back from Francine's face. "You're right," she said, laughter still in her voice. "We'll do it your way and get a good sleep. And in the morning we'll see Rodney. He is to be here at the hotel for a nine o'clock breakfast." The lilt in Belinda's voice indicated she could hardly wait.

"I wonder what he's like now," mused Francine as she removed her small hat and traveling coat.

"What do you mean?" Virginia responded.

"I wonder what he's like now? How much he's changed?"

"He's only been gone a little over two months."

"I know. But he'll be different. I just know it. University does that to people."

"Don't be silly," Virginia chided, but a strange little fear twisted somewhere inside. Was it true? Did one really change that quickly when off to university? Had Rodney changed? And if Rodney had changed—might Jamison change, as well? A little shiver passed through her. She didn't want Rodney to change. She liked him just the way he was. And she certainly didn't want Jamison to change. He was almost perfect, so any change would not be for the better, she was sure.

CHAPTER 2

$\mathcal{A}$ctually, I like the chemistry classes best. I mean, just to study how things are constructed, what holds them together— it's amazing. I think it has strengthened my faith in God, though our professor certainly doesn't put God in the picture. But there has to be a God. Such . . . such spectacular things couldn't just happen."

They were in the hotel dining room having their breakfast together. Virginia had witnessed her mother's relief that Rodney had not lost weight since leaving her table, and her father's consolation that his firstborn still stood without a slouch and had a decent haircut. Danny, totally unaware of his parents' unspoken observations, openly admired his older brother and groused over the delay in being shown around the campus. He was convinced Rodney had the whole place under his full control. Francine, in between bites of French toast with peach syrup, was still studying him carefully. Virginia was sure she was looking for those subtle but inevitable changes that happened to university students.

Virginia found herself watching for changes, as well. Little things now caught her attention, and she found herself puzzling over whether they had been there before or had developed since his university admittance. *Did he always part his hair on that side—or was it the other? Is he wearing his tie looser? That brushing of his hand over his cheek—did he do that before?*

The truth was, she wasn't sure. She had never paid that much attention to Rodney before.

But Danny had quickly wolfed down his plate of hot cakes and sausage and was fidgeting in impatience to be off for their tour.

"More coffee, ma'am? Sir?" the waiter was asking. Virginia saw Danny grimace when Drew nodded and moved both cups forward.

"Tell me more about this church you're attending," Belinda encouraged.

"It's great. It really is. They have a nice bunch of kids my age. They really want to make an impact on other university students. I'm the only one from the U at this point. But I'm working on my roommate and the fellow just down the hall. They come from Christian homes, and I know they feel they should be going to church somewhere. They just haven't settled on one yet. Then there is this fellow from my physics class. He tries to act like a tough guy, but he's not been feeling well, and the doctors can't find out why. I think his bravado is just a bluff. That under it all he's scared. I've been trying to befriend him, but I'm not getting much encouragement yet. I'd appreciate your prayers. His name is Austin."

Virginia watched her father push back his coffee cup. "Let's take a moment to pray for Austin," he suggested.

Right here? Right now? Virginia wished to question her father, but she knew exactly what he intended. Right there, in the middle of the busy hotel dining room, they would all bow their heads as their father led them in a sincere prayer for Rodney's needy new friend. Virginia wanted to hide under the table.

The prayer was made quietly in a few short, earnest words. Virginia did not know whether to open her eyes when it ended or to just stay as she was so she couldn't see the astonishment—or amused smirks—of other diners. When she did manage to find the courage to peek around the room, she was surprised to discover that the other diners seemingly had paid no attention to them at all.

"I say it's time to be getting out there," Danny blurted. "We are going to be missing half a day if we don't get started."

Rodney smiled and reached over to give his younger brother a playful punch on the arm. "Let's go. I'm looking forward to showing you around. Things are always a bit quiet on Saturday, but you can still get a good feel for the place. Who knows?" he added with a grin. "We might even catch one or two in the library studying."

As they left the hotel, Rodney fell into step beside Virginia. "So are you still hearing from Jamison?"

Virginia was surprised. "Of course," she answered.

Rodney nodded.

But Virginia could not dismiss his question so lightly. "Why do you ask? Like that?"

Rodney half turned to her, his shoulders giving a careless shrug. "Like what?"

"Like . . . I don't know. Like you thought that just because Jamison is away that we'd . . . well . . . stop caring or something."

"I didn't say that."

"No . . . but you sort of hinted at it or something."

"No. No, I didn't mean it that way."

"Then what way did you mean it?"

Rodney placed a lanky arm over her shoulders. "Look, I didn't mean anything. I was just making conversation, that's all. So how's the guy doing?"

Virginia's eyes lit up. She loved to talk about Jamison, and here was a fresh, uninformed listener to whom she could boast freely. "You know he's the quarterback," she enthused.

"And they've been doing very well in their games. Think they might even be able to win the championship this year. They have never won it before. So far, their record is seven and one. And Jamison says—"

"And his studies," Rodney interrupted. "How're they going?"

"Oh, Rodney," said Virginia, shrugging off his arm with a mock frown. "You're always thinking of studies. Jamison thinks he might even be able to make a professional team if things continue to go well. They do make good money. More than he would ever make as a lab technician—or whatever—like you plan to be."

Rodney nodded. "True" was all he said. Then he added with a bit more enthusiasm, "He always did like sports and was especially good at football."

Virginia nodded, appreciating Rodney's acknowledgment of the things Jamison was good at.

"He had a hard time deciding between football and baseball," she continued. "But he picked football. Next year he hopes to receive a scholarship."

"That's great. Has he found a good church group?"

"He meets with a small interdenominational group just off campus. He likes the young minister, and he says they've a good group of young people. They have some real fiery discussions. Coming from many church backgrounds, they find they have different opinions—on many things. Jamison says it's good for him. Makes him think through issues that he has just blindly accepted as truth in the past."

"Such as?" Rodney wondered.

"Not . . . not basic things like who God is or if Jesus is really divine or anything like that. Just . . . small things. Baptism or communion."

"They're not small things."

"I didn't mean like that. But different churches do treat them in . . . in various ways."

Rodney nodded.

"Jamison says that it is good to understand why other churches take different views. It opens one up to thinking through things and making Bible-based decisions."

"Bible-based decisions are good," agreed Rodney.

Rodney sounded sincere, and Virginia was about to continue on concerning Jamison's church and spiritual journey, but Danny dropped back beside them and broke into the conversation. "You know that fox kit that I had last summer?"

Rodney nodded.

"I was out in Grandpa's field a couple weeks back and I saw him. I'm sure it was him. He stopped and looked right at me like he couldn't decide whether to come to me or run off. Then he trotted away and looked back twice before he disappeared. I'm sure it was him."

"Really?"

"He had that funny little crimp in his left ear. Remember? Well, this one had it. Right up top." Danny indicated where the crimp had been located.

"And he didn't bolt?"

"No. Just stood there and studied me. I . . ."

Virginia hastened her step. She knew she had lost her audience. She might as well walk up beside Francine.

———

The university campus was interesting, and Virginia thought about her own college experience less than a year away. But in spite of being used to walking, she found that she was tiring as the day wore on. There were just too many walkways. Too many buildings. Too much to see and too great a distance separating them all.

Francine complained first. "My feet are whining. Besides,

all these buildings look the same. Can't I just sit down somewhere and wait for you?"

"Not alone . . ." began their mother.

Virginia saw her opportunity. "I'll stay with her," she was
quick to offer.

"There's a little shop with a soda fountain just up ahead,"
Rodney informed them. "You can get yourselves a cool pop
and wait for us there."

Rodney ushered them in and indicated an empty seat. He
even ordered frosty Cokes and saw them settled before moving off with Danny and their parents. Virginia stretched out
her legs under the table and even slipped off her shoes. Like
Francine, her feet were aching.

It was fun to just sit and sip, watching the young and chat-
tery university students. Virginia envisioned herself as one of
them and could hardly wait for her upcoming graduation so
she might join the friendly, laughing crowd. But she would
not be attending this university. No, her plans were already
made to be with Jamison. What fun it would be to be in college together. How wonderful it would be to watch him play
football. Already she saw him as the star of the game. People
would be cheering, "Yeah, Jamison," and she would be cheering
more loudly than all the rest. She could hardly wait.

And she would go with him to his little church and share
in the discussions on faith and how to live it in a world that
showed indifference. She would listen to the various ideas
presented and be free to express her own thoughts on subjects.
Jamison said that anyone was welcome into the discussions.

Another little cluster of students entered the shop and
took seats not too distant from Virginia and Francine. Virginia tried not to stare, but it was hard not to watch them.
They were rowdier than other groups had been. Loud laughter
punctuated most of their remarks, and Virginia heard speech
peppered with words that her friend Jenny Woods might use.

Words that Virginia often had not understood but knew were
not appropriate for a Christian to use. Inwardly she cringed
and diverted her attention back to her Coke. She would focus
her thoughts back on her future days at college with Jamison.
Jamison would . . .

"I think that fellow is trying to catch your eye," whispered
Francine, nodding toward a seat somewhere behind and to
the side of Virginia. "He's been staring at you ever since he
sat down."

"Don't be silly," responded Virginia, jerked back to the
present. In spite of her words, she felt her face flushing.

"He is," insisted Francine. "He keeps waiting for you to
look his way."

"I have no intention of looking his way," muttered Virginia
with determination and a lift of her chin.

"He's rather handsome."

Virginia's chin lifted higher.

"He has dark wavy hair, deep brown eyes, a little cleft in
his chin . . ."

It sounded as though Francine was describing Jamison.
It was all Virginia could do to keep from spinning around to
look.

"And a scar—just above his eyebrow."

Jamison had no scar above his eyebrow. Unless . . . Surely
Jamison had not been hurt playing football. In spite of herself
Virginia turned around and met the brown eyes that Francine
had described. They were not Jamison's. The young man nodded, gave a triumphant smile and a slight wave of his hand.

Virginia's cheeks flamed as she whipped back to face her
sister.

"Francine," she whispered harshly, "stop looking at him.
You are just encouraging him. . . ."

"He's coming over."

"Don't joke."

"I'm not joking. He's coming over. Coke and all."

Virginia did not even have time to respond.

"Excuse me," a smooth voice said. He was right beside her. "Can you tell me where the Chem Lab is?"

Virginia was forced to look up into the brown eyes again. She felt her face flush and reached self-consciously to slip her feet back into the shoes she had discarded. One toe found its desired destination, but stretch as she could and reach as far as she might, Virginia's other searching foot came up empty.

"I . . . I don't know," she fumbled and wasn't sure if she was describing her predicament in locating her shoe or her ignorance regarding the Chem Lab.

"You don't take Chem?"

He was sliding into the booth beside her. Virginia had never experienced such forwardness.

"No," she managed.

"So what do you take? I thought you might be in the nursing faculty."

"No."

"Education?"

Virginia shook her head.

"We are just visiting," put in Francine, seeming to have more sense and better use of her tongue than her older sister.

"Visiting?" The young stranger's eyes had not left Virginia's face.

She nodded and tried to swallow. He was making her nervous, though he seemed harmless enough.

He smiled, showing even, white teeth. "For a long, long time I hope."

"Actually," said Francine, "just for today."

"That's a shame."

He pushed his unfinished Coke aside. "Then if your stay

is so short," he continued in his easy manner, "perhaps I could have the pleasure of showing you around."

Virginia began to shake her head but no words came.

"The Chem Lab?" asked Francine coyly, tipping her head to the side and giving him a knowing look.

His attention focused on the younger sister. He looked genuinely amused. He even laughed, a cheery, chuckling laugh. "Okay," he said, throwing up his hands. "So you caught me. Yeah, I know where the Chem Lab is. And lots of other things, too. I'm a junior. Been here long enough to know my way around campus."

He turned back to Virginia. "So how about it? I even know a few places that aren't on the campus map."

Virginia was still shaking her head.

"Our brother has already shown us around," Francine informed him. "He showed us around until my feet felt ready to fall off."

But the young man was still looking at Virginia. "And you? Are your feet still okay? I know a real good place to rest them."

Virginia thought of the still shoeless foot under the table. For a frantic moment she feared he might take a peek under the table and discover her secret. She drew her foot back, hoping that it was hidden under her skirts.

"We're to wait here," said Francine. "Dad, Mom, Rodney, and Danny will soon be back, and we are going out for dinner."

"Whew. You sure don't travel light." He seemed about ready to stand to his feet. He turned to Virginia again. "Is . . . is one of those guys your . . . boyfriend?"

Virginia shook her head. "Brothers," she said with some emphasis.

"Good," he replied and settled back again.

"Her boyfriend attends Webster College," filled in Francine.

Virginia finally found her tongue. "He's a Webster Webspinner. Quarterback."

The fellow cocked an eyebrow. "Figured there would be a boyfriend somewhere." He shrugged. "But Webster is a lo-o-o-ng way from here. My offer still holds. Like to see a little of the town tonight?"

Virginia was shocked.

"Of course not," she responded indignantly. "Even if . . . even if I knew you—which I don't—and . . . and liked the places you'd take me, I still wouldn't . . . wouldn't step out on Jamison."

"Jamison?" He reached out a hand to twist his Coke glass. "Jamison," he repeated. Then he lifted his eyes as he hoisted himself up from the seat and looked directly at Virginia. "The way I see it, it's really okay. I mean, I've got a girl back home, too. But that's not much help to me now, is it? Guy has to have some fun. Can't sit around like a monk. And she doesn't expect me to. She's more realistic than that." He shrugged. "But then—guess some girls can be pretty narrow-minded."

Then he was gone before Virginia could gather her wits to vehemently respond.

CHAPTER 3

They attended Rodney's church the next morning, and the experience provided conversation for much of the train ride home. Virginia knew her parents were impressed with the pastor and his morning message and were relieved to know that Rodney and his faith were in good hands.

Virginia herself felt exhausted. The weekend had been a busy one, and they were all tired. But that was not the only reason she felt edgy and drained. There was something about this new crowd of youth that disturbed her. Something in the riotous laughter that sometimes rang false. In the coarse language that was bandied about, not even hushed out of deference for nearby ears. Something about the whole scene unsettled her. Not the least was her experience with the young man at the soda fountain. She could not follow his reasoning. Had never been exposed to such thinking before. Did some people really think it didn't matter whether one was true to one's commitments or not? It was a distressing thought.

Virginia tried to push aside her uneasiness and think instead about the fun it would be to share her adventures with Jenny the next day at school.

Jenny wavered between university and moving to the city

31

for a job. One week she would be all enthused about going out to some big school and sharing in the experiences of other young people. The next week she declared that she was through with books and classes. She was just going to get herself a job and take control of her own life. Virginia felt constant confusion where Jenny was concerned. Virginia longed to see Jenny settled—at peace with God, with life, with herself. Only a deep, true faith would do that for her friend, Virginia was sure. But Jenny, who did go to church sporadically, pushed aside all of Virginia's pleadings and invitations.

Virginia often grieved over Jenny and her careless, carefree attitude about life. But she would not give up on the girl, and it was to Jenny that she went with her bits of girl-to-girl sharing. At least Jenny could get excited over girl things.

Should I tell Jenny about the fellow in the soda shop? she debated.

Yes. Jenny would certainly be intrigued by the whole event and probably would squeal with excitement.

No, she changed her mind. Jenny would wonder why in the world she hadn't responded to his open and unexpected invitation.

She would not talk about the incident with Jenny. Jenny saw their world through different eyes. Much like the young man who had slipped, uninvited, into the booth beside her. Had Jenny been given the invitation by a good-looking young man . . . Virginia squirmed on her train seat. Suddenly some things fell into place in her thinking. What she had seen as so abnormal and inappropriate was quite normal for one sector of society. What she always had been unable to understand about Jenny would be totally accepted in many quarters by a vast number of their peers.

It was difficult for Virginia to come to terms with this new standard. Protected as she had been in her own family and small town, she had never really had to face truly immoral behavior.

Now she realized that what made Jenny and her outrageous speech and action stand out in their hometown crowd would also make her a good fit with other groups of young people. Jenny was not unusual in her attitudes and actions. Perhaps—just perhaps—Jenny was more in step with the world at large than she herself. The thought was a new and startling one and made Virginia cringe.

Oh, God, she inwardly cried. *I don't think I want to go to college. It's so . . . so scary. So wicked.*

Immediately Virginia realized that God was not absent from the university campus—even though many of the attendees were unaware of His presence. Rodney was doing fine. He had found a church home. A good pastor. A great group of young people. He was growing in his faith and finding his own basis for what he believed, even when the professors presented different teachings. Rodney knew God was with him.

And Jamison was fine, too. He wrote about how he prayed before each football game—not that he would win, but that he would play well and not get hurt. That no one would get hurt. Why, a few other players even slipped over beside him now and asked him to pray for them, also. And Jamison had a church family. Rather unconventional perhaps, but they were stretching him, forcing him to strengthen his faith. That's what Jamison said. Jamison was doing fine. No—it wasn't the place—it was the individual. One could find God on the university campus just as easily as anywhere else if one had a mind to search for Him.

Virginia's thumping heart was quieted. She need not fear. God would be with her wherever she went. The secret was in being conscious of Him and remembering His promises. *Proverbs 29:25*, a little voice deep inside seemed to be saying. *Remember the verse? Grandma Marty taught it to you when you were afraid of the dark. Oh yes. "The fear of man bringeth a snare: but whoso putteth his trust in the Lord shall be safe."*

Of course she need not fear—wherever she was—if she just followed the admonition of the verse and trusted the Lord.

If only she could help Jenny to understand that.

————

Virginia said very little to Jenny about her trip to the city university. She stated that they had gone to visit Rodney, and before Jenny could start plying questions, she had quickly moved on to another topic of conversation. "Are you coming to Youth Group? We're having an autumn party at the pastor's house. Well . . . yard, actually, if Indian summer stays around. I expect a good turnout. All the kids love the autumn party. There's lots to eat—that usually brings the fellows. And that," she laughed, "usually brings the girls."

Jenny laughed too. "Sure, why not?" she responded. "I've been bored out of my mind lately. There is absolutely nothing to do in this dead town. I'll be so glad when this school year is over and I can get out of here. Some place where people actually *live*."

Virginia thought of the university crowd, and a funny little fear shot through her again. She shrugged her shoulders to dismiss both Jenny's comment and the thought, and then decided to speak. "You know—I've been thinking. For those who don't have faith—don't know God is with them—there seems to be, well, an emptiness they need to try to fill with *something*. Excitement. Adventure. Pleasure. Anything, really. I don't find this little town boring at all."

Jenny gave her a scathing look. "You are one strange creature, Virginia Simpson. I've no idea why you're willing to substitute your God for all those other things."

"When you know God—He *is* all those things," she said simply.

"Your God is about the furthest thing from excitement

or adventure or pleasure that anyone—or anything—could get."

The fire in Jenny's eyes and voice made Virginia tremble inside.

"But you're wrong. You've never tried to find out."

Jenny sniffed her disbelief. "He's God," she said emphatically.

"Of course He is."

"Then you tell me how the God who considers anything that is fun as evil can bring any pleasure."

"Jenny, there are lots of fun things that aren't evil."

"Name one," Jenny challenged.

"Well, the autumn party, for example." Virginia was relieved to have come up with one so easily.

Jenny snorted her disdain. "You call that fun? It's childish, that's what it is. Pure child's play. Food. A few silly games. Maybe a little harmless flirting. You don't even know what real fun is."

Virginia was taken aback. "And you," she threw back at Jenny, "are so . . . so blinded that you can't enjoy simple, pleasurable things. You think that you need . . . need . . ." But Virginia could not come up with the needs of Jenny. In truth she had no knowledge of what the likes of Jenny might be needing to make something seem fun. It was totally foreign to Virginia. She flushed at her own ignorance.

"You are such a child," responded Jenny. "Someday you need to grow up, Virginia."

Virginia wanted to respond with as caustic a reply as Jenny's, but suddenly her concern for Jenny's spiritual state swept through her being and stopped her angry retort. With a great deal of feeling she replied softly, "And I pray that someday you might become as a little child," she said instead. "Jesus said that we must if we are to enter the kingdom of heaven."

Jenny's answer was another indignant sniff before she flounced away in a huff.

———

Virginia's next letter to Jamison was much different than her abbreviated report to Jenny about their trip. Page after page filled up with the visit to Rodney. She told of the poky train, of the disappointing hotel, of the campus with its long walks and confusing, same-looking buildings. She shared her feelings about the soda fountain and the noisy students who poured in and out, seeking company from like-minded souls looking for empty amusement. She still was too confused and embarrassed by the incident with the fellow who was so forward and brash to make more than a vague mention of it. She told of visiting the church where Rodney attended and how pleased her mother and father had been to know that Rodney had found one similar to their own hometown church.

Then she wrote of Jenny and her reaction to the invitation to Youth Group. "She still doesn't understand," Virginia wrote. "If only I could find the right words to explain it to her. She thinks that life is all about fun and doesn't know where real enjoyment can be found. Sometimes I get so angry with her, and yet I feel so sorry for her all at the same time. It rather frightens me. I wonder just what might happen to her in life if she doesn't change her thinking and her ways. Really, I am scared that Jenny might destroy herself. And I feel helpless to do anything to stop her."

As always, she ended by saying that she could not wait until Christmas break when he would again be home and they could spend long hours together, sharing their thoughts and feelings in person rather than by mail.

By the time Virginia folded the letter, it was all she could do to get it into the envelope.

———

Clara's pregnancy was not going well. The first months were spent being so sick that she lost weight rather than gained. Doc Luke, their uncle, was concerned enough that he decided she should go to a city clinic to see if she could get some help. The arrangements were made, and Troy, her husband, took her by train to see what could be done.

Five days later she was home again. "The doctors said there is nothing to do but to wait," she announced disconsolately. "Hopefully things will settle down before too long."

But things did not settle down. Clara seemed to look thinner and weaker by the day. At last she was forced to spend much of her time in bed, and Virginia rotated with her mother in dropping over to prepare meals and do the laundry and cleaning.

And then one night Virginia was returning home, tired after spending the evening with Clara, when she overheard a conversation from the back hall that brought her steps to a halt and her heart to pounding.

"If that baby ever makes it, it will be a wonder," Virginia heard her father say.

"I worry about Clara. She is so thin and pale," her mother responded. "If the baby comes to term, I fear she will not have the strength for delivery."

"What does Luke say?"

"He is as concerned as we are. He's been making phone calls and reading all the material he can get. He still has no answers. He doesn't know what can be done."

"We'll have to keep praying."

Virginia heard her mother sigh, then her muffled voice. She knew her father had pulled her mother close and that she was speaking from the comfort of his embrace.

"I'm so scared. I admit it. I know that God is in control. I know that. But—" She sounded about to cry. "I also know that sometimes His plans are not our plans. Sometimes He does not answer our prayers the way we ask. He . . . He might take her, Drew. And the baby." Her voice broke. "We have to face that—and somehow accept it. But it would be so hard. I don't know if I'm brave enough—strong enough."

She was crying now.

Virginia's own wild thoughts took over, drowning out the sounds of her father's attempts to comfort her mother. *Lose the baby?* Yes—she had known that might happen, though she still fought against it. *But lose Clara?* Never. No. She'd never be able to accept that. Never.

From the next room the muffled sounds told Virginia that her father was praying with her mother. But she did not stay to hear and understand his words. Instead, she took flight and ran down the hall to her own room, where she threw herself on her bed and sobbed.

———

Jamison did come home for Christmas, but Virginia was so busy that she felt cheated. Her mother did all she could to free Virginia from nursing duties so she and Jamison could spend time together. But Virginia felt guilty if she didn't feel she was doing her fair share.

Besides, Jamison acted fidgety and distracted. He was full of thoughts and conversation about college and his church group and all the sports activities he was engaged in. Like Jenny, he seemed to find the small town a bit boring—though for a far different reason.

"I wish you were done with school so you could come with me now," he told Virginia.

With all of her heart she wished so, too. "It won't be long. Just one more term," she assured him. "Besides, you will soon be home again for the summer."

"I'm not sure I'll be coming home this summer, Virginia. I have an opportunity for a job. It would pay much better than anything I could find around here. It seems like I should take it."

Virginia nodded, but her heart sank in disappointment.

"Besides, there's football. We want to spend a lot of the summer months sharpening up our game. We came so close to the championship this past year. If we work hard we can make it next year. Several from the team are getting jobs in town, and we plan to keep right on practicing through the summer months."

Virginia nodded again. But it was hard for her to think of the long months ahead without Jamison and no summer reunion to look forward to.

"Then in the fall—" Jamison did not finish his sentence but held his arms out to Virginia, and she accepted the invitation for a warm embrace.

"It won't be long until you'll be joining me," he whispered into her hair. "I have so much to show you. So many people to introduce my girl to."

He released her but continued to hold her hand and look into her eyes. "I'll be proud to show them the one I've been telling them about all year." He gave her hand a squeeze.

Virginia forced a trembling smile. She could hardly wait.

———

When spring finally came, it was not any too soon to Virginia's way of thinking. The long winter and Clara's long confinement made Virginia feel totally exhausted in mind and body. Then she mentally chastised herself for even thinking of complaining, when her mother and Clara were bearing an even greater burden.

With the arrival of the songbirds and spring flowers, a bit of her melancholy seemed to melt away with the drifts of tarnished snow by the roadside.

Clara was not regaining robust health, but she did not

seem to decline further, either. That was something that kept Doctor Luke and her mother hoping for the best.

The baby is growing, Virginia reminded herself as she trudged home from Clara's late one afternoon. *Quite normally, under the circumstances. That is something to be thankful for. Indeed an answer to our prayers.* Perhaps it was helping that Belinda spent a great deal of time and energy making nourishing broths and puddings to try to tempt Clara's lagging appetite.

And it seemed to be working—at least to some extent, though Virginia, watching Clara, felt that she often choked down the food more in an effort to save her child than because she found it inviting.

"So how is Clara doing?"

Virginia's thoughts were interrupted by their neighbor, Mr. Adamson. He leaned on his freshly painted fence and peered at her from under his grubby, battered hat. He had already spent many spring hours out in his garden uncovering plants and coaxing forth blossoms.

Virginia tried to smooth the worrisome frown from her face and let her lips relax into a smile. Mr. Adamson's care and interest in her during her early teenage struggles made a special warm spot in her heart.

"She's still holding her own," she responded, hoping it would sound like good news.

The elderly man nodded.

"And the little one?"

"Uncle Luke says he—or she—seems to be growing just fine."

He nodded again.

"Think Clara would like a little bouquet of those tulips and daffodils? Got a few new colors this spring. Look at the creamy pink ones. Pretty little things, aren't they?"

Virginia's eyes followed the dirt-encrusted finger. The

flowers were pretty. She was sure Clara would enjoy them immensely.

"I'll fix up a little bouquet for you to take on your next trip over. When you going?"

"Right after I get my load of books home. It's my turn to get supper for Troy and Clara tonight."

The frumpy hat nodded. "I'll have them ready for you to pick up on your way by."

Virginia gave him a genuine smile. "She'll love them, Mr. Adamson. They'll brighten her day."

The faded blue eyes misted. "Missing Clara," he said simply. And he turned away to survey his flower garden.

Virginia knew what he felt was not expressed adequately in his few, simple words. And yet . . . yet, maybe it was.

CHAPTER 4

As graduation time drew near, Virginia found her excitement growing in spite of her busy days juggling housework and homework. She would soon be done with high school. Soon off to college to join Jamison. Soon considered an adult rather than a teenager.

Even with Clara's situation as difficult as it was, Virginia could not keep the lightness from her step. Surely, surely with all the good happening in her world, things would work out for Clara and her baby, as well.

So Virginia went through each busy day dreaming and planning along with her classmates. The whole world stretched out before them, and each one sought to fulfill dreams in a little different way.

Jenny was almost beside herself with anticipation to "be done with this grubby little town," but every remark she made caused Virginia further concern. Jenny had again decided she would go to university after all and had applied and been accepted. Now she talked of nothing but her impatience to finally be a part of dormitory life. But the scenes she always painted were not of students with serious interest in preparing for a future career, but of frolicking young people intent upon making up for all the fun they had been missing when constrained by home and family.

This was not at all Virginia's perspective on college life. She expected to spend far more time in the library than in the fraternity house or nearby confectionary. Of course, in between times she would be with Jamison—discussing ideas from a class, going to church events, enjoying a soda together.

Jamison had made up his mind about the offered job and would not be home for the summer. Another three months of letter writing rather than sharing experiences firsthand sounded rather bleak to Virginia, but she wrote that she understood and wished him well both in his work and in his football pursuits. "When I get there I will be your biggest fan," the letter concluded. "I am so proud of you."

But Rodney was coming home. Virginia could hardly wait to see her big brother; Francine still brought up the changes in him they might have to face. Virginia tried to push those thoughts aside, but they continued to nag at her.

One Saturday while she and her mother were taking a quick break from housework over cups of tea, Virginia broached the subject. "Do you think people change when they go off to university?"

"Undoubtedly," Belinda replied without a moment's hesitation.

Virginia felt an uncomfortable feeling deep in the pit of her stomach.

"Why?" she responded, hoping her mother might give it further thought and retract her statement.

"We change all through life," replied Belinda easily, reaching to pour herself another cup. She leaned back in her chair and took a sip. Virginia waited.

"But I suppose the late teen years might hold some of the biggest, fastest changes."

She seemed so totally unconcerned that it puzzled Virginia.

"Do you think Rodney will have changed?"

"I'm sure he has."

Still no concern in her voice.

"Aren't you—don't you sort of wish that he'd stay like he is?"

Belinda smiled, but she turned to look directly at Virginia. She put her teacup down on the saucer and leaned toward her daughter.

"No," she said with a brief shake of her head. "I do love Rodney—just the way he is—the way he was. But I have watched many changes in Rodney's life over the years. Do you think I would want him to stay as that little preschooler I walked to school on his first morning? Or as that preteen a bit scared over his first job delivering the paper? Or as that high schooler with concern over his problem with skin blemishes and a first date?" Belinda shook her head again.

"No. I love him. Have loved him through each of his growing stages. But I do not want him to stay the same. I want him to grow. To mature. To become everything God has in mind for him. To be a man. Accept responsibility. Be a leader.

"And he will. I have every confidence he will. He's on the right track—your brother. Following the leading of his Lord. I want him to change, but I never want him to leave behind the solid base he has already established for who he is deep inside. But I also want him to build and develop and carefully nurture that inner self. And as that happens, there will be changes."

Virginia nodded. But she did secretly hope that in the growing and maturing, the brother she had always known would still be recognizable. There was so much that she did not want to lose.

And of course this also was true of Jamison.

———

Graduation day started rainy and looked as though it would stay that way. Virginia groaned as she stared out her window. She had been named class valedictorian. Her mother had helped her to sew a new dress. Now the dripping weather threatened to drown all her excitement over the special occasion.

Jenny, too, was to have a part in the ceremony. She would be speaking on behalf of the graduating class, summarizing the years spent within the halls of Hugh Carson High. Virginia did hope she would use wisdom in preparing and presenting her speech. Jenny had constantly tormented her on the way to and from school with bits of satire or downright rudeness that she claimed would be a part of her address.

Virginia knew she was teasing, or at least sincerely hoped she was. But she still felt nervous and irritated whenever Jenny came up with a new line about this teacher's ratty toupee or that teacher's foul-smelling breath. She had informed Virginia that she intended to say Miss Crook was such a constant natterer that, upon retiring for the night, her false teeth continued to chatter even after she deposited them in their container. Or that Mr. Noraway once got his beard and his tie mixed together and trimmed two inches off of both, which he then pasted on his bald pate as replacement for his hair loss. She concluded with a flourish, "Town folks thought he had taken to wearing a ribbon in his hair!"

Virginia was sure—or nearly so—Jenny would not be so foolish as to include such ridicule in her graduation address. But Jenny certainly was having a lot of fun teasing the class valedictorian.

Now, as Virginia donned the new dress and carefully combed and pinned up her hair, a queasiness gripped her stomach that she had never felt before. Her hands were moist, her throat dry. She was nervous. Out and out nervous. Regrets that Clara would not be at her graduation—or Rodney, or her beloved Jamison—quickly vanished. Indeed, she took to wishing that no one would be there. Not her parents, her grandparents, her uncle Luke—or any other member of their small community. Even her concern over the dreary weather was forgotten. She could not remember a single line of her carefully prepared speech. Frantically she grabbed up the well-fingered note cards for one more perusal. She was sure she would never be able to deliver the address in any kind of coherent fashion.

And Jenny? Would she really dare to present some of her outrageous material? Suddenly Virginia did not care. If Jenny really, really made a scene, perhaps folks would forget that she, Virginia, had disgraced the family name with her faltering presentation.

She bundled up in the coat she had earlier declared she would not wear for fear it would crush her dress and gloomily followed her parents from the safety of her home.

"I will arrive there dripping wet," she mumbled to herself. "My hair will be a sight, my dress all wrinkled, my stockings splashed with dirty rainwater and my shoes soppy. I will likely catch my death of cold."

Her final regret was that the cold would not develop quickly enough to rescue her from her present dilemma.

But none of the dreadful predictions came true—thanks to the care of her father, who managed to deliver her in a dry and unwrinkled condition. Her mother reached out to do a last-minute pat of her hair—more because she was a mother than because the hair needed it. "We're proud of you," Belinda whispered and leaned forward to plant a kiss on her forehead. Virginia felt a spark of confidence being reborn.

The ceremony proceeded in accordance with their program. Jenny's father had printed up the sheets as his contribution to the community and the special event. The principal included thanks to the local newsman in his opening remarks.

Jenny gave her address. It contained some bits of humor but nothing that brought embarrassment to anyone. Virginia heaved a sigh of relief when it was over, and Jenny cast a glance of victory her way.

A group of junior students sang a song dedicated to the graduating class, and the principal exhorted the graduates about reaching their full potential.

Then it was Virginia's turn. She walked to the podium on trembling legs, but once she began, she forgot her nervousness. Looking out into the audience and seeing the proud grin on her grandfather's face and the quiet nodding of her grandmother in agreement gave her added confidence. She finished to a fine round of applause.

And just as simply as that, it was over. She was no longer a student in the local town. She was a graduate. An adult. She thought she should feel something. Older. Wiser. But she felt nothing but a strange emptiness. An inner knowledge that she was now on the edge of the nest, ready to try her own wings. That she would need to find her own place in the world. Reestablish herself in some way that she didn't yet fully understand. It was a bit frightening. She felt a sudden thankfulness that college would wait for a few months. She needed some time to make the adjustment. To discover, like Rodney, just who she was and how to establish her identity before becoming a responsible adult and leaving the safety of the home she loved.

She thought she might understand—just a little bit—about what her mother had said about changing. College would change her. Would force her to change. She would never be a child again.

———

Jenny found a summer job and began to tuck away money for the upcoming college year. Her father would be paying her tuition and board, she told Virginia, but she intended to make sure that she would also have money for clothes and parties. She was sure her father would not be providing adequately in that department. And Jenny intended to do a good deal of partying.

Virginia knew there would be no summer job for her. Clara's baby was due any day, and as things now stood, no one could expect Clara to take over immediate care of the newborn. Virginia only hoped that there would be no complications with the birthing. Each day Clara and the new baby took a good share of the family prayer time.

Their mother had seemingly gotten over her earlier fears and, with the help of their father, had placed her confidence in the fact that God was in total control of the situation. Whatever the outcome of the impending birth, God would be with them and help them to face whatever they must face. It was in the middle of the night that the knock came on their door. Belinda was up and at the door so quickly, Virginia wondered if her mother had been lying awake anticipating it.

Virginia heard the murmur of voices even before she could stand on shaking limbs and work her arms into her robe.

Then she heard her mother hurrying back down the hall to be met midway by her father. "Luke and Dr. Braden have gone over to Clara's," she heard her mother say just as she exited her room.

"How is she?" asked Drew, tying his own robe around himself.

"So far they have no concerns. Things seem to be . . . normal."

"Are they taking her to the surgery?"

"No. Luke thinks that under the circumstances she will be better if she is not moved. They plan to deliver the baby at home."

"I'll get dressed."

The final statement from her father was an acknowledgment that Belinda would need to be there. He was prepared to get her there as quickly as possible.

Francine came sleepily into the hallway. "Is it—"

"Yes," her mother answered without waiting for the complete question. She stopped long enough to brush Francine's hair back from her face, cast a quick glance Virginia's way, and then moved hurriedly on.

Virginia turned to Francine, who had suddenly dissolved into tears. "Don't," pleaded Virginia. "We should pray—not cry."

She felt in no condition to try to comfort a sobbing sister.

"I have prayed," wailed Francine.

"Then trust," Virginia responded almost severely. Then she thought better of it and reached out to pull Francine's head against her. She said no more, just stroked the trembling shoulder of her younger sister until the sobs subsided.

"I have a feeling it is going to be a long night," Virginia whispered into the darkness. "We should try to get some more sleep."

"I'll never sleep now" came the sniffing reply, and Virginia feared that Francine might start crying all over again.

"Then let's go to the kitchen and have some warm milk," she quickly suggested and led the way.

"I wish Rodney were home," Francine snuffled.

"He is to come tomorrow."

"I wish he were here now."

Virginia wished that, too. But Rodney, who normally would have arrived home already, had been given permission to spend a couple of weeks on a camping trip with some of his new friends. One was Austin, who had finally warmed to Rodney's friendship and had admitted that his unknown disease had him worried and scared.

"This time could be very important," Rodney had said over the phone. "I feel that Austin needs me."

And his parents had readily agreed that the time in the outdoors, away from college pressures, would be time well spent.

"He will be here soon," Virginia repeated. "Maybe he will even get here before Clara's baby."

Francine's eyes widened. "It takes that long to have a baby?"

"Sometimes."

"But that's hours."

"I know. Sometimes it takes hours."

Francine began to cry again. "I don't think I can stand it for that long," she cried.

"*You* stand it?" Virginia asked abruptly. "What about Clara?"

The cries grew louder, and Virginia knew she had said the wrong thing.

"Blow your nose. Here." She handed Francine a fresh hankie. "Are there any more of those muffins left?" she went on, hoping to distract her sister.

"In the pantry," sniffled Francine.

"Get a couple."

Francine went off to the pantry just as their parents came in the kitchen, fully dressed and anxious to be on their way.

"You'll watch out for Francine," Belinda was saying in a low voice as she drew on her light coat.

Virginia nodded. Her mother knew that she would, but Virginia guessed she had to say the words anyway.

"I expect to be back soon," said her father. "I'd be useless and in the way there."

Virginia nodded again.

"Let us know . . ." began Virginia. Those words were not necessary, either, but she had to speak them.

Francine emerged from the pantry carrying a muffin in each hand. At the sight of her parents, she burst into tears again, and her mother gave her a quick hug. "Tell Clara—we're praying," Francine sobbed out to the backs of her departing mother and father. "We love her. She was a . . . a wonderful sister. I really—"

"Stop it," cut in Virginia. "You're talking like . . . like she's dying or something."

"Well . . ." blubbered Francine.

"She's only having a baby. Hundreds—thousands of women have babies every year."

"And some of them . . ." began Francine, but Virginia refused to let her say it.

"Get the butter," she ordered more loudly than necessary. "I'll put the milk on."

Francine blew her nose and moved to the pantry once more.

"This is going to be a long, long night," Virginia said again under her breath. She felt like weeping, too.

———

News came long before Rodney's eleven-o'clock train pulled in at the local station the next morning. Clara had a baby boy. Mother and baby both seemed to be resting comfortably. The doctors in charge felt no reason to be concerned about the new arrival, and Clara seemed to have weathered the birthing much better than they had dared to hope. The good news traveled fast. Belinda insisted on taking it out to the farm herself to inform the great-grandparents.

Virginia breathed a sigh of relief. God had seen them through another crisis. And if the news hadn't been so good, she told herself, God would have seen them through that, too.

Rodney's train was met with extra enthusiasm as he was greeted with the news that he was now an uncle. Virginia shared his emotions as his cap soared high into the air and he gave a whoop of delight.

"Have they named him yet?" was his first question.

"He's Anthony Clark," Francine announced before Virginia had time to answer.

"Anthony Clark. That's nice. Real nice."

"And Clara says that he is not to be called Tony," added Francine importantly.

"And how does she plan to stop that?" laughed Rodney.

"She says she will pummel the first one who calls him that," spoke up Danny.

"And the others?"

Danny shrugged. "I suppose she will pummel all of them."

Rodney laughed again, then gathered his suitcases, passing some to Virginia and Danny to carry. A small parcel was handed to Francine as her allotment.

"Don't drop that," he admonished her. "I've been nursing it all the way home. There's something for Mama and that new baby in there."

"How did you know what to buy?" asked Francine, attempting to get a peek into the parcel.

"For Mama?"

"No, silly. For the baby."

"What do you mean? Babies aren't too particular, so I've been told."

"But you didn't know if it was a boy or a girl."

"So? I bought a toy and a couple of bibs. I don't expect him to complain."

They all joined in Francine's laugh.

"Now, let's get out of here and go get a look at him," said Rodney, picking up the remaining suitcase.

"We can't." The short directive came from Virginia.

Rodney stopped short. "What do you mean?"

"We can't. Not yet. Clara has to rest. Mama says that it may be two or three days before we can see him."

Rodney's face showed his disappointment. "Haven't any of you seen him yet?"

"No," they all said in unison.

"And Danny didn't even know he was on the way," accused Francine. "He slept right through the whole commotion."

Danny shrugged again. "Nothing I could have done about it anyway," he excused himself.

Rodney reached out a hand and ruffled Danny's hair. "C'mon," he said. "Let's get on home. I'm starving."

Virginia picked up the case she was to carry and followed her two brothers from the station. A smile played about the corners of her mouth. Rodney didn't seem to have changed—at least much—at all.

CHAPTER 5

$\mathcal{U}$ncle Luke says you can pay a visit to Clara," Belinda announced the next day as she entered the kitchen where her family was having their noon meal. They had not expected this news to come so soon, so excitement followed.

"Is Clara well again?" asked Francine.

Belinda withdrew her gloves and removed her hat. "No, she's still not strong, but she is so anxious to show you her new son that Luke thinks her agitation may cause more trouble than your visit. If you stay only a few minutes, Luke says it shouldn't cause any harm."

The enthusiasm of the little group was tempered by the reality that Clara had a ways to go to full recovery.

"But she will be okay, won't she?" asked Francine.

"We hope so. But it may be a long, slow process. If we only could discover what it is that has bothered her, we might be able to do something about it."

"You still don't know?" asked Rodney with a frown.

"Luke thinks now that it may be some infectious bacteria— not connected with her pregnancy at all."

"Will the baby get it?"

Belinda shook her head slowly. "We don't have any answers. We certainly hope not. But it is something to pray about."

Belinda was the one to break the silence that had fallen. "He's a beautiful baby. You are going to love him. He's already stolen my heart."

She was smiling as she moved to pour herself a cup of tea.

"Well, Grandma," teased Rodney. "I didn't expect anything else. He would have stolen your heart if he'd been purple with one eye and a green tail."

They all laughed, but they knew it to be true. Belinda was bound to be taken with her first grandchild.

"Well, he has two beautiful dark eyes, he's creamy white, with a reasonable amount of dark hair—and no green tail," she answered Rodney's banter.

"Oooh! I can hardly wait to see him," exclaimed Francine. "Virginia, are you going to take all the things you've made for him?"

Virginia thought of the little garments she had sewn whenever she could find a few spare moments. And the sweater set and baby shawl she had knitted. "I've already given most of it to Clara. She was feeling so down because she wasn't able to be up sewing and getting ready, so I took the things I had finished."

"Bet she was glad. . . ."

"She cried."

Virginia herself had to choke back tears just thinking of the emotional moment.

"I'm going to take my gift," spoke up Rodney.

"Hey, I don't have anything." Danny looked up, concern on his face, as though the whole event had caught him totally by surprise and he had suddenly realized that he was actually an uncle. He turned to his siblings. "Can I run quick and get something?"

"No," responded Francine. "I don't want to wait. You can get him something later, Danny," she informed him with sisterly aplomb.

But Danny had already risen from the table and was heading for his bedroom. "I'll meet you there," he called back, his words muted by a mouthful of food.

Virginia was busily clearing the table. Francine jumped up to help her.

"Remember," Belinda warned, "don't stay long. And try not to tire her with questions."

"How long is long?" asked literal-minded Francine.

"Ten or fifteen minutes. But Luke will be there. He'll shoo you out if he sees Clara tiring."

"I can't wait to hold him," Francine enthused as Virginia prepared the water for the dishes.

Virginia was thinking the same thing. In fact, she had fully expected to be the first with the honor of holding Clara's new son.

"Don't bother with the dishes," Belinda said. "I'll wash up."

Virginia wheeled away to remove and hang her apron. "We won't be long—promise," she said to her mother. "Leave the dishes and we'll do them when we get back." Already she was walking briskly toward her bedroom to gather the last of the baby things for little Anthony.

It was an excited group that hurried through the streets bearing their gifts for the new nephew. But as they neared Clara's little house on the edge of town, their pace slowed and their voices became hushed. Uncertainty as to what they might find made them somber and silent.

They did not bother to knock but cautiously let themselves in the back door. Their uncle Luke sat at the kitchen table, coffee cup nearby, his hands busy writing out some report. He

greeted them brightly, the first indication to Virginia that their
fears might be unfounded.

"So you've come to see the new baby?"

They nodded their answer.

He rose from his chair. "I'd prefer to bring him out, but
Clara would throw something at me. I know she'll want to see
your faces when you get your first peek."

"How is Clara?" Virginia whispered over a lump in her
throat.

"Clara?"

Luke's voice was strong and loud to Virginia's ears. She
almost hushed him.

"Like every new mama. So excited she can't sleep. Her eyes
are always on that crib. C'mon, I'll show you."

They tiptoed down the hall behind him. To Virginia, his
masculine steps thumped and echoed on the hardwood floor-
ing. Again, she wished to hush him.

Clara lay pale among her pillows, her hair fanned out over
their whiteness, her thin arms limp beside her body. But her
eyes shone with a light that Virginia had never seen there
before.

"Come in," she welcomed them with a smile. Her voice
sounded no stronger than her frame looked.

Rodney had stopped short. It was the first he had seen his
older sister since Christmas, and the shock of her illness and
its effects on her body caught him totally by surprise. Virginia
nudged him quickly. He regained a measure of composure,
swallowed hard, and moved forward again.

"Hi, Clara." Virginia quickly filed in and hurried over to
press a kiss on her sister's cheek. "We couldn't wait to see
little Anthony."

"He's beautiful," the new mother managed, and the spar-
kling eyes misted.

"How are you?" Virginia whispered for Clara's ears only.

Clara lifted a tired hand, but the smile did not leave her face. "I'll be fine once I . . . once they find out what's wrong."

Virginia gave the hand a squeeze.

A squeal behind her told her that Francine had beat her to the baby. "Look at him."

Virginia wheeled around to see that Francine already had the new nephew in her arms and was gazing down at him with flushed cheeks and glowing eyes. The bundle of blankets around the wee baby hid everything but blue wrappings. She felt a bit cheated that she had not been the first to hold him. Hadn't she been the one caring for Clara over the past several months?

Rodney pressed close to Francine and reached out a hand to push back some blanket. Virginia got a look at the child for the first time. He did have creamy white skin. Creamy white with a gentle flush when he squirmed. Round, soft cheeks, and the tiniest bit of a nose above the puckered mouth. His eyes were closed, but even in his sleep his mouth worked slightly, as though he might be searching for food but a little unsure as to where and how to find it. Hair covered the top of his perfectly round head like a small dark cap.

Virginia held her breath. So this was Anthony. Her nephew. The one they had all been waiting for.

She laid the gifts she had brought on Clara's bed and tiptoed slowly over to Francine. "Can I . . . ?"

"Not yet. I just got him."

"But I . . ."

"Then it's my turn," said Rodney.

Virginia wanted to protest. He was her baby. She had looked after his mother. In some strange, unexplained way she felt that she had some rights where this new baby was concerned. But as quickly as the feelings came, they were dismissed. Of course that was silly. He was Clara's baby. She was just an auntie. No more or no less than the one who now held him. And Rodney, as an uncle, had as much right as she.

Still, it was very hard to step back and wait her turn. She hoped that Danny would not suddenly burst into the room and announce that he was next in line.

Francine at last relinquished the baby to Rodney's waiting arms, and Virginia was one step closer to her goal. Francine retrieved the small parcel she had dropped on the table by the door and moved to the bed to greet Clara.

"I brought him this," she said as she placed the package on the bed and leaned to kiss her sister.

Clara murmured her thanks and with shaky hands began to tear the wrapping from the gift.

Virginia, watching, felt further concern. *She is so weak. I hadn't realized just how bad things have gotten. Will she ever be able to care for her baby?*

Clara was smiling, a weak, yet excited smile as she drew forth Francine's gift. "A romper. It's sweet. He'll be needing this before we know it. Thank you, Francine. Did you make it yourself?"

"Mama helped me," Francine admitted.

"It's lovely."

Virginia turned back to Rodney, her impatience barely in check. Just then, as she had feared, Danny came thumping down the hall and into the room. He was puffing from his run to the store, and his cheeks were flushed from his hurry and excitement. In his hand he held a brown paper package. Without waiting for any kind of greeting, he placed it near Clara on the bed.

"It's not wrapped proper. I didn't have time," he panted out.

Clara managed a weak chuckle. "Thank you, Danny."

It was a tan-colored teddy bear with a red bow tied askew around its neck. "He'll love this," said Clara, her eyes filling up again. But Danny had not stopped to hear her response. He had moved to Rodney and was carefully taking the baby into his own arms.

"Hey, little fella," he said as he looked down. "This is your uncle Daniel." His eyes softened as he gazed at the child in his arms. Virginia was reminded of the same tenderness he showed when he was nursing one of his injured animals. "I'm gonna teach you all about creatures—and things. You can go with me to the woods and the creek, and we'll see bird nests and rabbit burrows and . . ."

"Danny," laughed Francine. "He doesn't understand. . . ."

Danny's head jerked up. "How do you know?" he flung back at her. "Lots of folks think that animals don't understand, either."

Luke, who had left the room after admitting the family, crossed to Clara's bed and reached a hand to her forehead, watching her with a doctor's steady gaze. Virginia had not even heard his footsteps return.

"Time's about up," he said softly but cheerily.

Virginia felt a moment of panic. She did not wish to jeopardize the health of her sister, but she had not yet had a chance to hold the baby. Her eyes turned to her uncle, pleading.

"I'd like—I'd like Virginia to stay a few moments." Clara's voice was weak but it held authority.

Luke nodded, seeming to understand. "Not too long," he cautioned Virginia, and taking the baby from Danny's arms, he placed him in Virginia's, then ushered the other three from the room.

Virginia looked down at the bundle she held. He was so little. So weightless. It was as if she were holding a bundle of blankets. He squirmed and searched with open mouth. One eye partially opened. Then both. Wide and seeking. They were dark. Just like her mama had said. They seemed to look right up into her face. Virginia wished to introduce herself—like

Danny, but she couldn't say a word. Just stood and stared at this little miracle in her arms.

Had she been able to talk, she would have told him of the love that was washing through her whole being as she held him close. She would have let him know that she had prayed over and over for his safe arrival. Now that he was here, she would go on loving him. Caring for him. Protecting him—if possible—from all of the hurts and bumps of an indifferent world. But Virginia said none of these things. Her heart was too full to be able to speak.

"Come here," whispered Clara and patted the bed beside her.

Virginia moved over to the bed, bearing her precious bundle. Carefully she placed herself on the edge of it. She felt Clara's hand lift to her arm, but she did not take her eyes off the baby.

"I think . . . I think you might understand a little of what I feel when I hold him," Clara said softly. "I can see it in your face."

Virginia looked at Clara and saw that her eyes were again full of happy tears.

"Someday," Clara went on, "it will be your turn. To hold a baby of your own. It's . . . it's something indescribable, Virginia. Something so precious that you can't put it into words. If I never . . . never do another thing in my life, I will feel that I have really lived."

Virginia looked from the small child to his weak mother. Fear gripped her heart. Did Clara mean . . . ? Surely not.

But Clara looked so totally at peace that the tightness began to leave Virginia's chest.

"And you've helped to give me this, Virginia," Clara went on. "All of those months of nursing and cooking and cleaning so that I could reach this moment. And all of the sewing. He wouldn't have a thing to wear if it weren't for you."

Virginia smiled, knowing that was an exaggeration, but she didn't care. Willing, for the moment, to overlook the many items that her mother and grandmother had added to the baby's chest of drawers.

"I can never thank you enough. Never. You've given me the most precious gift that one could ever give," Clara finished.

The baby began to squirm in earnest. Clara reached out a hand to pull back the blanket. She chuckled softly again. "So you want to eat again, do you, Anthony? All right. Come to Mama."

Virginia reluctantly relinquished the baby into Clara's open arms.

She stood. "I must go," she whispered, "or Uncle Luke will come throw me out."

"I know."

She reached down to kiss Clara's cheek, then pressed a kiss on the top of Anthony's soft baby head, as well. Her eyes flashed a silent message to her sister, then she tiptoed from the room.

When she entered the kitchen, her uncle Luke looked up from his writing. "The others went on," he told her. "Said they hoped you didn't mind."

Virginia shook her head. She did not mind. In fact she was glad. Glad to be alone. She was filled with so many emotions that she looked forward to some private time to try to sort them through. The walk home alone was just what she needed.

———

"Seen a lot of scurrying around your house lately," a voice greeted her as she passed Mr. Adamson's fence. He was there, stooped and tottery, his wrinkled face showing deep interest and concern.

Virginia stopped. "Clara has a son. Born yesterday," she informed him, her face breaking into a broad smile.

"How is she?"

Virginia's smile faded but did not entirely disappear. "She . . . she's very happy . . . but not strong yet."

He said nothing. Just nodded. One hand reached up to remove the battered hat, and his eyes dropped to the ground at his feet. Virginia wondered if, in the short silence that followed, he was praying.

Then he lifted his eyes again, and the dirt-covered hand pushed the hat roughly back on his darkened silver hair. He nodded, seeming to have all of the information he needed. "I'll send her some of these early roses," he said as he turned away.

Virginia noticed how unsteady he had become on his feet and how his hands trembled slightly as he picked up his garden trowel from the fence post where he had placed it.

"She'd like that," she answered before she moved on toward home.

———

In the days that followed, much of Virginia's time was taken with duties at Clara's or filling in at home while her mother helped Clara. Clara was not regaining strength as they had hoped.

Virginia loved looking after small Anthony. Even the washing of the baby items seemed much more fun than hanging the home laundry out on long lines in the summer sun. She loved watching Troy and his loving pride in his tiny son.

Clara tried to push herself as she choked down nourishing food or attempted simple bed exercises to improve her strength. She was determined that she would be able to care for her own baby. She insisted on changing diapers and burping after feedings and singing him lullabies. Virginia often was concerned that Clara might be trying too hard, pushing too fast, but she knew that her uncle Luke was keeping a sharp eye on Clara.

By the end of July there had not seemed to be much improvement. After a family conference, it was decided that it would be wise to bring Clara and the baby to the Simpson home to make the nursing care easier for those involved.

Clara and her infant son were moved back into Clara's old bedroom, and a cot was set up for Francine in with Virginia. Troy, who ran his father's store, had his days full with the business, the home garden, and trying to also help his wife. Virginia felt that poor Troy was always on a run, coming and going between work, checking on things at their own little house, and spending time with Clara and Anthony.

The work had increased for all of them, but Virginia did not fret under the load. It became more and more of a pleasure to care for her young nephew. She could not believe how quickly he grew. How quickly he changed. In no time at all he was smiling at her as she gave him his morning bath. Then he was giggling as she played little piggy with his toes. He seemed to know her the minute she entered the room to pluck him from his crib in the morning to deliver him to his mother for nursing.

In fact, the summer slipped by with Virginia scarcely noticing. She did not have time to chafe over the fact that she was spending those long months without Jamison. Oh, she missed him. She even had her dreams of what it would be like to have a home of their own with a baby that was really hers. But her hours were so filled with small Anthony, caring for Clara, and helping her mother with house and garden duties that she really did not have time or energy for moping.

But as August moved toward September and Jenny popped in and out with her wild excitement over soon leaving for college, Virginia's tension began to mount. Did she, or did she not, want to leave and go away to college herself?

Yes. Yes, she did. It was true that it would be hard to leave young Anthony. But she couldn't wait to begin her own college experience—and to be part of Jamison's life again.

CHAPTER 6

Once she had made the decision, Virginia began in earnest to make her own preparations for college life. She had already been accepted at Webster College. Whenever she found a few extra moments, she went over her wardrobe, assessing and repairing and sewing complementary pieces. Her mother smiled and offered her assistance, and even Clara, from her sickbed, asked for small projects she might sew by hand. A few selected books, a favorite quilt for her dormitory bed—with each bit of progress Virginia's excitement grew. It wouldn't be long now.

One late summer evening, after Anthony had been tucked in for the night, Virginia decided on a drink of milk before retiring herself. She thought that all family members had already gone to their rooms, so she was surprised when she saw her mother sitting alone at the kitchen table, her back to the doorway.

Virginia stopped short and watched as Belinda rubbed a hand back and forth over her neck. Her head drooped. Her shoulders sagged. She looked exhausted—and old. It was a shock to Virginia. She let her eyes study the figure before her. Was her mother *really* getting old? Or was it the strain of the heavy burden she had been carrying? Would her mother have a return of her former vigor and cheer when Clara improved?

Virginia did not enter the kitchen as planned but stole silently back to her own bedroom, her thoughts tumbling about in troubled chaos. What was happening? Her mother never complained of fatigue, but she was clearly showing it in the unguarded moment. She looked utterly spent. Why had Virginia not noticed it before? Did the others know? Shouldn't something be done about it? Surely her uncle Luke must be aware. Why hadn't he done something? Said something? What about her father? Wasn't he concerned?

If her mother was already worn out, how would she be when she had to manage alone? Francine tried to help, too, but her youth and the fact of school starting soon made her efforts too inconsistent to count for much. Perhaps, as her mother had cheerfully noted, they might be able to find a neighborhood woman who would be willing to come in two or three times a week to help with laundry or floor scrubbing. But there was so much more to be done. Virginia knew that. Daily meals and baking. Shopping. Cleaning. Baby care. Clara's care. It all added up to a very heavy load. And it didn't look to Virginia as if all the responsibilities would be lessening any time soon.

She had been so unaware. In her plans to go off to college, she had missed all the signs. How could she have been so blind?

Virginia sat at her window, staring into the dark as Francine peacefully slept on her cot. She shouldn't go. She couldn't. There was no way that it was right for her mother to try to get along without her. Virginia could see that clearly—now. All her plans—all her dreams of joining Jamison—shifted and dissolved as she buried her face in her hands and wept bitter tears.

Oh, God, she prayed, *help me do what I need to do*.

By morning, after a fitful sleep, she had herself well in hand and her resolve in place. She would put her plans aside until Clara was well enough to return to her home. And Virginia would pray, even more earnestly, that it would not take too long.

"I've done some thinking and praying," she commented to her mother as the two of them worked side by side in the kitchen. "I've decided to wait a bit longer for college."

Belinda's surprise showed on her face. "Whatever do you mean?"

"It isn't the right time just now." Virginia kept her voice carefully matter-of-fact.

"But you had your heart set—"

"I know. But it will wait. Clara seems to be getting a bit stronger. Maybe I'll be able to go next year. Maybe I'll only have to miss one term and can go after Christmas. But now . . ."

"Are you sure?"

"I'm sure."

Virginia watched as her mother's whole body seemed to relax. She knew without doubt that her decision had been good news for her mother. She could see the relief written all over her face.

But then Belinda said, "You think about it a bit more. Pray about it. I don't want . . ."

"Mama, I have already prayed and thought," said Virginia with finality. She didn't add that she had also cried well into the night.

Belinda's eyes searched her face, then she nodded. She sighed deeply and lowered herself to a kitchen chair.

Virginia was afraid she was going to start crying again. Determinedly she held her emotions in check.

"I won't pretend, Virginia," Belinda said slowly, her own emotions making her voice shaky. "I didn't know how we would ever make it without you. But I so much wanted . . . I mean, this is . . . so difficult to ask you to put aside your plans for us."

"You didn't ask me, Mama."

"I know. I couldn't. Really. I have wanted you to be able to follow your own dreams. Not . . . not be forced to lay them aside for us. For me. And Clara. I know how excited you have been about going to college. About being with Jamison."

Virginia managed a smile. "That will wait," she said, speaking the words as much to convince herself as her mother.

"Jenny goes off in a couple of weeks."

"Jenny isn't even going to the same college."

"I know, but—"

"It's all right, Mama. I am convinced that this is the right decision."

Belinda smiled and reached out a hand to brush back a strand of hair from her daughter's cheek. Virginia needed all her willpower to keep tears from overflowing her eyes.

She did know she had done the right thing, but still it was very hard to put her own future on hold.

Later that night her father sought a few minutes with her alone.

"I can't tell you how proud I am of you," he began with a warm hug. "I know how much you wanted to go to college. I didn't want to deter you from doing that, but frankly, I have been so worried about your mother. She's pushed herself to near exhaustion. I've tried to find help, but so far every woman I can think of seems to have all she can do to keep up with her own household. Thank you, Virginia, for making this sacrifice. I don't suppose there's anything you could have done to convince me of your . . . your maturity and selflessness more than this has."

It was enough for Virginia.

————

Jenny was shocked when she heard the news.

"How could you?" she demanded. "I can't wait to get

out of this dumpy little town. I wouldn't stay on here for anybody."

Virginia could have responded that if that was the case, Jenny did not understand about family. But she held her tongue.

"I can't imagine why you want to stay," Jenny ranted on. "This place is—"

"It's not that I want to," Virginia finally broke in. "My family needs me, Jenny. Mama is going to collapse if she doesn't have help. And, anyway, I wasn't going to college to escape this place. I like it here. I was going for an education."

"Hah," scoffed Jenny. "You were going so you could keep your eye on your Jamison, and you know it."

"I was not."

"You were, too. You couldn't wait to be there with him. That's the only reason you chose Webster. For Jamison!"

Virginia flushed. "I admit I want to be with Jamison. What's wrong about that? But it wasn't so I could keep my eye on him. Jamison doesn't need . . ."

But Jenny "hahed" again in a very loud voice and tossed her red hair. "You don't think there are other girls after him? I would be if I were there."

Truthfully, Virginia had never entertained the thought before. Of course there would be other girls after him. Jamison was a very attractive young man.

"Jamison wouldn't . . ."

Jenny's "hah" was accompanied this time with a loud, brassy laugh.

Virginia, too, tossed her head. "He told me he's much too busy with football to even think about social things. He's been worried how we would find time to be together when I got there."

Jenny swore and exclaimed, "I'd dump a guy who thought more of his football than he did of me."

"It's not that."

Jenny cocked her head to one side and gave Virginia a knowing look. "No?"

"No, it isn't. It's just that it's very important that he do well. If he wants a career as a player, then he has to give football his full attention right now. It's not that he's forgotten me. He writes. . . ."

Jenny gave a dismissive sniff, so Virginia let the words trail off. Jenny could never be convinced of anything once she had made up her mind. But then Jenny surprised her by completely changing her tone.

"I'm sorry, Virginia. Really sorry. It would have been good for you to get away and find out what the world is really about. Have a little fun. Learn to live a little. You are so . . . so staid and . . . and responsible."

Jenny spat out the last word as though it were something disgraceful. Virginia could feel her hackles rising again. "I wasn't planning to let college change that, Jenny," she threw at her friend.

Jenny gave her a long, hard look. "Then you have completely missed the point of what college is all about, Virginia," she said scathingly and turned and walked away.

———

It was the hardest letter Virginia had ever written, but she had to let Jamison know she would not be joining him for the fall term.

In his own letters, Jamison always asked about Clara and the new baby, so Virginia was confident that he shared her concern, at least as far as he was able, being so far away and so busy with his job and football. She was sure he would understand her decision, would even support her in making the choice to stay to help her mother. Yet it would be disappointing to him, just as it was to her. He had to know immediately so he could make the difficult mental and emotional adjustments before classes started.

It was hard to strike a proper balance in her letter. Hard to let him know her deep disappointment without making it sound like she felt herself a martyr for making the decision that she had. She didn't want him to believe that she was thinking, *Poor little me—I'm giving up so much to be a good little girl*. Yet she did not want him to think that she didn't feel deep sorrow over more long months apart.

Virginia wrote and tore up four copies before she was satisfied that the words on the pages properly conveyed her feelings without sounding maudlin.

She delivered the letter to the post office herself and slipped the envelope into the letter slot. Inwardly she worried about what her missive would do to Jamison. It was not just her plans she was disturbing. It was his plan, as well. In fact, he was the one who had chosen the college he felt to be right for both of them.

Virginia felt very close to tears again as she made her way back home to the stack of baby laundry.

———

Jenny was bubbling with enthusiasm, as if they had not ever had the recent exchange. "I've come to say good-bye. My luggage has already been dropped off at the station. My pa took it over."

Virginia had never seen her so excited. "I thought you weren't leaving until Saturday," Virginia questioned.

"I talked my pa into letting me go today so I'd have lots of time to look over the campus."

"You've already visited the campus."

Jenny shrugged. "I know, but Pa fell for it. Besides, I do want time to settle in. Sort of watch others arrive. Check out the hangouts, et cetera."

Virginia felt emptiness gnawing at her insides. Jenny was off to college and she was not. The reality of her situation hit her fully.

"I'm going to miss you," she said simply, knowing that she really was.

"I was hoping you'd walk with me to catch my train."

Virginia nodded and moved into the living room, removing her apron as she went. "Mama, Jenny is here. She's leaving for college."

Belinda looked up in surprise. "Now? I didn't think her classes started until next week."

"She's going early."

"I was planning to have some baking to send. . . ."

"She needs to catch her train, Mama."

Belinda hurried into the kitchen to say good-bye to Jenny and wish her well. Virginia watched as she gave the girl a warm hug and remembered with a lump in her throat how her mother had filled in for Jenny's mother over the years.

"I'm going to walk with her to the station," Virginia said to Belinda.

Virginia watched her mother dab at her cheek, a look of motherly concern shadowing her eyes. She knew that her mother's prayers would follow Jenny to the distant campus. It made her own heart ache just a little bit.

Virginia did not stop for a wrap since the late afternoon was warm, with only a slight wind blowing.

They were not even out the door before Jenny's excited chatter began. "And Pa said to go ahead and do my own shopping. So I did. Not here, of course. I took the train into the city and, boy, did I shop. You should see all the things I bought. I wanted to show them to you but there wasn't time. I was so anxious to get them packed when Pa agreed that I could go early—I never thought I'd ever be able to talk him into it—so I had to quickly throw things into the cases before he changed his mind. I might have to take a hotel for a couple of nights. The dormitories aren't even open yet. But that will be fun. I've never stayed in a hotel alone before. Have you?"

Before Virginia could even shake her head, Jenny was hurrying on. "I sure hope my roommate turns out to be fun. I'd hate to be stuck with some small-town prude who doesn't even know—"

"Like me?"

Jenny looked just a bit sheepish, then nodded and kept right on. "We were friends in a small town, Virginia. It worked here. I'm not sure it would work at college. I mean, things are different there. Things are moving. Here, everything is d-e-a-d. Dead!"

Virginia was shocked that Jenny could discard their years of friendship so casually. *And she used the past tense. We were friends. If this is how she feels*, Virginia found herself wondering, *why in the world did she come get me to walk her to the station?*

But Jenny was still talking. "The skirt is the most gorgeous material. I'm sure if Pa saw it he'd think it on the short side, but skirts are getting shorter now. No more of this covering up the ankles. When I was in the city—wow—I couldn't believe how far behind we are in fashions.

"This one shirtwaist I bought. You should see it. It is the most gorgeous shade of green."

Virginia wondered if everything Jenny had purchased was gorgeous.

"Really makes my hair look—well—frankly, like burnished copper. Gorgeous! It's fantastic. Even the saleslady said so. Then I got this evening dress for going out that's this gorgeous shade of blue, with a shaped bodice. I mean—really shaped." Jenny rolled her eyes. "And the material is real clingy and you should see it. Even I feel daring—"

A car went by and honked the horn. Virginia recognized the driver as a new fellow in the area. He leaned on the horn again and honked long and loudly, then waved his hat in the air as he passed. Jenny squealed and waved back. Virginia frowned and fanned the dust from her face.

"I wish he would have stopped," said Jenny. "I could have told him that I'm going today."

"Have you said good-bye to your father, or do you need to stop by the paper?" Virginia asked, shaking her skirt to dislodge the settling dust.

Jenny looked at her as though she had lost her senses.

"He knows I'm going. He bought my ticket."

"But have you . . . ?"

Jenny gave her a withering look. "We don't say good-byes, Virginia. That is sentimental tripe."

Virginia could not imagine leaving home without a family good-bye.

"And this other dress," Jenny rambled on, "is a cream color. You remember how good I look in cream? It's sleeveless, with a scooped neck and a slightly flared skirt."

Sleeveless. Fitted. Shorter. Scooped. Clingy. Virginia could not believe her ears. What was the world of fashion coming to?

"Did you buy anything for classroom wear?" she asked, just a hint of sarcasm edging her voice.

"Oh, Virginia. You are such a prude. Of course I bought clothes for classroom wear, if you must know. But they really aren't very exciting to talk about, are they?"

And suddenly Virginia knew why she had been invited to accompany Jenny to the train. Jenny was about to explode with the excitement of her new purchases. Her new life. And she had no one to share it with. No one, that is, except for her old, now discarded, old-fashioned, prudish friend of her school days.

Virginia was tempted to turn around on the spot and go home.

She quickly pushed aside her disappointment and anger. In her own way, Jenny did need her. Maybe when Jenny got to her college, she would forget that they had ever been friends. That Virginia Simpson even existed. But Virginia had no intention of forgetting Jenny. She would pray for her every day.

———

Jenny even allowed a quick hug. Virginia was surprised at her brief moment of clinging. "Good-bye, Virginia. Thanks for standing by me all these years," she whispered to Virginia's unbelieving ears. "I'm sorry you can't go to college. Really."

There was no use for her to ask Jenny to write. Jenny had already made it quite clear that she expected to have no time for writing letters. "Take care," Virginia said instead. "I'll miss you. And I'll pray for you."

Jenny withdrew from the embrace and gave Virginia a half-teasing, half-reproachful look. "Don't waste your prayers, Virginia. I don't plan to spend my time in the local pews."

And then she was gone in a flash of green skirt and bright red hair.

Virginia found herself crying. She wasn't sure why. Was it because Jenny was leaving? Because she, herself, was not? Or because Jenny had, with such firmness and finality, dismissed any interest in the faith she had tried to share for so many years? Maybe it was all those things.

Virginia turned away, wiping her eyes on the hankie she pulled from her pocket.

"Virginia."

The call of her name spun her back around. She could not trust her ears, but it had sounded so much like Jamison.

And there he was. Standing on the platform, his arms held out to her. Dumbstruck, she could not move. Just stood and stared, fresh tears spilling unheeded down her cheeks.

He moved quickly toward her, speaking her name again.

"How did you know I was coming?" he asked. "I wanted it to be a surprise."

It really was Jamison. Virginia blinked and gave her head a quick shake to clear away the confusion. "I . . . I didn't. I never thought—I mean, classes start in a few days. I never—"

"Then what are you doing here?"

"I came to see Jenny off. She just left for college. On this train."

She still had not moved. Her feet seemed bolted to the wooden platform.

He reached for her and looked deep into her eyes. "If we weren't out in public I'd . . ."

Virginia smiled through her tears but shook her head. Half of the town population seemed to hang around the railroad station. There would be no kiss in public. But she did move into his embrace for a warm hug.

"Why are you home?" she asked when she could speak.

He leaned back and looked at her. "Do you really need to ask? I just got a letter from my girl that she won't be joining me. I've waited all summer for you to come, and now . . . Well, I decided to take a few days and come home before classes start. I had to see you. I get really lonesome, my Virginia."

Virginia closed her eyes and leaned against him. She felt his hand on her hair. "I get lonesome, too" was all she was able to say.

CHAPTER 7

Virginia and Jamison sat on the Simpsons' back porch trying to catch up on all of the details of the summer that had not been shared through letters.

"I feel really good about our chances for the championship this year," Jamison was saying. "A number of the fellows stayed close enough so we could keep on playing. 'Course there were those who had to go home for jobs, but those of us who could get jobs in the city spent almost every night practicing. A couple on defense had shift jobs, so they couldn't always join us, but we got in a lot of practice time anyway. Even came up with a few plays we think will impress our coach. Can't wait to show him."

Virginia smiled. She still couldn't believe that he was actually home, beside her on her own porch swing.

"You'll do well, I just know you will," she assured him.

He squeezed the small hand he was holding.

"You know," he said. "I really could've used you in the stands. Your confidence would be a real boost."

"I'll be cheering you on from here," she promised. "Honest."

He slipped his arm around her shoulders. "Well, that isn't what I would have preferred, but I guess it will have to do."

"How is your church group? Any interesting discussions lately?"

He hesitated for a moment. "Well, I've missed a few Sundays because of work and practice and all, but . . . yeah. We've had some real interesting discussions. Wild debates at times."

Virginia waited for him to go on.

"What do you think it means to be without sin?" he asked finally.

"Sinless?"

"Yeah. Sinless. Like in First John Three. 'Whosoever is born of God doth not commit sin,' and all those other verses. That kind of thing. How would you interpret that?"

"I don't know. I've never thought much about it. What possible ways can you interpret it—except just as it is? Without sin."

"And how can a human be without sin? What is sin? What would you put on the list?"

Virginia shrugged. She was no theologian. "Well," she began somewhat tentatively, "disobedience. I'd say that if you went against something that Scripture says—that God has commanded—you'd be sinning. Like lying, cheating, murdering—all those things."

"That's what I've always thought."

"So . . ." Virginia pressed, "does someone else think it means something different?"

He shifted slightly. "Yeah. Well, sort of. Several people. We had quite a discussion about it."

Virginia turned to him. "How can they argue about that?"

"Some said that those actions are not wrong if they don't hurt someone else."

"But sin always hurts someone else," Virginia reasoned.

"Not always. Say, for instance, I lie. Not to cover up anything or put down someone else—just lie."

"Why would anyone do that?"

"I don't know. I was just using a 'for instance.' " He stood and walked to the edge of the porch and stared out over the yard.

Virginia shrugged again. "Okay," she agreed. "So . . ."

"So some people think," he said, turning to look at her, "that as long as you don't directly hurt someone with the lie, it's not wrong."

"Directly?"

"Yeah."

"How directly?"

"I don't know. It's just an example."

"I'm not trying to be difficult," Virginia said. "It's just that I don't see why anyone would lie if it didn't either protect or advance him in some way. And if it does, it's false. Wrong."

"But what if you lie to protect someone else?"

This was getting tougher. Virginia thought for a moment.

"It would still be wrong," she concluded.

"That's what I've always thought," agreed Jamison.

"And others don't think so—in your group, I mean?"

"Some of them say that there's nothing wrong unless it was intended to hurt someone else. Build your own case, or something. They feel that way about cheating, too."

"Cheating?"

"Yeah—on papers and tests and things. They say as long as it doesn't hurt the other guy, it's not sin."

"But it does hurt the other guy. He has to compete against you for grades. If his grades are deserved, and yours aren't, he has had an unfair disadvantage."

"But they argue that he has the freedom to cheat, as well, and if he doesn't do it, then it's his own choice."

Virginia stared at Jamison in bewilderment. "And these people are in your church group?" she asked incredulously.

He nodded and then was silent for many minutes. Virginia wondered if her comment might have offended him. She was about to try to make amends when he spoke again.

"They really have dived in, so to speak. They discuss lots of things."

"Like?"

"Like whether God really did create the world, and was it the way it's presented in the Genesis account?" Jamison rejoined her on the porch swing. "Is Jesus really God, a created being, a special prophet, or just a good man? Is it possible to have a triune God—three persons in one? After all, the Bible does not use the word *Trinity*. Is there a real heaven somewhere or do we make our own heaven or hell here on earth?"

"But the Bible is clear on all those things," Virginia argued. "Do they honestly think they can pick and choose what to believe?"

"We all have free choice, Virginia."

It was a sobering thought, but it was true. Jenny certainly had, to date, made her own choices.

"Does this disturb you?" he went on after a moment of silence.

"Well . . . yes . . . I guess it does. I mean, it wouldn't disturb me so much if this was . . . was just fellows talking in the dormitory. But a Christian church group. How can they call themselves Christians and not have settled those issues? I guess I just don't understand it."

"I reacted the same way at first."

"And now?"

He was slow in answering. "Now I think . . . I don't know. We do have to be open to other points of view. We have to be willing to explore other possibilities. Discuss things. If we don't know what our faith is all about, how can we ever be sure of what we believe?"

It sounded reasonable.

"Have these discussions ever . . . ever helped anyone in your group to understand more clearly? Be strengthened in their faith? Have doubters been encouraged to . . . to embrace the faith?"

"You mean—conversions?"

"Conversion? Commitment? Have the discussions helped anyone to know who God is and what He expects of us as His followers? Have the standards for Christian living been raised—or lowered?"

He did not answer her questions. He tightened his arm about her and whispered against her hair, "I sure wish you were there with me, Virginia."

———

The visit passed far too quickly for Virginia. Long before she was ready, she was walking to the train for another good-bye. This time her companion did not chatter all the way to the station. They were both strangely quiet. Maybe they had already said everything that was on their hearts. Maybe they were afraid to speak for fear their words might expose feelings too painful to share at this time.

"I plan to come home for Christmas," Jamison said as they rounded the corner of the last block.

She nodded, tears threatening to come. Christmas seemed like such a long way off. Why, little Anthony would be six months old by then.

They mounted the platform, and he set down his single suitcase. The wind tossed her hair about her face, and she reached up to push it aside so she wouldn't miss a second of their last few moments together. In the distance she heard the long, low whistle of the train. It seemed to echo the mourning in her heart.

Jamison's few days at home had meant enjoying ecstasy and enduring agony. It had been so good—so unexpected—to have him home for this time. Yet it had also cruelly reminded her of just how much she missed him, what she had given up in not joining him at college, and what a long time it would be until they were together again.

And she was worried. She couldn't put her finger on it, but there was something different—something deep inside that troubled her. He had changed. Subtly. She had been forced to accept that he would change. Had she? Was she still in step? But what troubled her most was that she couldn't define the changes. They were there, and she didn't know where they were or what they were or how it would eventually affect them. She clung more tightly to his hand.

The train, bearing down upon them now, meant that their final seconds together were closing in on them.

She realized that she had to speak. It was hard to make him hear the words with the train hissing and grinding as it came to a halt beside them. She stood on tiptoe to be nearer to his ear. "Jamison," she called above the noise. "I've been wondering. Do you think maybe you should find another church?"

He had heard her and he seemed not to take offense. His arm around her shoulder drew her closer. "I've tried," he shouted back. "I haven't found one—at least one close to the college."

With a tightness in her chest, Virginia leaned toward him. She did not even object when he pulled her to him and kissed her in front of half the town.

―――――

Virginia was not sure if Jamison's time at home had made her days easier or more difficult. It seemed that she had to find the rhythm of living all over again. She felt out of step, agitated, unsure of just where and how she fit.

Baby Anthony proved to be her one source of solace. No one could fault a person for hugging a baby. Whenever she felt particularly lonely or distressed, she found excuses to pick up the little one and hold him close.

On some days she was encouraged to see that Clara was gaining some strength. On other days she despaired over Clara's continued frailty. It was all so frustrating.

Autumn slid into winter, and the leaves stopped tumbling. Empty tree arms waved in winter winds and then were blanketed with snow as Christmas neared. Jamison kept her informed about his football season, though because of his busyness, he did not find time to write as often as he had in the past.

But his team did win the championship. Virginia was so proud of him. She could hardly wait for Christmas, when he would be home, so she could properly tell him so.

But then a letter arrived. Jamison would not be home for Christmas. The coach wanted him to stay and work with some freshman players. He would be paid for his time. It was too good an opportunity to miss. Virginia was devastated, but she wrote back quickly telling him that she understood.

"I hope Clara is much better so that you can come second term," his letter also said. But Clara was not better. Not that much better. She was able to be up for a portion of each day now. Could sit in a chair and nurse her growing baby. But she certainly wasn't ready to return to her own home and assume the responsibility of wife and mother. Virginia knew that she wouldn't be joining Jamison anytime soon. She sadly wrote to tell him so.

By the time the holidays were over, Clara could be up for hours at a time. At the end of January there was more color in her cheeks and further strength in her body. February ended.

Clara could sweep a floor. Get a meal. She still needed to rest off and on throughout the day, but everyone was encouraged with her progress.

The traditional March winds came in gale force. Virginia had looked forward to getting out, taking Anthony for walks in the carriage. Maybe even getting Clara outside for some fresh air. But the wind prevented that.

Anthony, nine months old now, was a happy, energetic baby who felt entitled to the full attention of everyone in the household. With six people to care for his needs—and most of his wants—he had no reason to be out of sorts. He was now pulling himself up to stand on his own feet and thinking about the possibility of advancing from creeping to walking. Virginia fleetingly wondered why he would even bother as she rescued him from another exploration of the kitchen cupboards. It seemed he already got everywhere he wanted to be, in short order.

Rodney was having a good junior year at university. He still had glowing reports about his church group. In fact, one name from the group seemed to be cropping up in his letters fairly often. Grace Featherstone. Virginia noted that every time he wrote about any church activity, Grace was included in his description of the event. So far Rodney claimed no special relationship with the young lady, but those at home smiled whenever they read her name.

Jamison's sporadic letters did not include references to what his church group had recently been discussing. Virginia wondered if he feared her displeasure or if he had been missing church. In her own heart she wasn't sure which was preferable. She feared that Jamison's new church group might be doing more to destroy his faith than to build it. But not to go to church at all—that seemed destructive, as well.

April's showers and the resulting flowers brought smiles of pleasure to the whole family. Clara could be up for most of the day now, and she was talking more frequently about getting back to her own home. Virginia was glad for her sister's return to a more normal life, but she dreaded the thought of losing little Anthony. He was daily lengthening his journeys on those short, uncertain legs.

In May they all agreed that Clara was well enough to be on her own. With great care, she was moved back to the little house on the edge of town. Belinda insisted on continuing to prepare the evening meal, which was delivered by one or another of the Simpsons. Virginia went over twice a week to help with the cleaning and the laundry. Things seemed to be getting back to what they should be.

There never was a proper diagnosis for Clara's strange malady. It troubled Doctor Luke and worried Clara in spite of her efforts to put it in the past. Virginia knew she wanted more children and was fearful that the debilitating situation might be repeated.

Jenny actually had written a couple of letters over the winter months. Even that much correspondence surprised Virginia. Jenny's breezy notes were full of trips and weekend parties and new experiences that Virginia could in no way understand. Her heart ached for Jenny. It sounded as though the girl had chosen the wrong friends and taken a foolish path.

Virginia stopped in to the newspaper office to ask Jenny's father when her friend would be home, and he just shook his head.

"She won't be home," he said gruffly. "Says she's gonna get a job."

Virginia should not have been surprised at that, but the news disturbed her.

"She might as well have stayed home in the first place," the father went on with a scowl. "Flunked most of her courses."

"Jenny?" Virginia could hardly believe it. Jenny had been

a good student when she'd made up her mind to be. She certainly was bright enough.

"Been doing nothin' but partying. Well, it's her life. But I've told her I'll only pay for one more year. If she doesn't settle down and get some good grades, I'm through. She can make her own way in the world."

He turned back to his presses, and Virginia knew she was dismissed. She walked home feeling dejected. Jenny's class failures had not been good news. Besides, Virginia had been counting on her being home for the summer. In spite of Virginia's frustration and discouragement over Jenny's attitudes, the two girls had many years of friendship and experiences between them. Virginia truly cared for her wayward friend.

———

When Rodney came home, Virginia noticed more changes in him than she had the year before. But they were not differences she didn't like. He seemed much more mature. More thoughtful of others. More concerned about his faith and God's plan for his life. And there were those occasional references to Grace.

Virginia concluded that Rodney was growing up and that their days of having him living at home, sharing the household, might indeed be drawing to a close. She didn't much like that idea. It had been hard enough when Clara got married and left the Simpson household. They had at least kept her in their small town. Virginia had the impression that when Rodney left, God's plan, when discovered, might lead him on an entirely different path. She felt a knot in her stomach when she thought of the future. Things were changing too much. Too fast.

Even young Danny was quickly approaching high school graduation and was making plans to be off to college in the fall to study veterinary medicine. Danny seemed so much younger than Rodney had been when he went off to start college. But then, Rodney and Jamison had both decided to work a year before leaving for school. Danny was planning to plunge right in. So when Virginia also went to college in the fall, there would just be Francine left at home. As excited as Virginia was about her own future at college, the thought was staggering. Such a short time ago there had been seven of them around the supper table. In a few short months there might be only three.

Her world was changing far too rapidly. But there didn't seem to be much she could do about it.

————

When Jamison wrote that he would not be coming home for the summer, Virginia had expected it. He was going to stay and take up the job he'd had the summer before.

"But I do hope to get home for a weekend before I start," his letter assured her. "I really do need to have a talk with you. I don't want to put it in a letter."

Put what in a letter? Surely he was not going to propose marriage when they both had schooling still ahead of them. Though the idea was not unwelcome, that kind of start to married life would be very unwise. She was sure both sets of parents would object. No, she really didn't think Jamison could be thinking of that.

Was it about his church then? Had he found a new one as she had suggested? No, he would have felt free to tell her about that in a letter. He knew she would be happy for him.

Surely he hadn't discarded his faith. Surely not. Jamison was much too devout and settled to do a thing like that.

Was it about football? Had he changed his mind about being professional? Or had he been told that he'd never make it? Had there been an injury he had not explained that would stop him from his dream?

Virginia fretted about Jamison's letter. She felt that

something was wrong. Something was troubling him. It could not be good news, or he would have poured it out on the paper, unable to wait to share it with her.

It caused a strange ripple of fear that tightened her stomach and made her heart beat more rapidly.

But there was nothing she could do but wait.

CHAPTER 8

Rodney arrived home and took a summer job with his brother-in-law, Troy, in the Dunworthy family store. Troy's father had decided to take the summer off. He and his wife would make the long-desired trip back to England to visit her family. That left Troy needing help to run the business. Rodney was pleased with the arrangement. He could start working immediately and could put in as many hours as he desired. He plunged right in, stocking shelves, doing clean-up chores, and waiting on customers. Soon Troy was appreciating some free time at home with Clara and little Anthony. Rodney seemed to be a natural in running the place, and the store did not suffer with Troy's absence. Rodney even kept the accounts and balanced the monthly statements, a chore that Troy detested. He began to joke that he had no intention of letting Rodney get away for school again.

Danny's summer job was with a local farmer, and his days were spent driving a team of horses, first planting and then haying. They began at five each morning with the choring and milking, and ended that way after a long, tiring day. Danny didn't mind the long hours or hard work. He was earning money for college, and as long as he could be handling animals he was quite happy.

For Virginia, it felt like a lazy summer after the extra responsibility and time helping Clara. At first it was strange to have no baby in the house. No invalid sister. But they all seemed to quickly adjust. Virginia learned to enjoy the lovely warm days and moments by her beloved creek without the pressure to keep up on all the chores for two households.

She still made frequent trips to Clara's, but her sister was feeling fine now and was quite specific in her desire to be keeping her own house and looking after her own "two men." So Virginia's little jaunts over to Clara's became social visits with her sister and Anthony rather than to take over household tasks.

She did put in a few hours each week in her father's law office, keeping accounts and filing. But she still found time for sewing and needlework that she tucked away in the cedar chest she had received for her seventeenth birthday. Danny teased her about her growing collection in the hope chest, but Virginia just smiled, tossed her head, and enjoyed the ribbing. After all, Jamison would not be attending college forever, and even the wife of a professional football player needed housekeeping items.

So the summer months blurred one into the other. Life seemed to rather drone on, neither particularly difficult nor exciting. Belinda remarked that people needed such times. It gave them opportunity to regroup. If simple routine continued for too long, it would certainly become a rut, but it seemed to agree with them after the months that had preceded it.

The weather, too, suited the ordinary atmosphere. Neither extremely hot nor cold. Not rainy nor arid. Just—natural. Days mixed with rain and sunshine, periods of clear skies and cloud. Times of wind and times of calm. Like life itself.

Little Anthony continued to grow in personality and size,

becoming not just a member of the family but the hub of their entertainment. Virginia wondered how they had imagined they were really living before his coming. His first steps excited them. His first words delighted them. They laughed and frolicked and coaxed and encouraged. And shared every new discovery that he made with one another, repeating every little anecdote to anyone willing to listen.

Mr. Adamson seemed to take special delight in the small boy, so Virginia made sure she took him to the fence for frequent visits. Anthony was even invited into the yard and allowed to collect bouquets for his mother or grandmother. He squealed with delight, holding the tender stems in tightened baby fists, anxious to get home with his treasure.

———

"I feel like . . . like a bumblebee," Virginia remarked to her mother one day as they sat on the front porch doing needle-work together.

"A bumblebee?"

"Fat and lazy. Like that one over there." She pointed with her needle to a nearby flowering bush.

"Bumblebees are far from lazy," Belinda responded with a chuckle.

"Well, they look lazy."

It was true. The one in question did seem to take its own sweet time, testing out each blossom, hanging midair or drop-ping for a sip from this, a drink from that. Or just crawling in and out of the large blooms, in no hurry to go anywhere at all.

Belinda laughed again. "I'd hate to put in the miles that bumblebee does in a day."

Virginia shrugged. "Well, it is so different not having to race through the day and still not be able to keep up with all that needs to be done. I mean, look at us. We've just washed up the supper dishes and here we sit. We have the whole evening to do nothing except what we feel like doing. It's so different."

Belinda nodded her agreement. "I like to think that this is the normal way to live. Not the other," she responded.

Virginia considered that idea for a few moments. "You know, it might be fine—for a while. But I think it might get boring."

"Don't borrow trouble," her mother cautioned.

Virginia stood and stretched. "Trouble I can do without, but a little excitement wouldn't hurt."

"Frankly, I'm enjoying the change of pace. But it is rather dull at times for you, isn't it? Rodney and Danny off working all hours. Jenny gone. Jamison . . ."

"I think I'll go write to Jamison. I've no idea what I'll tell him. Nothing has happened since . . . since the Pickerly's pig got loose and rooted up Mrs. Tingle's garden."

Belinda laughed. "That was two weeks ago."

"That's my point."

Belinda laughed again. "I'm sure your summer would be much different if Jamison were here."

Virginia did not comment. She was sure that was correct. But Jamison was not here. He still hadn't come, even after his letter had stated that he planned to be home to discuss something personally. Whenever Virginia thought about that planned discussion, her stomach tightened. Jamison had not referred to it again, but she had the feeling that it was still there. Still needing to be addressed—whatever it was. Jamison's subsequent letters seemed different somehow. Rather—stiff and stilted. But maybe she was imagining it. Perhaps it was just that he was so very busy. Virginia was only too happy to mark it down to that.

———

A mid-August knock on the front door, and Virginia found Jamison standing on the porch. With a glad squeal she flung herself into his arms, and he held her close for a long time.

It was Virginia who pulled away, needing to see his face. His smile was a little crooked, maybe a little uncertain?

"When did you get home?" she asked, for something safe to start with.

"About twenty minutes ago."

"You didn't tell me—"

"I wasn't sure I would make it."

She gathered her emotions—surprise, joy, a little fear—and reached for his hand. "Come in. Everyone will be so—"

"No, I'd rather not. Can we take a walk—or something?"

Virginia felt momentary bewilderment. Jamison always came in to greet the family—even if he was anxious to see her alone.

"Sure," she nodded. "I'll . . . I'll just tell my folks I'll be out for a while."

Jamison nodded and stepped back from the door to wait.

When Virginia joined him, he was silently gazing off into the distance, his hands stuffed in his pockets. When he saw her, he gave a quick smile and reached for her hand.

"Where do you want to go?" she asked.

"How about the creek?"

She nodded and fell into step beside him. It seemed that Jamison intended a rather lengthy stroll.

They walked quietly until they reached the last street of the town. Virginia could stand the silence no longer. "How is football going?"

"We haven't been doing as much this summer. I don't know. It's hard to get the fellows motivated. Guess winning the championship last year sort of took away their drive or something. Not many of them even stayed around."

Virginia could tell that it had disappointed him. Jamison was keen on more than one championship.

Silence again.

"How's work?"

"It's going okay. Pretty routine."

More silence. They were almost to the creek. As they walked through the neighboring woods, they could hear its soft murmur as the water gently slid over the rocks and fallen trees. At this time of year the creek was anything but a torrent.

"How's your summer been?" Jamison asked.

Virginia looked up into his face. Here was someone to whom she could express her innermost feelings. Here was someone who would understand.

"At first it was wonderful. It was so good to not have to be on the run all the time. To actually be able to slow down and take a breath. But after a few weeks of that I—well—I'm bored. Quite simply, restless and rather weary of the sameness. Mama and I get the work done and then just sit and sew. Oh . . . we drive out to Grandpa's now and then and have tea with Grandma, or I go over to Clara's and play with Anthony. But it's . . . it's rather dull. I mean, most of our friends are off somewhere . . . or working. I'm just putting in time."

He gave her hand an understanding squeeze.

"Maybe you should get a job."

"I work a few hours a week for my father. It's not the most exciting job in the world. Adding numbers and shuffling papers into proper files." She shrugged.

He chuckled. "Sounds like you have the malady of youth."

"Malady of youth?"

"That's what my ma calls it. Says every young person goes through a time when life just isn't exciting enough—no matter what happens. She calls it Malady of Youth. Says it's a disease we all outgrow—in time."

"So have you outgrown it?" Virginia asked teasingly.

He stopped, bringing her to a halt beside him. "I don't know," he said and his voice was low, haunted.

It frightened her for some reason she did not understand. She looked up at him. His face matched his voice. Strained—yet empty.

"Let's sit down." He led her to the fallen tree that had provided them with a seat for talks in the past. Happy talks. Exciting talks. Talks that laid out plans for the future and dreams to be shared.

Virginia wished to ask what was wrong, what was troubling him, but she was afraid. Afraid to even express her concern.

He sat beside her—yet a little distance away—running a hand through his thick dark hair, looking pained and troubled. She reached for his hand again, and he held hers tightly, seemingly to try to find the will to express what was on his mind or the right words with which to say it.

"So much has happened this past year, Virginia," he began. He licked his lips, looked at her briefly and then off into the distance.

She waited, her hand tightening until she felt her fingers ache.

He began again, but he did not look at her. Instead he gazed out in the distance. Not at the creek, not at the trees, but beyond—beyond to nothing. Or to something else, something unseen.

"I don't know, Virginia. I've been so . . . confused. Everything used to be so . . . so clear. So plain to me. So planned out and right. Now everything seems blurred."

She didn't understand his words. Hoped that he would go on to explain them. She wanted to know what he was thinking and feeling.

He glanced at her briefly, then turned back to that unseen world out there. "When I first went to college, I had my plans

all made. I was going into business. Accounting. I started playing football because . . . because I like sports, and I thought I
needed a little exercise—a little relief from studies."

He hesitated again.

"I didn't know I was good," he said quite simply. "I had no
idea I could make the team. And certainly not as quarterback,
but the coach—he saw 'potential,' so he started spending time
working with me in the evenings and on weekends. . . ." He
shrugged. "The rest is history, as they say."

Virginia gave his hand a little squeeze to let him know that
she was proud of him.

"Well, I hadn't planned for football to take over my life.
I—under the coach's urging—changed my major. Picked up
easy classes so I wouldn't have to spend as much time studying. Sort of just . . . skimmed by. Chalked up a lot of credits
that don't amount to much."

His free hand began to work through his hair again.

"You don't like football anymore?" Virginia finally dared
to voice the question.

"I love football," he was quick to respond.

"Then what's the problem?" She asked the question before
she had thought it through. Was Jamison telling her that he
was not good enough to make a professional team? Was he
depressed because he now had neither a business career nor a
football career ahead of him?

"Isn't it working out?" she timidly asked.

He looked at her then, his head shaking a negative response,
but when he spoke, his words surprised her.

"I think I can make it. I honestly do. Coach is sure I
can."

"Then . . . ?"

"I'm not sure that is what I want. You've no idea of the
pressure. The control of others over your life. You don't feel
like a person anymore—just a machine. One that the coach

screams at and the fans cheer on. Girls flock all around, wanting autographs, flirting, making eyes. Other guys your age envy you and call you names. Teasing, sure. But they don't treat you like a friend. Not a real friend."

Virginia had no idea. She reached her other hand to enfold Jamison's big one. For the first time she realized how large Jamison's hand was compared to her own. No wonder he could handle the football with such skill.

"Doesn't your church . . . ?" she began.

"I'm not going to church," Jamison said abruptly.

His words and the tone of his voice shocked Virginia.

"We have a lot of Sunday games and practices," he explained. "And—quite frankly—I was scared. I mean, that church—not a church really, it was a debate gathering—well, it shook me. I was getting to the place where I was questioning everything I had believed. I didn't know where I was at anymore. I had to get out of there."

"But couldn't you find another one?"

"I tried. There was none that I could get to—not with my hours."

"So you don't go anywhere?"

He shook his head.

How can Jamison ever manage without a good, solid church? her heart cried.

"And the classes," Jamison said, shaking his head. "The professors—I don't think there's one in the lot who has any kind of faith. And they keep . . . just keep on hammering at it. Evolution. Existence by chance. Religion is a crutch of the weak. That sort of thing. They laugh at what they call myths of Christianity." He rubbed a hand through his hair. "It just goes on and on."

Virginia had not realized how awful it must be for the Christian students. No wonder Jamison was confused. She did not know what to say to be of help to him. She switched back to football.

"I . . . I certainly don't know how to advise," she began, "but if you are unsure about football, then . . . then maybe you should give it up. Go back to your other major. Accounting. You were always good in mathematics. Play your sports as a pastime. For fun. There are always ways to be involved. In any community. Even as an accountant. You love working with numbers. Switch back."

"I'd have to start all over again." He sounded so dejected. "It would mean two years of college—wasted. I don't know where the money would come from."

"But you must have some credits?"

"Filler. Junk stuff."

His words jarred Virginia.

"But didn't your college—the counselor advise . . . ?"

"He wanted a winning team, too. They all did."

"You mean they were willing to . . . sell you out for . . . a winner?"

"I wouldn't be that condemning. Sure, they wanted a winner. But I think they considered being a professional player would be an advantage to me, as well."

"But you don't like it?"

"I don't like it. It's taken all the fun from the game."

They sat in silence, their faces reflecting their troubled thoughts.

"Oh, I admit it has its advantages," Jamison finally said. "At first it rather went to my head, I think. I mean, here's everyone on campus noticing the big guy. The quarterback. The winner. Guys slap you on the back and want to buy you drinks. Oh, don't look so shocked. I haven't started drinking."

Virginia's horror changed to relief.

"Girls hover around and let you know they would be free on Saturday night. Hero stuff. As long as you are a winner. But it's all so false. It soon gets old. And empty. I wasn't raised to wallow in that kind of stuff, Virginia."

She nodded. It was true. Jamison's small-town background did not lend itself to celebrity status.

"Have you talked to your folks?" she asked.

"I wanted to talk with you first."

She tightened her grip on his hand again. She was pleased, but she also felt so helpless. She had no idea how to advise him.

"I think we need to talk to them," she said. "And to my folks, too."

"My folks will be so disappointed," he admitted. "They encouraged me to be an accountant, and I threw that away. Now if I throw away a football career, too . . ."

"There's a way out of this," Virginia assured him, trying to make her voice light and promising. "You're young. You can start again."

"Yeah" was all he said, but he didn't sound convinced.

He reached for a pebble at his feet and, with a quick flick of his wrist, sent it skimming across the creek. It pinged when it hit another rock on the other side.

The woods were already becoming shaded. Virginia stood up. The summer sun was leaving to light another part of the universe. *Always on duty, the sun*, she mused distractedly. *Moving from one needy area to another. Shining the light. Warming the earth. Supplying crops. Sustaining life.*

God is like that, Virginia concluded. *He's always on duty. Moving from one need to another. Always there—for everyone. He'll get us through this. He has a way.*

She reached out a hand to Jamison to pull him to his feet, but he did not respond. So she lowered herself to the ground beside him. She even tried a smile.

"Don't worry," she encouraged, maybe for herself as much as Jamison. "We'll get through this—somehow. Mark it down to a learning experience. Someday we might even see good come from it.

"For now, it'll be different once I am at college with you. We'll find a good church. There must be one somewhere. And if you decide to go back into accounting, we'll work it out. I could even get a job and—"

"That's the hardest part, Virginia." He looked up at her, and his eyes looked so filled with pain they frightened her. "I . . . I don't think that I am ready for . . . those kinds of plans. Any kind of plans with you now."

CHAPTER 9

"What do you mean?" Virginia's bewilderment made her voice shaky. "We already have plans. We've had since—"

"I mean, not anymore."

"I don't understand. What are you saying?"

"You and I. Our plans for our future. The future has changed. . . ."

"But that's all right. It doesn't bother me. I—"

"It bothers me."

Virginia stood up, the world spinning about her. "Just what are you saying, Jamison? I don't—I'm afraid I don't understand. When you left for college we . . ."

He stood then, his face drained of color, his eyes still shadowed with pain.

"When I left for college . . ." He dropped his head, then lifted it to begin again. "When I left for college, we were both kids. Our worlds have changed, Virginia. We've changed."

"I haven't changed," she argued quickly.

He lowered his head. "Maybe you're right. Maybe that's part of the problem. I don't know. I'm so confused. . . ."

Virginia stepped forward and laid a hand on his arm. "Look, Jamison. Everything is all topsy-turvy for you right now. I can

103

understand that. But you'll get it sorted out. I know you will. I can wait. I'll help you. Honest. When the fall term starts we can . . ."

"I don't think you understand," Jamison said, brushing her hand gently aside. "It's not 'we' anymore, Virginia."

The words finally struck home. Virginia began to understand just what Jamison was trying to tell her. She stepped back, her face white, her body beginning to tremble.

"You mean, you don't want to . . . to be a couple anymore."

Jamison worked at swallowing. He managed only a nod.

"Why?" Virginia's demand for an answer came out in only a whisper. "What have I done?"

"No, it's not like that," he was quick to say, and then he stepped forward to place a hand on her arm. "You've done nothing. I still respect . . . and . . . and love you, Virginia. Believe me. It's just that with . . . with everything that is happening in my life, I don't . . . don't feel like the same person anymore. We don't . . . don't fit like we used to. Can't you see it? Don't you feel it? We're not . . . connecting."

"No," said Virginia, shaking her head. "No, I don't feel it. I . . . I still care, Jamison."

"I care, too," he answered, his voice low and muffled.

"Then what is the matter?"

He turned from her.

"Is there someone else?" Virginia addressed the question to his back.

He whirled around. "No. There is no one else. Don't you think I would have told you if there had been? No."

"Then why?"

He took her by both arms and pulled her closer to him, looking deeply into her eyes. "I wish I could make you understand," he said. "This is not . . . not my choice. Not how I had planned this to be. My whole life is . . . is out of control right now. I've got to step back, sort it out, find out who I am again."

"Then . . . then once you get it figured out, we'll be—"

"No." He spoke very softly now and looked pleadingly into her eyes. "I know, deep inside, that when I get this sorted out, I'll be an even more different person than I am right now. I'm not sure yet just who I'll be, but it won't be the little schoolboy from Hugh Carson High, Virginia. I know that. Please. Please try to understand. This wasn't my intention. My desire. I would have done anything to keep from hurting you. Anything but lie to you. I don't feel the same way anymore, Virginia, and I can't let you go on thinking that I do."

Virginia could no longer deny the truth she was hearing. Jamison, her beloved Jamison, was stepping out of her life. Pushing her away. She lowered her head so he couldn't see her eyes and the tears that were spilling down her cheeks. He drew her close and held her. She could feel his own tears wetting her forehead where his cheek rested. He was weeping, too.

Why? her heart kept crying. *Why has this happened? What has made us grow apart? Would things have been different if I'd been able to go to college as planned? Yes. Of course. That's it. Things would have worked out if I had been there with him.*

But would they? Could she really have kept Jamison from the exposure to life in the bigger world? The making of tough decisions? The calling to account?

No. Likely not. It was true. They had changed. Jamison much more than she. They were not in step anymore. Jamison had moved on to a new life. A new world. Whether he became an accountant or a football star, he would never be the same again. There was no way she could hold him back. Make him return to being that hometown boy she had learned to love.

But she would always love him.

That realization brought a fresh burst of tears. He let her

cry, and when the worst of it had passed, he lifted her chin and forced her to look up.

"Virginia," he said through tear-filled eyes, "I never wanted to hurt you. Believe me. This has been the most difficult thing I have ever done in my life. I have loved you, Virginia. Still do, but in a different way. Maybe always will. You've been the best thing that has ever happened to me. But I know—just know that all those plans—those dreams—they wouldn't work out now. Not for us."

With his thumbs he wiped the trail of tears on her cheeks, then continued, "I want us to be friends, Virginia. I would be so . . . so saddened—would lose so much—if that is taken from me. I need you, Virginia—as a friend."

Virginia reached up to brush aside his hands from her face. Her back stiffened and her head lifted. She couldn't find the words to express her hurt. Her anger. Maybe there were none. She just looked at him. Straight and steady. Then she shook her head and turned and fled.

————

Virginia did not know at what hour she stopped weeping and fell into a troubled sleep. She still could not believe it. Did not understand it. Surely . . . surely Jamison would be back to tell her that he had made an awful mistake. That he still loved her. Really loved her. All through the following day she kept one eye on the street, one ear tuned to a knock on the door.

But Jamison did not come.

She was tempted the next morning to plead a headache or an upset stomach, something—anything to excuse herself from the morning church service. She was sure Jamison would be there with his family and knew she could not face him.

But even though her head did ache and her stomach did feel upset, it was not enough to keep her from church. With a great deal of determination, she forced herself to be ready when her folks ushered the family out the door for the trip to join the local congregation.

"Virginia, you look pale," her mother commented. "Are you feeling all right?"

Virginia nodded numbly. She was glad her mother had not overheard her nighttime weeping. There would have been questions, and she did not feel ready to talk about it.

But with Jamison at church, sitting apart and aloof, everyone would soon know their circumstance. Virginia cringed at the very thought. She wondered if she would be able to bear it.

But Jamison was not with his family. Word soon passed that he had already left for college. Something came up that was pressing. Something he needed to tend to. Virginia felt relief at the same time that she felt deep disappointment. He was gone. Really gone. Now her only hope was a letter. A letter saying that he was sorry. He had been all mixed up in his thinking. Virginia promised herself that she would not write until she heard from him. He must be the one to make the first move toward reconciliation.

But day after day passed and no letter came. Virginia kept telling herself, "Maybe today," as she went to the local post office and faced another disappointment. Jamison was not going to write. Night after night her pillow muted her sobs.

———

Rodney and Danny were making preparations for university. Belinda bustled about assembling bedding, checking over clothing items, and ticking off lists. The whole household seemed to pick up speed as the days for their departure neared. Once again, there didn't seem to be quite enough hours in the day.

"Virginia," Belinda exclaimed one morning, looking at her daughter in consternation. "You have been so busy helping with the boys that you've had little time to prepare for your own departure. I appreciate your help, but I think things are under control. You go ahead and work on your own packing," she encouraged as she folded a towel into a case.

Virginia paled. Before her mother could make further comment, she hurried to speak, hoping that her voice was controlled and casual.

"I'm not sure I'm going."

"What?" Her mother's full attention was on her now.

"I've been doing some thinking," Virginia hurried on. "I'm not sure Webster is the place for me. At least not . . . just now."

Belinda looked surprised but answered calmly, "Well, you don't need to choose Webster, dear. I had no idea you were having second thoughts. We could have been making arrangements elsewhere. Have you spoken to your father?"

Virginia shook her head. Her mother knew full well that if she had spoken to her father, he would have passed word on to Belinda.

"So what has . . . ?" Belinda stopped short, looking at her daughter's anguished face. "Has something happened?"

Virginia began to cry, the hot, salty tears running freely down her cheeks. Her mother was there in an instant, holding her close, caressing her hair, pressing a kiss to the top of her head.

"What happened?" she asked when the sobs began to subside.

"I'm not sure," said Virginia, accepting the offered hankie. "Jamison just feels that . . . that we've changed. Grown apart. He's . . . he's so confused about a lot of things."

"Why didn't you say something?"

"I kept hoping—maybe—he'd . . ." The tears started again.

"I'm so sorry," said her mother, running fingers over her hair again.

Virginia blew her nose.

"When?" The question from her mother was short and direct.

"When he came home a couple of weeks ago."

"And you've carried this . . . this burden alone for all that time?"

"I kept hoping . . ."

"Oh, Virginia, I feel so bad for you."

Her mother finally released her, still holding one of her hands. "Come," she said, indicating the nearby sofa. "Sit for a minute and talk to me."

Virginia moved to the sofa, wiping her eyes and blowing her nose.

"So what do you want to do?" was her mother's first inquiry.

"I don't know. I've been thinking about it and praying about it. But I just don't think that I can go to Webster."

Her mother nodded in understanding.

"Do you want to join the boys?"

Virginia thought about that for a moment and then shook her head. "I don't think so. For one thing, I haven't applied. I doubt I would be accepted at such a late date. Besides, the boys might not want a sister there spying on them."

"Nonsense!" exclaimed Belinda with emphasis. "On the contrary, they would likely be having you do their laundry."

Virginia managed a smile.

"I don't think that I . . . that I want to try to get in anywhere this term. I have never really decided what I want to pursue anyway. I had always thought that I would . . ."

But she couldn't finish. The truth was, she had always wanted only one thing. To be Jamison's wife.

"Well, I certainly will be glad to have you here with me," Belinda said, pulling her close and stroking her shoulder. "I was worried about your father and me with this empty nest."

"You still have Francine."

"Yes. I've been thanking God for that. But another plate at the table will be nice, too."

They were silent for some time.

"We will need to speak to your father. He is expecting to have three offspring piling up the college bills this fall."

Virginia pulled away and nodded. She knew her father would need to know her change of plans, but she dreaded telling him.

"Could you? Could you sort of talk to him? Let him know?"

"Of course. But then he'll want to have a chat with you. You know that."

Virginia nodded. At least she would not need to explain the whole thing again.

————

But Virginia found herself explaining—or partially explaining—her change of plans many times in the next few days as other college young people packed bags and bedding and gathered at the local train station for sometimes teary send-offs.

It was the hardest with her own family, for they asked further, more personal questions. And even worse than the questions was the genuine sympathy they offered. Virginia did not want sympathy. It made her feel like a victim. But she did wish for understanding and was glad when they nodded their agreement to the change of her plans.

"What do you plan to do, dear?" her grandmother asked, an arm protectively around Virginia's shoulder.

Virginia shrugged. "I'm not sure," she admitted. "Help Mama. She always has so much to do. Maybe get a job."

"A job? With your father?"

"I don't suppose he's got enough work to keep me busy

more than the few hours a week. I might try something full time."

But even as Virginia spoke the words, she knew she was being optimistic. There were very few jobs in their small town for people like her.

"We'll pray about it," spoke Grandma Marty with a pat on Virginia's shoulder.

———

There was more than one awkward moment. The people of the church, and the little town in general, were so accustomed to thinking of Jamison and Virginia as a pair that they naturally assumed it to still be so. Virginia could not count the times she was asked about Jamison in some cheery voice that expressed interest in his welfare and indicated that they fully expected Virginia to be up on any latest news.

At first she tried to respond in an easy manner. Jamison had been just fine the last they had been in touch. He was extremely busy. Doing well on the football team. In her heart, she still hoped there would be a reconciliation.

But as the days and weeks went by, Virginia began to realize she wasn't being totally honest with others—or with herself.

When the kindly minister smiled as he shook her hand one Sunday and asked, as he often did, "And how is that young man of yours doing?" Virginia could not brush the question aside with a half-truth. Jamison was no longer her young man.

She looked directly at her pastor, and with a calm voice she forced herself to actually say the words, "Jamison and I are no longer corresponding."

He looked startled but quickly recovered. The hand that held Virginia's in a friendly handshake tightened slightly. "I'm sorry," he said.

Virginia could tell from his eyes that he truly was.

———

With Francine back in classes at the local school and the boys away at university, the autumn days seemed to fall into an easy routine. Again Virginia felt boredom. Boredom and a sense of loss that settled over her like a great, smothering blanket.

There were no longer letters from Jamison to look forward to. There were no longer the hours of writing to him, bringing him up-to-date on every ordinary little happening of the small town, or sharing deep feelings and future dreams. Virginia turned her letter-writing attention to her brothers, not expecting too many answers in reply but needing the sense of keeping in touch just the same.

She also wrote to Jenny with regularity. Here again, the answers came sporadically. She didn't really care. At least there were people in the world to whom she was still connected.

She was walking up to post her little bundle of letters late one afternoon when her eyes spotted a sign. "Wanted," she read with great interest. "Someone to train for work in the post office." Virginia could have clicked her heels with excitement. Instead, she walked in and very calmly asked to apply. The very next week she was in training, a little overwhelmed at first, but excited about actually being "on her own"—in some way.

She learned quickly and the job went well. Soon she was enjoying every minute of it. Her dreary days began to have some sort of meaning again. She began to feel that she had weathered her own personal storm. She had her life back in control. She could go on.

Until one day, when sorting the mail into the boxes, her eyes spotted an envelope clearly bearing Jamison's handwriting. Excitement washed all through her. She was about to tear open the envelope when it registered that it was not addressed to her. It was written to his parents.

The tears started again. Virginia was thankful she was not observed and secretly wondered if she would ever really get over the pain of losing her first love. She missed him more than she ever could have expressed.

She pushed the letter roughly into the proper box and hoped Jamison was not in the habit of writing his folks too often.

————

Then Jenny actually wrote back. The tenor of her letter had not changed. She was still in a whirlwind of activities. Taking in sporting events, dances, and far and wide excursions to parties. Virginia wondered how Jenny ever found time to study and then remembered her distraught father's words. Jenny did not study. She felt it interfered with college life.

Her hurried scrawl told only of good times and partying friends. Virginia laid aside the letter, feeling a little sick inside. Jenny seemed to be getting further and further away from any desire for a faith to live by.

————

Jamison did not come home for Christmas. Virginia did not know whether to be relieved or disappointed. On the one hand, she dreaded seeing him again. On the other, she still hoped that another meeting might bring a reconciliation. Even the passing, silent months had not completely buried her hope.

But Jamison's mother stopped her on the church steps and informed her, rather quietly and discreetly, "Jamison has plans to visit a friend over Christmas. He still is confused, I think. He misses your letters, Virginia. He said so quite openly."

Virginia did not know what to say, and his mother moved on. *If he misses them, why doesn't he write?* Virginia asked herself, feeling irritated. *It was his decision to end our relationship. Not mine.*

But for some reason, Virginia could not feel as angry with him as she had in the past. Instead, she found herself worrying about his welfare. Had he found a church? Was he still trying to sort through his confusing life? Did he still pray, asking for God's help in his decisions?

She found Jamison creeping back into her prayers again and realized that it was now much easier to think of him as a friend who needed her support. She wondered if the day would ever come when she would be able to express those feelings to him.

———

A phone call came from Rodney.

"I know this is short notice, but do you think it would be okay if I brought a friend home with me for the Christmas break?"

Belinda assured him that they would be able to accommodate that request. "Who is he?" she followed her agreement.

"She," corrected Rodney.

"She?" There was silence on the other end for a brief time. "Grace?" asked Belinda.

"Yeah. Grace."

Now it was Belinda who fell silent.

"Mama? Are you still there?"

"I'm here."

"Is that a problem?"

"No. No, not at all."

"It's . . . rather important for you to meet her."

"You mean . . . ?"

"We'll talk when we get there. Okay?"

"Of course."

"You're okay with this, Mama?"

"Fine. It just caught me by surprise, that's all. We'll be happy to meet your Grace."

"Good," he sounded relieved. "We'll see you on Friday."

"On Friday."

When Belinda turned from the phone, Virginia saw tears in her eyes. "Something wrong, Mama?"

"No." She stopped to sniff. "Nothing. Rodney is bringing Grace home. I'm not sure, but it sounds like they might have some plans."

"Plans?"

Belinda nodded and reached in her pocket for her hankie.

"We don't even know her," Virginia protested.

"We soon will."

"But . . ."

"I know. I'm not prepared for this, either. You all are growing up far too fast. I'm just not ready to send another one off on his own. Before I know it, it will just be your father and me."

Virginia almost reminded her mother that they might be stuck with her—forever.

CHAPTER 10

$\mathcal{V}$irginia had thought they were ready for Christmas, but after Rodney's call a flurry of activity was initiated by her mother. What had been considered quite in order now needed some extra polishing. Baking that was sufficient for boyish appetites now was set in the back of the pantry while daintier Christmas treats were produced. Virginia heard her father teasing, but that did not deter Belinda. "First impressions are always important," she replied firmly.

"I think her first impression of this family has already been formed," he answered, "and it has nothing whatsoever to do with you or me—or even your cooking."

It was bone-chilling cold the night Rodney's train pulled into town. Belinda fretted a bit about it, but her Christmas preparations could not include the weather.

Danny, who had been nearly forgotten in the course of events, came off the Pullman car grinning widely, though staggering under extra luggage that Virginia was sure had been loaded on him by his older brother.

"Where's Rodney?" Belinda asked as she hugged her younger son. "Nothing happened, did it?"

"He's there," said Danny, jerking his head back toward the train car. "Gathering up her things."

Belinda's eyes anxiously searched the train, as though afraid that it might chug its impatient way into the night before her son and his guest could disembark.

Virginia pulled Danny to the side. "What's she like?" she whispered quickly as she gave her brother an unusually welcoming embrace.

Danny just lifted a shoulder. "She's okay," he answered in an offhand manner.

Their father had stepped forward to greet his son and relieve some of the load he carried. "So how's the future vet?"

Danny grinned. "Lovin' it," he replied.

Virginia smiled and knew they would hear much about Danny's studies over the few days he would be home.

"Where's Rodney?" repeated the impatient Francine, bouncing from one foot to the other to stave off the cold.

"He's coming."

"My word," Virginia joined in. "How much does she have to gather up anyway?"

"Just the usual girl stuff."

"So when did you get to be such an authority on girls?" Virginia couldn't help but ask, surprised at his implied knowledge.

Danny gave her an all-knowing look that turned into another grin. "Don't forget. I grew up with three sisters."

And then Rodney was coming down the steps, his arms filled with parcels, his free hand holding the arm of a young woman.

Virginia strained forward, but the girl's face was shaded by a brimmed hat. She was looking down to watch where she would place her exquisitely shod foot, so Virginia could not yet see her face.

Virginia did notice that she was rather tall—almost as tall

A Searching Heart *

as Rodney—and slim. She carried herself with regal bearing. An elaborately fur-trimmed coat and matching muff spoke of elegance and—yes—money.

"I can't believe it," said Virginia under her breath. "He's gone and fallen for some City Susie."

Her mother must have shared her impression, for Virginia heard her sharp intake of air. Even her father seemed caught off guard. Virginia watched as he reached up and swept off his hat, in spite of the bitterly cold night air.

When the dainty shoe took the final step to the snow-covered platform, the young woman lifted her head and the light from the platform played across her face and her smile. But it looked uncertain. Hesitant. Her eyes were beautiful as they swept quickly over the entire small assembly, wide open and beseeching. Other than those eyes, Virginia thought her face somewhat unremarkable.

She thinks she has fallen in with a bunch of small-town yokels, Virginia thought to herself. *I'm glad Mother did all that last-minute fussing. At least we won't look totally uncivilized. Still, she will likely be wanting the first train out.*

The ride home was a rather quiet one. It seemed no one knew exactly how to start a conversation with their visitor.

Once inside, heavy wraps removed and hung in the front hall closet, a warm fire glowing in the fireplace, and Belinda's offer of hot cider and her special ginger cookies made and accepted, the girl seemed to relax a bit. Virginia saw her give Rodney many little glances and wondered exactly what they were communicating.

"This is wonderful," Virginia heard her whisper. "Just like you said."

Rodney nodded and gave her a warm smile, edging just a bit closer to her.

"Rodney's in love," Francine whispered giddily into Virginia's ear. Virginia gave her a stern look to hush her up.

119

"Grace has a few things to add under the tree," Rodney informed them, and they left together to bring the items from the parcels they had carried from the train.

Gifts? That's what all the parcels were? Oh, dear, worried Virginia. *I wonder if Mama thought to purchase something for her. I certainly didn't.*

"I know you must be tired," Belinda told Grace when the two returned. "It must have been a long day for you. Rodney, you can take Grace's things to Clara's room. Please"—she turned back to the young woman—"please make yourself at home. Sleep as long as you wish tomorrow morning, if you can. I know how exhausting university life can be. Especially exam week."

The girl smiled one of her delightful smiles again. It made her face come alive and illuminated the color of her large blue-green eyes. "I am tired," she admitted. "If you don't mind, I would like to retire early."

Rodney rose to get her luggage and show her her room. He was soon back to join the family before the fire. Drew threw on another log and picked up the long poker to stir up the blaze. Belinda sat down with a cup of cider, a pensive look on her face.

Virginia was so full of questions that she thought she would burst, but she dared not voice any of them.

Francine had no such hesitations. "Is she rich?" she blurted out as soon as Rodney had seated himself beside his mother on the long sofa.

"Francine!" chided Belinda.

But Rodney responded without seeming to take offense. "Grace?"

"Yeah."

"No. Well . . . yeah . . . sort of. I guess. I mean—"

"Tell them about her," Danny prompted.

"Yes, tell us about her," Belinda seconded quickly. "We

know nearly nothing about this girl. I think, perhaps, we could have been a bit more informed if things are as they appear to be."

Rodney flushed slightly. "I've told you about her," he defended himself.

Belinda nodded, but Rodney's expression acknowledged the fact that that wasn't good enough.

"She's from the church I attend," he began.

Belinda nodded again. That much Rodney had disclosed.

"A city girl, obviously," Drew added, though Virginia knew her father's observation did not mean he would hold that against her. "What does her father do?" he asked.

That seemed to be a standard question for one father to ask about another.

"She doesn't have a father."

Several pairs of eyes turned to Rodney, expressing surprise and interest.

"Both her father and mother were killed in an accident when she was four," he hurried to explain.

"She's an orphan?" exclaimed Francine.

Rodney nodded.

"She sure doesn't look like an orphan."

"Orphans aren't always people in rags begging on the street, Francine," Rodney said a bit impatiently.

They waited.

"Her father had been an investor—his family's business. Mostly real estate and lumber, I think. When they were killed, she was left with a maiden aunt as guardian. She has been with her ever since—until a year ago last May. Her aunt Sadie died then, and Grace has been on her own. She decided to go to college. She's taking nursing."

"Nursing?" Belinda's voice conveyed her feelings. Virginia

121

supposed no chosen occupation would have surprised—or pleased—her mother more.

"If she's rich . . . ?" began Francine.

"Please, Francine, let's let Rodney tell us," broke in Belinda. Francine held her tongue.

"She is rich," admitted Rodney. "At least she has potential to be rich. But she doesn't want to live a rich, idle life."

Belinda's satisfied nod reflected Virginia's approval.

"Her aunt was quite strict," went on Rodney. "Real strict. She kept Grace quite confined. Almost like . . . like a monk."

"Girls aren't monks," murmured Francine under her breath. Rodney only glanced her way before continuing.

"She's never had family—that she clearly remembers. She thinks I am so lucky. So blessed." He lowered his gaze and rubbed his hands vigorously together. "And she's right," he went on, raising his face again. "I *am* blessed. I want to share that with her. That's why I brought her home with me."

"So you don't have plans?" asked Belinda hesitantly.

"Oh no," Rodney was quick to say. "I still have to finish school. Grace has two more years. We haven't even talked about . . ."

Virginia could feel her mother's relief as she smiled warmly at her oldest son.

Rodney picked up the conversation again, his face flushing with his confession. "I . . . I really like her a lot, Mama, but we haven't—I haven't . . ." He paused, then closed his mouth. He didn't seem to feel the need to say any more.

"We're glad you brought Grace home," Belinda said for all of them. "We'll make her visit just as pleasant as we can, even though it's quite obvious she is not used to living quite like we do."

"Mama," said Rodney, "she realizes she hasn't been as blessed as we have, but she is more than willing to try to fit in. To learn."

Virginia blinked. She knew that wasn't quite what her mother had meant.

———

Grace did try to fit in, though Virginia was sure it was not easy for her.

By nature Grace was shy, and living with the maiden aunt with her strict disciplines could not have helped her confidence in new situations.

She knew how to do very little around the house and admitted that the first she had ever made her own bed or cleaned her own room was when she moved into the university dormitory. "But I'm rather good at it now," she noted shyly.

But when it came to kitchen duties, she knew nothing. Virginia, who had grown up with an eggbeater or a dish towel in her hand, could not believe that one Grace's age could be so ignorant of simple procedures.

But Grace did want to learn and hovered near Virginia, her big eyes fixed on every move. She was full of questions. *Why do you do that? What is that for? How does this work?* It was like teaching a willing child.

Grace caught on quickly, and Virginia could see that she had a bright and eager mind.

"Why nursing?" Virginia asked as they prepared an evening meal together.

The large eyes opened even wider, then she nodded as though she understood the purpose behind the question.

"I wanted a profession where I could be of help to people," she said, her voice soft but clear. "I've been alone all my life— except for Aunt Sadie."

Yes, I've heard about "Aunt Sadie," Virginia thought to herself. Already she had decided she didn't care much for the elderly dowager.

"And the staff, of course, but Aunt Sadie did not want me

'hobnobbing' with them. I was banned from the kitchen and even the gardens unless supervised."

It must have been dreadful, thought Virginia.

"When I decided to go to university—I was of age and could make my own decisions—I decided to take a course that would not only let me be with people, but would also let me help in some way. I felt I understood a little bit about suffering."

"Do you remember back before you moved to your aunt's house?" Virginia asked, trying to be delicate.

"Oh, I didn't move to hers. She moved to mine. Well, my parents', really."

"So it wasn't her . . . ?"

"Home? Her wealth? Oh my no. She had nothing really. There was no way she could have cared for a child. She just had a little place on a back street."

Virginia must have showed her surprise.

"We were not a big family. Great-aunt Sadie was the only living relative I had."

Virginia felt further sympathy.

"I don't know what I would have done without her," Grace went on and the blue-green eyes misted with unreleased tears. "She was good to me. She was old—and arthritic—even from the first. It must have been hard for her to care for a child."

Virginia began to readjust her mental picture of the elderly woman.

———

When Christmas had been celebrated and the time came for Danny, Rodney, and Grace to return to the university, the whole household was sad to see her go. Even small Anthony had taken to her quickly, and he begged her not to leave when she said her good-bye.

"I'll be back," she promised him with another warm hug for the sturdy little boy.

He changed his tactic with "Me go, too." He reached his arms around her neck. "Tony go, too."

Virginia smiled at the irony that Clara had managed to require that he be called by his full name, only to have Anthony choose to call himself Tony.

"Maybe someday I will be able to take you for a train ride. But not now. Your mama and papa would be too lonesome if you came with me."

Anthony looked back at Clara, then held out an inviting hand. "Mama—come," he insisted. Soon he would have the entire family traveling the train with Grace.

Troy rescued his son and freed Grace to board the train. They all waved one last time, then stepped back to watch the train pull from the station.

Not much was said as they returned home, but Virginia knew the whole family likely felt as bereft as she herself. There was something about Grace that warmed your heart. Maybe Francine, a bit too candidly perhaps, said it for all of them. "You know, after she had been here awhile, I forgot about all her money and her fancy clothes and just thought of her as . . . as normal."

They would miss her.

Virginia thought forward to the months ahead. Her mother had given Grace an invitation to come back anytime she had a break in her class schedule.

———

The cold weather remained, but Virginia paid little attention to it, even though she had to face it every day walking to and from work. She probably had become used to it, but perhaps it was because she genuinely enjoyed being a postmistress, and the walk in the cold seemed a small price to be doing something that brought her satisfaction.

She had not discussed it with her parents as yet, but she

had quite decided she would not pursue any further schooling. As far as she was concerned, she had already established her career.

Though it was far from glamorous and didn't pay high returns, it would be steady employment. She should never need to venture from her own hometown or the family that she loved. Perhaps one day she would even get her own little suite of rooms or maybe even a very small house of her own. If she saved every spare penny, she should be able to care for her own needs. She did not want her parents to think she expected them to support her all her life.

The thought of one day marrying never even occurred to Virginia. She took no notice of any of the young men of the town and naïvely did not catch the little signals of interest that were sent her way.

Jamison had not written. Many evenings Virginia had to resist the impulse to sit down and write to him, sharing the events of her day and the small-town news that she felt might be of interest to him. *His parents keep in touch*, she told herself. He would know all the news from the town.

Pulling out a sheet of paper, she would then begin a letter to Rodney or Danny or often Grace.

But even as she wrote, her heart still felt empty. Lonely. If Jamison should ever change his mind, she knew she would have no hesitation in taking him back. She missed him so much that it was a constant, conscious pain in the depth of her being.

Church did little to alleviate the pain. Every time she looked toward the pew that he had shared with his parents as a boy, or the one they had shared for so much of their growing-up years, the pain became fresh again. She wondered just how long it took for a broken heart to heal.

Her Bible and its familiar passages offered comfort and

hope for the future, and she clung to its truth of God's love and care for her when her heart was especially heavy.

———

The big news for the family in the new year was Clara's announcement that Anthony was to have a new sister or brother. At first there was deep concern, even on Clara's part. She was closely observed by the two doctors in town and watched even more closely by her mother. But no signs of recurring illness developed in the first few months of her pregnancy, and everyone began to relax.

Virginia let herself be excited and once again began a new round of purchases for baby things. This time she was hoping for a niece.

———

Virginia was on her way home from work late one afternoon, her coat collar pulled up about her face, her scarf securely tied to keep out the cold, when she almost collided with a man hurrying down the sidewalk.

She stepped aside just in time, excusing herself but thinking that the near miss was mostly because of his carelessness. Then the man spoke.

"Virginia?"

It was Jenny's father.

"Yes," she replied in a faltering voice. Was he intoxicated again?

"A call just came," he said, his voice strained. Troubled. "It's Jenny. She's been hurt in an auto accident."

CHAPTER 11

Virginia stared at Jenny's father, trying desperately to make sense of his hurried words. *Jenny. Hurt. Auto accident.* Her mind processed the words, but she still fought against what they meant. At last she spoke, but her voice was choked. "Where is she?"

Not, *How is she?* Virginia didn't know if she was ready to hear that part.

"In the hospital—there in Almsburg. A doctor called."

Virginia was busy sorting through the information. Mr. Woods started to move on. She reached out a hand to detain him and spoke again before he could hurry away.

"Is she—is it serious?"

He nodded then, and Virginia thought she saw tears in his eyes. "It's serious." Then he was gone.

Virginia bowed her head, her own tears streaming down her face. "Oh, God," she prayed, "be with Jenny. I know she's rejected you, but give her another chance. Please. Please don't let her die now. She's not ready. Help the doctors. And, Father, be with Mr. Woods. He loves her, too. I could see it in his face. Please, God. Don't let Jenny die."

Virginia did not add an amen. Though she lifted her head

and hurried toward home, her heart did not cease its continual prayer. Over and over she whispered, "Please, God, be with Jenny. Don't let her die. Please don't let her die."

When she reached home, she pushed open the kitchen door and called for her mother. From somewhere near the front of the house, Belinda answered, "I'm here."

"Where's here?" The agitation and alarm in Virginia's voice was met with the sound of hurried footsteps coming to meet her. Belinda's expression showed her concern when she entered the hall leading to the kitchen. One look at Virginia's tear-streaked face and she rushed forward. "What is it?"

"It's . . . it's Jenny," Virginia managed before she burst into uncontrolled sobs.

Belinda reached out for her daughter and pulled her close, then pushed her back to look into her face. "What happened?" she insisted. "Tell me what happened."

"An auto accident," Virginia said with trembling lips.

Belinda's eyes reflected the horror in Virginia's. She paled and pulled her daughter back into her arms again.

"Is it . . . is she . . . ?"

"She's in the Almsburg hospital."

Belinda's relief that the young girl was not dead was apparent.

Silently she held Virginia, stroking her hair, patting her shoulder, kissing the top of her head. The shoulders soon stopped shaking, and the muffled sobs subsided.

"How did you hear?" Belinda asked.

"I met her father on the street. He was rushing toward . . . toward the train station."

"He's going?"

Virginia thought about that. "He must have been," she answered. "He had a little . . . little valise in his hand."

Silence again.

"I'm glad he's gone to be with her," whispered Belinda.

Now that she thought about it, Virginia was glad, too. She leaned back in her mother's arms. "Do you think I could go?" she asked her mother.

"To Almsburg?" Belinda sounded surprised, but she did not give an immediate and negative reply.

"We'll see," she said thoughtfully. "We need to talk to your father. He should be home soon." She glanced at the clock on the mantel through the open archway. "You'd never make today's train. It should be pulling out anytime now."

"But there's another train tomorrow," Virginia commented.

Belinda seemed a bit shaken. "Almsburg is a long way from here. We know no one in the city. I have no idea how you'd find your way to the hospital—or accommodations—or anything."

"They must have streetcars or taxis," replied Virginia.

They were moving down the hall, back toward the kitchen. Virginia realized that she still had not removed her coat. She did so now, hanging it on a peg behind the door.

"We'll talk to your father," Belinda said again. "In the meantime, we'll pray."

"I've been praying." Virginia sounded about to burst into fresh tears.

"I know you have," responded Belinda lovingly. "Come. We'll pray together. The Lord will show us what to do."

———

The discussion with her father concluded that he would look into the possibilities in the morning.

Virginia got little sleep that night. Every time she stirred from troubled dreams, she found herself praying for Jenny again. In the morning she bathed her face in fresh cold water and tried to disguise the puffiness of her eyes.

It was difficult to go to work, but Virginia did. She was sure she'd never be able to concentrate on the tasks at hand, but once she was there with a job to be done, she found she was able to put her mind to it.

The news traveled quickly through the small town. Several morning customers to the post office asked Virginia about Jenny, knowing the two girls had been friends for many years. A few had their own information. Which of Jenny's bones had been broken or how many young people had been in the auto. Virginia wondered where they had learned it and discarded the conflicting accounts as hearsay. One lady even told Virginia that Jenny was the only one to survive the crash, and she was hanging on by a thread.

I will not believe any of this until I have the facts, Virginia told herself, firmly keeping her emotions in check.

The facts came in the person of Virginia's father. His face was somber when he entered the post office. He spoke first to Mr. Manson, the postmaster. "May I have a moment with my daughter, please?"

Mr. Manson took one look at Drew Simpson's face and nodded in agreement. He indicated a small supply room off to the side. Virginia did not wait further but moved toward the room, a big lump in the back of her throat. As soon as the door was closed, she turned to her father.

"Virginia," he said, "I've been on the phone for most of the morning. I wasn't able to get through to Jenny's father, but finally one of her doctors talked to me."

Virginia held her breath. She knew it was not going to be good news.

"Jenny is still fighting for her life. But she is alive," he continued. "We can be thankful for that. She's unconscious. She has internal injuries. They are not sure yet just how extensive. The bleeding has the doctors greatly concerned. She had a nasty bump on her head. That, too, is a big concern."

"Broken bones?" Virginia heard herself asking.

"Broken bones, but bones heal." Her father's dismissal of

the broken bones with such casualness sent another tremor of fear through Virginia. If broken bones could be shrugged off so easily, then Jenny's condition was extremely serious.

"Jenny is unaware of anything that is going on around her right now."

So I'm not to go, thought Virginia. She waited for those words from her father.

"But I think that you should leave on today's train," her father said instead. "I'm sure in this situation Mr. Manson would be agreeable."

Virginia looked at him, her eyes wide with surprise. He seemed to read the question she did not ask and went on simply, "You may not be able to help Jenny at this point, but I think her father needs you."

Virginia swallowed. How could she help Mr. Woods? That would be a pretty big task. He was likely holed up in some hotel room with a bottle for solace. The very thought frightened her.

"But I don't want you in Almsburg on your own," her father went on. "I've asked our pastor to contact a minister in one of the churches there. I have talked with him directly, and he will meet you at the train station. You are to stay with them. He'll see that you get to the hospital. If anything—*anything*—concerns you, you can call on Pastor Black."

A stranger. I am to stay with a complete stranger was Virginia's first thought. She recoiled at the idea. But as her father continued to speak, she felt she understood his reasons. He, as well, knew that Mr. Woods often sought his consolation from a bottle. Many bottles. Yes. Her father was right. She would feel much more at ease staying in the home of a minister whom she could turn to for help.

She managed a nod and whispered, "Thank you, Papa."

Drew reached out with his one remaining arm and pulled her against his chest. "Virginia," he said into her hair. "I'm so sorry. For a young person you have had more than your share of life's hard knocks. We'll be praying. Telephone us. Anytime you have need. And remember, God is still in charge. He's still great. He can turn this whole thing around and use it for good. This might be the very thing that brings Jenny to Him."

It was a new thought to Virginia. She had not recognized any possible good that could come from such a tragedy.

"If you are in agreement, I will talk with Mr. Manson. See if it is possible for you to have a week off."

Virginia nodded. Yes, she was in agreement. Even if Jenny could not recognize her, was totally unaware that she was even in the room, she would be there. She could pray with her, even talk to her. But as to Mr. Woods, Virginia was sure she would be of little comfort to him.

"I'll talk to Mr. Manson," she told her father, stepping back from his arm. "I'm the employee. It's my responsibility."

He nodded and patted her shoulder again. "I'll get your ticket," he informed her and opened the storeroom door.

———

Virginia's heart was beating hard as she boarded the afternoon train. She had never traveled alone before, and the reason for her trip added to her uncertainty and nervousness. All sorts of "what ifs" ran through her mind. Her mother already had covered most of them, with continual, "If . . . , Virginia, then . . ." Her father had managed to chuckle in spite of the circumstances. "You'll have the poor girl afraid to breathe," he teased his wife.

Belinda chuckled and kissed Virginia on the forehead. "You're right," she said to her husband. "She's quite able to handle things properly on her own. It's a habit of mine. This . . . this mothering and fretting over my young. I'm sorry, Virginia."

But Virginia had not resented the extra hovering from her

mother. In her heart she wished she could take Belinda with her into this rather frightening, undesired circumstance that confronted her. She never would have confessed as much. Now she boarded the train, selected a seat, and leaned to the window for one last wave to her family standing on the platform.

As the train began to slowly move forward, squealing a protest as iron wheels ground against iron rails, the tears gathered in Virginia's eyes. She wasn't sure if they were brought on by her continued concerns for the welfare of her friend or because she was traveling alone into the unknown. What would await her at the other end of this rail line? Would the minister be friendly—or stiff and frightening? Would Jenny's father be glad to see her—or resist her intrusion? Would Jenny be totally unaware of her visit to the hospital room—or stir from her unconscious state to welcome her? Or would—would Jenny die before she could even reach her side?

———

The rambling train seemed to travel at turtle speed. The sun went down and darkness engulfed them. Virginia sat stiff and silent on the maroon plush. A few times the weathered conductor with the handlebar mustache, blue suit, and brimmed cap passed down the aisle, moving easily back and forth with the sway of the train, nodding her way and passing on. An occasional passenger stirred from time to time, finding footing much more difficult than the seasoned railman had. Mostly, folks just sat. Virginia heard a baby's cry and a mother's hush. Two old gents near the middle of the car carried on a rather loud conversation. She idly wondered if they both were hard of hearing—or only one of them. She made no effort to understand the words tossed back and forth in the closeness of the railcar.

It was almost ten o'clock at night before her rumbling stomach reminded her of the lunch her mother had packed.

Carefully she unwrapped the little package, thankful that her mother had insisted, and began to eat. A small bottle of milk finished off the meal.

She was sure she would never be able to sleep, but she rolled an extra sweater into a ball and placed it beneath her head, resting up against the coolness of the window. The next thing she knew, someone was gently shaking her shoulder. "Miss. Miss," a voice was saying, "your stop is just up ahead."

A uniform was bending over her. Virginia's sleep-filled eyes traveled up past the blue and braid chest, past the curling mustache and into the eyes of the conductor who bent over her. She shook her head to clear its fog and nodded.

Once fully awake she began to gather up her things. The minister was to be meeting her train. But it was the middle of the night. How had her father ever persuaded a total stranger to get up from his bed to meet the train for an unknown girl?

Virginia decided that anyone willing to do such a service must be a person of unusual caring and worth. Perhaps she would not need to be so fearful after all. She picked up her case and coat so she would be able to disembark quickly once the announcement was made.

———

"Watch your step, miss."

The conductor took Virginia's arm to assist her down the steep, narrow steps into the night. She blinked in the glare of lights that lit the platform and murmured a thank-you to the man as her foot reached for the last step. Adjusting her luggage, she followed the other passengers to the station.

For the hundredth time, her mind busily engaged itself in wondering, *How will I know him?* Her father had told her that the minister's name was Reverend Thomas Black, but that was all she knew.

Upon entering the large room full of benches and people,

Virginia immediately began to scan the crowd. Off to the left a group of young people, probably students from the college, huddled and laughed and shared some hilarious news or joke. On the seats ahead, a few loiterers lingered, some slumped in sleep, others eyeing the incoming passengers with varied degrees of curiosity. Virginia turned to her right where several people milled about, some seeming to have purpose, others just aimlessly on the move. Among them was an elderly, respectable-looking man who seemed to be peering into the crowd. Just as Virginia began to move forward, certain that this was the minister she was to meet, he was greeted by an equally elderly woman. The two smiled at each other, gave a preemptory embrace, and started off together, he taking the small valise from her hand.

Virginia sighed. This might prove to be difficult. She didn't know whether to comb the crowd or just pick an unobtrusive seat and wait.

Just then her eyes caught a sign, held up high above the heads of others. There was her name. Virginia Simpson. With another sigh, now of relief, Virginia moved confidently toward the sign carrier.

As a path cleared before her, she saw the sign lowering, its bearer moving in her direction.

Good, she thought to herself. *He's spotted me.*

One last person moved to the side, and Virginia prepared a welcoming smile. She was so thankful for the wisdom that prompted the signmaker to simplify this meeting.

Then Virginia stopped abruptly. *There must be some mistake. No minister could possibly be this young*, she thought frantically.

———

"Miss Simpson?"
Virginia managed a nod. Her throat felt dry.
"I'm Pastor Black."

He must have seen her bewilderment. "Your father, Andrew Simpson, called me," he explained. "Made arrangements for me to meet your train. He said you have a friend in the hospital, badly injured from a car accident."

He had all the facts. Surely he must be the right man.

He moved forward to take the suitcase from her hand. Virginia didn't know whether to let it go or not.

"I have a car waiting—this way."

She still did not speak or move.

"I hope your journey was not too stressful," he continued with a kind smile. "This way," he said again.

Virginia knew he expected her to fall in step. She did, her legs moving woodenly forward.

"This must be very hard for you," he was saying as they moved from the building.

Virginia nodded.

"I understand your friend is a student at the university."

She nodded again.

"We have several university students who attend our church. I know she was not one of our usual group, but perhaps she had been an invited guest at some time."

Virginia shook her head. It was highly unlikely.

"I haven't had opportunity since your father's call to make a hospital visit, but I certainly plan to do that first thing tomorrow. Just to let the family know that we will do all we can to help them through this difficult time."

Virginia nodded again, wondering distractedly how welcome his services would be.

"I understand her father has come."

Virginia knew she must find her tongue.

"Yes" was all she managed.

"I must look him up," he continued.

They had reached the auto, and he was storing her suitcase in the backseat and opening the door for her to be seated.

Before she could check herself, she blurted out, "Are you married?"

He looked totally surprised by the question, then seemed to nod in understanding. He looked solemn for a moment, then he threw back his head and laughed. Virginia had never seen so many changes of expression pass so quickly on anyone's face before.

"I am not," he answered through his chuckles, "but you are quite safe. I live with my mother—or rather, she lives with me." He helped her in and closed the door.

He chuckled again when he climbed in beside her and started the engine.

He soon sobered and eased the auto from the curb and out into the street.

"Are you uncomfortable in an auto?" he asked, all of the laughter gone from his voice. "I can imagine that you would be uncertain—"

"No," Virginia put in quickly. "I'm all right."

"Good. I just thought—with your friend's accident and all—some people get very fearful."

Virginia shook her head again, sure that driving with a minister was much different than being with Jenny and her friends on the night of the accident.

"You might not meet my mother until morning," he informed her. "I encouraged her not to disturb her sleep. But she is there—let me assure you." He smiled reassuringly. "If you are not certain about me, a stranger—trust your father. You can be sure he checked things thoroughly before he made this arrangement."

Virginia relaxed. Of course her father would have checked.

CHAPTER 12

They were prepared to tiptoe their way into the house where a cheery light awaited them, but a middle-aged woman met them at the door, welcoming Virginia with a pleasant smile.

"Do come in, my dear," she invited.

"Mother. You were to stay in bed," her son reprimanded gently.

She seemed to pay little attention to his fussing. "How was your trip?" she asked Virginia. "Miserable time of the day to be traveling. But then, train travel is an adventure at any time. Never did care for the train. All that rocking to and fro makes my stomach queasy."

Virginia managed a smile. "I slept part of the way," she offered, still surprised by the fact that she actually had.

"Oh, that's good. It makes the journey seem so much shorter if one can sleep. Well, come right this way. Your room is at the top of the stair. Tommy, take her suitcase up. Put it on the low stand by the door."

She turned back to Virginia. "I'm so sorry to hear of your friend's tragic accident. Have you any further word on her condition?"

Virginia shook her head.

Virginia watched as her suitcase moved up the stairs in the hand of the young minister.

"Well, we have our people praying. We haven't had one bit of time to do anything more. Tommy had to go to Trent this afternoon to see an ailing parishioner, and then he had a church meeting this evening, and by the time it finished it was too late to get over to the hospital. But he'll get you on over the first thing in the morning. He has cleared his day so he might be available to help in any way he can."

"Oh, he shouldn't have," Virginia objected. "I don't wish to interfere with his pastoral duties."

"Nonsense." She smiled. "That's what his pastoral duties are."

Virginia was relieved to find her hostess warm and talkative, though as weary as she was, she would have been quite content for the chat to take place after she had gotten more sleep.

"Do you want a cup of tea, my dear? Warm milk? Lemonade?"

With each shake of Virginia's head, the woman named something else.

"No, thank you. Mama fixed a lunch for me to eat on the train. I'm fine, thank you."

"Then it's off to bed with you then. You must be exhausted."

Virginia admitted that she was.

"Right up the stairs. Tommy will have your suitcase there for you."

"Thank you," said Virginia sincerely. As she turned to mount the stairs, she smiled at the "Tommy," sounding as though the minister were still a small boy. She wondered what Tommy himself thought of it. He had given his name as Thomas.

Virginia was so tired she could not wait to climb between the cool, white sheets. There was her suitcase, just where it was supposed to be. There was no sign of the pastor who had brought her from the train station. She did wish briefly that she'd had an opportunity to thank him and to ask him to please have her called in the morning in the event she should oversleep.

But Virginia did not sleep in. She was awake and dressed before she heard stirring in the rest of the house. She waited nervously until she thought the minister and his mother were both up and about, then cautiously opened her door. Yes, she could hear the murmur of voices. She took a deep breath and began her descent.

Through the open kitchen door she could see the breakfast table already set for three. The woman, bountifully garbed in a blue checkered apron, was working at the stove. The young minister sat on a chair near a window, an open Bible in his hand. His head turned toward her as she appeared in the doorway.

"Good morning." His smile greeted her.

The clock above his head said ten minutes past seven.

His mother turned also and graced Virginia with a warm smile. "Did you get any sleep, my dear?"

Virginia smiled, too. "I feel much better this morning, thank you. The bed was—just right. Not too soft, not too hard, just right. Did I happen to have 'baby bear's bed,' by any chance?"

The young man looked up again from his reading as though surprised that she could put so many words together in a row. The woman chuckled at the little joke. "Baby bear's?" she repeated. "Perhaps." Then she continued, "Sit down, Virginia. Take that chair right in front of you. Breakfast will be ready in a jiffy. I've just to dish it up."

"May I help?"

"Oh no, no. I've got it all right here. Tommy, put that hot pad by the milk pitcher. This breakfast casserole is too hot for the table."

Virginia had never had a breakfast casserole before and wasn't quite sure what to expect. The woman placed the dish on the table and went for the plate of muffins.

"Sit down, my dear," she repeated.

Virginia sat down, wondering if everyone in Tommy's church was "deared" by his mother.

The minister led in the morning prayer, which was considerably more than a simple table grace. He referred to the day they were facing, needs in his congregation, which included Mrs. Tiffany's gout, Margaret, who had fallen and broken an arm, Jack, who was confronted with bills he had no money to pay, and Mr. Sloan, who had lost his wife.

His prayer was sincere and earnest. He remembered the young girl in the auto accident and her greatly concerned father. He prayed for Virginia and God's needed presence and help to get her through the difficult day ahead. In the closing sentences, he thanked a loving God for bountifully supplying the daily bread to sustain their physical bodies.

The meal was much more than bread. The casserole was delicious, an egg and ham concoction with browned crumbs sprinkled over the top, and seasoning that made one lick one's lips. The muffins were a wonderful complement, and Virginia found herself eating heartily.

"It's a bit early to be heading to the hospital," the young pastor said. "Is there anything you want to do first?"

Virginia tried to think. There was nothing that she needed to do, and she did not know the city well enough to make any requests.

"No," she answered. "I just want to see my friend. I came for no other reason."

He nodded. "I understand."

"Did you want to get in touch with the girl's father?" Mrs. Black asked.

"I don't know where he is staying. I imagine I'll see him at the hospital," Virginia responded.

"Perhaps you'd like to call home. Let your folks know you have arrived safely."

"If you don't mind, I'd appreciate that."

But even before they had finished their meal, the telephone rang. It was Virginia's father. She was so glad to talk to him and then her mother. She felt connected, even though they were many miles apart.

"No, no, I haven't heard anything new yet," she said into the telephone. "We are just finishing our breakfast, and then we will drive over. It's a bit early for the hospital to respond to visitors. Yes, I'll let you know as soon as I learn anything. Yes, I will. I love you, too. Bye-bye."

Virginia returned the phone to its cradle and turned back to her host and hostess. "My mother says to tell you just how much she appreciates your kindness. They would not have let me come on my own without some . . . some connection here in the city."

"We are most happy to be of assistance," Mrs. Black answered for both of them. "Tell us about your family."

Virginia wondered where to start. Did they want a full account or just a briefing? She decided on the briefing. "I have two sisters, the older one married with a little boy, the younger one still in school. And two brothers who are both university students."

"Your father?"

"An attorney."

"Ah yes."

Virginia was not sure what Mrs. Black meant by "Ah yes." She let it pass. "My mother was a nurse, but since the family arrived, she has only nursed when needed to assist in some emergency."

Mrs. Black nodded, took another drink from her coffee cup, and then said, "This friend who was hurt. Tell us about her."

Again Virginia did not know where to start. To really give a full account about Jenny would sound much like gossiping. Yet to refuse seemed rude.

"She—we went to school together. They moved to our town when her father bought the local newspaper."

"A newsman?"

"Yes."

"I always think that newsmen have such potential to do good. The moral values of the entire community are often set by the local newspaper and the person who runs it."

Virginia had never thought of that before. She did not say that Mr. Woods certainly hadn't set the moral tone for their small town, nor did he represent the morals of the largest number of the town citizens.

"Is this her first year at college?" asked the Reverend Black.

"No. She attended last year, as well."

"Is there some reason her mother wasn't able to come, or has she had the sorrow of losing her mother?" This probing question from Mrs. Black.

Virginia paused. How could she answer without either gossiping or dissembling?

"She—I guess you would say she—she hasn't been in touch."

Mrs. Black exchanged a look with her pastor son. But there was no condemnation in her eyes. Only sympathy.

"Has she—the mother—been informed of the accident?" Virginia was sure it was the woman's mother-heart inquiring.

Virginia shook her head slowly. "I don't believe they have any idea where she is," she responded honestly.

Mrs. Black seemed about to make further comment, but she

lowered her head and pursed her lips tightly. Virginia appreciated her discreetness.

"If you'll excuse me, please," Thomas Black said, "I have a
few things to tidy up and then we'll leave for the hospital."

"Of course." Virginia nodded her assent.

"More coffee, my dear?" Mrs. Black asked as soon as her
son had disappeared.

"No, thank you. I am not much of a coffee drinker, I'm
afraid. One cup is quite sufficient."

"Well, if you don't mind, I think I'll just have my second
cup."

Virginia smiled and nodded without comment.

Mrs. Black poured her coffee, settled back in her chair,
and generously poured cream into her cup.

"People are often a bit surprised when they see Tommy for
the first time. They don't expect such a young man to be in the
ministry. This is his first parish, you know. But Tommy never
had a moment's doubt from the time he was eleven. Went
straight into Bible college for pastoral studies from high school.
That was all he ever wanted to be. All he felt God wanted him
to be. His grandfather was a minister. I think Tommy had a
special affinity with him.

"Oh, not that he chose the ministry because of his grandfather. No. He has always felt called himself. But I do think
my husband's father had a great influence on the young boy.
'Course, Papa Black—that's what our family always called him—
Papa Black influenced many lives. He was a good man."

She stopped thoughtfully for a moment and then continued. "We lost him two years ago. And the next year—almost
to the day—Tommy lost his father. He's had two very difficult
years, my Tommy, but he seems to have weathered it well. Says
it has made him far more understanding of others when they
go through the loss of loved ones."

Mrs. Black nodded her head, as though agreeing with her Tommy. "And it does. If one accepts it in the proper way."

Virginia, who had listened silently, supposed the woman to be right, though she had never had the sorrow of losing someone close to her. She thought of her own grandfather and her father, and wondered how she would ever face it if something happened to either one of them. She felt a great sympathy for the young Reverend Black. Her gaze traveled toward the partially closed door where he had gone after breakfast. She could hear his voice, muted by the door and the distance, and from the pacing of the conversation, she guessed him to be making a telephone call.

"I am so sorry for this young friend of yours," went on Mrs. Black. "To be going through the tragedy that she is going through and not to have her mother at her side . . . And for her father. I ache for him, as well. And his only child—that must be especially hard. Well, no," she quickly added. "I guess it wouldn't matter if a parent had one or three dozen. Each one would be too precious to lose."

The nearby door opened and Pastor Black came back into the room. His eyes addressed Virginia. "All set?"

"I just need to get my wraps and handbag."

He nodded as Virginia pushed back from the table and voiced her thanks for the meal, then he turned to his mother. "Mrs. Winston is down with the flu again. Do you suppose you could take her a bit of broth or something? The Hensley baby is over the croup. Another prayer answered. If there should be any emergency calls for me while I'm out, call the hospital and have me paged, please."

Virginia passed out of earshot, but a feeling of guilt made her face flush. Here she was in a strange city, usurping a pastor's time that should have been given to his parishioners. She wished her father had not made the call but had left her to fend for herself. Surely she was old enough and wise enough to find her way around a city, even a strange one. But on the other hand, knowing her parents, they would not have wanted her to "fend for herself."

They began their trip to the hospital in silence, and Virginia mentally searched for some way to express her chagrin at taking up his valuable time. She scarcely knew where to start or how to voice her feelings and hesitated for some minutes before making an attempt. At length she just blurted out, "I'm so sorry that I am taking your time. I'm afraid my father is a bit overly protective. I can manage just fine. There is no reason for me to tie up your day when you have so many folks to tend to. Please, just drop me off at the hospital, and I'll take a taxi or a streetcar back and forth from now on."

He looked surprised as she began but listened without interruption. When she was finished he did not argue, just nodded and replied, "Let's see what we find."

What we find, Virginia repeated in her mind. What would they find? Had Jenny regained consciousness? Was Jenny still with them? She had no idea what she would be facing when she walked into the hospital.

Then she remembered Jenny's father. What was the young minister expecting of him? That he was a stalwart Christian man, depending upon prayer to pull his daughter through her crisis? If Reverend Black was, he was in for a shock. Virginia wondered if she should warn him or let him take it as it came. She decided to hold her tongue. But concern made her tense. She did hope intensely that Jenny's father would not be intoxicated and abusive.

It was not a long drive to the hospital, and being a Saturday morning, the traffic was light. Before Virginia scarcely had time to collect her thoughts, Pastor Black was pulling into a parking space. Virginia took a deep breath. She had dreaded this moment all the way on the train. Hated to face it now.

What awaited her in the tall brick building beyond the heavy oak doors?

To her surprise the young man beside her reached over and took her hand. Under normal circumstances she would have quickly withdrawn it from the grip of a stranger. "Let's pray," he said. She felt her fingers wrap tightly about his as she clung to him for support and strength. She closed her eyes tightly and tried to quiet her heart for prayer.

She was never sure how much of his prayer she really heard or understood. It was enough to know that God had. By the time he said "Amen," Virginia's eyes were filled with tears, but a strange new quietness had reached her heart.

He released her hand and opened the door of the auto. Virginia took a deep breath and followed suit.

"I assume we'll find her on the third floor," he noted, "from your description of her injuries, but we'll stop at the front desk to inquire."

Virginia realized that she was with someone who knew his way around this city hospital. Thankfully, she was more than happy to fall into step beside him and let him lead.

The minute he stepped through the large oak doors, he removed his hat. It was the first time Virginia had noticed how blond his hair was.

"Good morning, Pastor Black," the lady at the desk greeted him.

"Good morning, Miss Davies," was his reply.

"I didn't realize any of your parishioners were in just now," she went on easily.

"No. No, none of mine directly, but a young woman was brought in with injuries from an auto accident. My friend wishes to see her."

Virginia did not miss the words "my friend."

"Her name is Jenny Woods. She is a university student," he went on.

The woman's expression turned serious. Virginia felt fear tighten her chest.

"She's on the third floor. You'll have to ask if she's allowed visitors."

Relief rushed over Virginia, making her feel suddenly weak.

"From what I understand, family members are the only ones allowed into her room. But ask at the desk on the floor. The situation may have changed."

Pastor Black thanked her and steered Virginia toward an elevator.

Again Virginia wondered if she should prepare the minister for his meeting with Jenny's father. Perhaps she should at least tell him not to bother informing the hostile man that he was a man of the cloth. Mr. Woods was likely to go into one awful tirade upon hearing that piece of news. Virginia wanted no scenes in the hospital corridor.

But before Virginia could think of a way to voice her warning, they had arrived at the third floor and the elevator door was opening.

Oh, dear, she rebuked herself. *It's too late now. I should have spoken when we were in the car.*

The nursing station stood right before them, with two capped heads bent over charts. Both heads came up as the visitors approached. One faced them with a smile, the other remained as rigid as her starched cap.

"We are here to see Miss Jenny Woods," Pastor Black informed the nearest nurse.

"Miss Woods? I'm sorry. Miss Woods is not prepared to see visitors at this time."

The words were curt and definite. Virginia knew they were dealing with a professional who would bide no stretching of the rules.

"Can you give us any report on how Miss Woods is doing?"

"Only the doctor can relay a patient's condition. And only at the behest of the family."

Virginia was feeling more and more discouraged. Had she come all this way to be refused admittance to Jenny's room? Even refused any knowledge of how Jenny was doing?

"Is her father with her?" Thomas Black asked.

"He was."

"He's left?"

The nurse looked annoyed at the continued questioning. She looked straight at this man of the cloth, probably feeling that she could not avoid his questions and she dared not lie.

"He has left her room. I do not believe that he has left the hospital."

He's been making trouble, was Virginia's first thought. *His daughter's life hangs in the balance and he's been making a scene—or worse.*

The young pastor turned to her. "Let's find him."

He took her elbow to steer her away, then turned back to the stiff nurse, gave her a pleasant smile, and thanked her sincerely for her assistance.

"Wait," said Virginia, stopping abruptly to face Reverend Black. "There's something you should know—about Mr. Woods."

But it was too late. There was Jenny's father.

CHAPTER 13

$\mathcal{M}$r. Woods was standing amid a small cluster of people in white coats, stubborn chin thrust forward, eyes bulging with rage. One of the medical men had a restraining hand on his arm, another appeared to be blocking the way with his body.

Even from where she stood, Virginia could tell that Mr. Woods was very angry. She also guessed, by his stance and his flushed face, that he was very intoxicated. His clothing looked rumpled and stained.

She wanted to turn around and flee, but the young minister still held her arm.

"Is that . . . Jenny's father?" he was asking in a quiet voice.

Virginia could only nod. Her knees felt weak and her stomach queasy.

"Did he know you were coming?"

Virginia tried to swallow and shook her head.

"How will he respond when he sees you?"

Virginia began to tremble. "I've no idea," she managed to answer.

"Do you wish me to go first—alone?"

Yes, she wanted to respond, but again she shook her head slowly. She steeled herself and swallowed again.

"No," she said instead, "I came to . . . to see if I could help. I . . . I'd best go myself."

But it took all of her resolve to force her shaking legs forward.

As she neared the little gathering, she heard Mr. Woods bellow in a belligerent voice, "No one tells me when I can see my daughter."

"Mr. Woods, sir," one young white-clad man was patiently insisting, "under normal circumstances, that may be so. Please try to—"

Mr. Woods responded with an outpouring of profanity. Virginia had never heard anything like it in her entire life. She felt faint. How could she—how could anyone deal with this totally unreasonable man?

She felt a presence by her side and realized that the young minister had stepped up beside her. It gave Virginia courage. Without hesitation she moved quickly forward and directly in front of the angry man. His hand came up as though to roughly push her aside. She spoke quickly. "Mr. Woods. It's Virginia."

To her relief the hand paused, then moved to pass over his eyes instead, as though he was sure he must be hallucinating.

"It's Virginia," she repeated. She knew that Pastor Black was close beside her. With further courage she reached out a hand to the distraught father.

"You came," he said, and the words of disbelief—was it also relief?—tore at Virginia.

The man's shoulders slumped. He rubbed the hand roughly over his face again. When he let it drop it was as though the face had crumpled. He began to shake as ragged sobs contorted his face. "They won't let me see my little girl."

Virginia could barely understand the muffled words. "I know. I know," she responded, moving closer, though the odor of stale liquor repelled her. "Let's sit down a moment," she said in a coaxing voice and gently steered the broken man toward a small alcove with seats. She heard "Well, I'll be!" from one of the hospital personnel, no doubt relieved at the turn of events.

"They won't let me see my little girl," Mr. Woods said again and again. "She's dying and they won't let me see her."

The last words shook Virginia. Was Jenny really dying? With all her heart she prayed that it was not so.

Virginia began to search her pockets for a handkerchief for the man, knowing she would not want to see that bit of linen back again after this use. But it was the young pastor who provided the needed hankie.

Mr. Woods blew noisily and stuffed the item in his own pocket. Virginia was quite sure Pastor Black would not protest over the lost fabric square, either.

Mr. Woods seemed to be pulling himself together. He looked up through watery, bloodshot eyes, now noticing the young man who accompanied Virginia.

"Who are you?" he asked frankly.

"He's . . . he's with me," Virginia quickly put in.

The man looked confused. "Him? This isn't your young man."

His words caught Virginia off guard. No. It was not Jamison. Would people never cease referring to Jamison as her young man?

"He's a friend from here in town," said Virginia, trying to gather her wits about her.

She saw the questioning look on the pastor's face and supposed he wondered why she had not introduced him as a minister. She would try to explain later. For now, it was important to keep Mr. Woods calm.

Then Pastor Black spoke. "Have you had breakfast, Mr. Woods? No, I thought not. Let's go out and find a spot for some. We'll talk over what might be done to get you in to see Jenny."

The words seemed to reach Mr. Woods. At first Virginia was afraid he was going to resist, but at last he nodded his head and stood on shaky legs.

Virginia looked around to see the hospital staff observing the scene from a watchful distance.

"We're going out to get some coffee and breakfast," she heard Pastor Black explain to them in a matter-of-fact manner.

The closest man, whom Virginia assumed was one of the doctors, nodded. "Thanks, Reverend," she heard him say softly. He stepped back and allowed them to make a quiet, though clumsy, exit with Mr. Woods.

They were almost out to the large oak doors before Virginia remembered that she had not gathered any news concerning Jenny's condition.

———

Even after consuming several cups of black coffee and a portion of his eggs and bacon, Mr. Woods was still in an emotional state. Virginia had never seen the hard man so unnerved. Pastor Black let him talk on and on, spilling out the facts about his troubled marriage, his departed wife, and his little girl. Now and then the pastor nodded in understanding or patted the man's shaking shoulder. At length, when there seemed to be a bit of a lull, he stood to his feet.

"Why don't you get a bit of rest," he suggested, "while I slip over to the hospital and see what I can do about arranging for you to see Jenny?"

Mr. Woods seemed to consider the thought for a moment, and to Virginia's surprise he nodded agreement.

"Where are you staying?" This from Pastor Black.

"Hadn't bothered with a room yet."

"Let's find you one then."

Shakily the man stood to his feet.

"Where's your luggage?"

For a moment Mr. Woods looked surprised—then confused. Virginia could see that he was trying hard to remember.

"I think I left it over at the hospital or somewhere."

It was plain he wasn't too sure.

"I'll check," said the pastor.

Mr. Woods seemed quite content to let the younger man take over.

They did not drive far before Pastor Black stopped before a small hotel. It was not in the least elegant, but when they entered, Virginia noted that it was clean and comfortable in appearance.

The young pastor stepped to the desk and made arrangements for the room. "Why don't you wait here," he advised Virginia. "I'll see him to his room and be right back."

Virginia agreed and moved to find herself a seat. Her eyes traveled to the clock above the desk. It was now ten minutes past eleven, and she felt the day had already been a week long. She sighed, feeling very weary.

Thomas Black was soon back. "He was asleep almost as soon as he hit the bed," he informed her. "I don't suppose he has slept since he got word of the accident. By what he has said, he drank most of the way on the train, got a little confused, and wandered the streets on foot looking for the hospital. I imagine he curled up in a back alley somewhere last night."

Virginia shook her head in pity rather than disgust.

"I've instructed the hotel staff to contact me when he makes an appearance. I think he'll likely sleep for several hours. Let's get back to the hospital and see how Jenny is doing."

157

Virginia suddenly felt restored to life. She was most anxious—yet fearful—to get some news about her friend.

———

Jenny's doctor recognized them immediately and drew them into a small waiting room.

The news was not good news. Jenny's condition was still serious. She had not regained consciousness, and the doctor, who spoke gently, did not offer any false hope.

"In the circumstances, you may see her if you like, but be prepared," Dr. Moore offered.

Virginia was confused. If they could see Jenny, why had they denied admission to her father?

"And as soon as her father sobers so we can trust him in the room, he can see her, as well," the man went on. "We are most grateful to you for defusing a difficult situation," he added. "We did not know how we were going to handle it—short of calling the police."

Poor man, thought Virginia. *I'm glad we saved him from that.*

"Does Mr. Woods have a drinking problem?" The doctor turned to Virginia to ask directly.

Virginia swallowed, then nodded. It was true. She could not deny it. Yet she felt like a gossip.

"He . . . he drinks . . . quite heavily, so I've heard. But he . . . he seems to be able to still . . . function. He works hard . . . runs the local paper alone."

The doctor nodded. "We'll be prepared" was his comment.

"I'll try to monitor him, Dr. Moore," put in the pastor. "See that he gets back and forth in a sober state."

"Thanks, Reverend."

There was a moment of pause. The doctor stood to his feet

and nodded his head toward a door down the hall. "Now, do you wish to see Miss Woods?"

Virginia took a deep breath. Yes, she wanted to see Jenny. But was she—could she—would she be able to endure the tragic sight that most surely awaited her beyond those closed doors? She felt the young minister take her arm and managed a brief nod. Yes, with him there for support, she would see Jenny.

"She is still unconscious," the doctor was saying as they moved forward. "But as we don't know too much about the unconscious state, we do ask that you try to control emotions. Talk to her, if you will. Tell her who you are. See if there is any response, but don't expect any."

He pushed open the door and stepped back to allow them to enter. Virginia's eyes took in a maze of monitors and connecting wires and hospital paraphernalia that surrounded a high, narrow bed.

She stood silently, wooden, until a hand on her arm prompted her to move forward.

A figure lay on the bed, looking so small. So vulnerable. So still. But it certainly wasn't Jenny. *No, it can't be Jenny*, Virginia's mind argued. *Not this silent, wasted figure with all the tubes in her nose and mouth. Not this empty shell.*

Virginia covered her mouth with her hand to keep from crying out. It was Jenny.

They had shaved off all her crown of red hair. In its place were a multitude of tubes and wires. Her face was so pale and battered it was hard to discern her features. One hand lay limp on the bed sheet beside her, as though it belonged to some strange rag doll. Virginia felt her knees go weak and thought she might have gone down had not kind hands been supporting her. She fought for control, scrunching her eyes tightly, praying for strength.

The faintness washed over her, departed. She paused for a moment, took a deep breath, and then stepped forward, taking the limp hand in both of her own. "Jenny," she said softly. "Jenny, it's Virginia. I've come. I'm here with you, Jenny."

Her voice grew stronger. "Jenny, do you hear me? It's Virginia. You're going to be all right. We're praying. All of us. Your father is here. He will be in to see you . . . soon."

There was no response.

Virginia gave the hand she held a squeeze. She wanted to wake her friend. To make her take notice. She wanted to force Jenny to determine to make it through this terrible accident. "Jenny," she said again, too loudly. She felt the young minister's hand tighten on her arm.

Virginia fought for control. In a voice that was calmer, she continued. "I'm going to come see you every day, Jenny. I'll be here. We need you to wake up. We need to fight this. Do you hear me? Fight."

Jenny had always been a fighter. It seemed strange to be bidding her to fight now. But Virginia repeated the order again, with a little shake to the limp hand. "Fight, Jenny."

There was nothing but the quiet hum of hospital machines.

Silently Virginia turned to go. There seemed to be little else to do.

———

Pastor Black drove her back home. It was a silent trip.

"Try to get some rest," he encouraged after she tried hard to swallow some of his mother's lunch. She was sure that the food was delicious, but she had no appetite.

Virginia nodded. She would try to rest. She felt drained. Maybe she should not have come. There was nothing she could do for Jenny. She knew that now. A miracle was needed for Jenny, and only God could perform a miracle.

"I'm going to the church to take care of some things, then I'll check on Mr. Woods."

Ah yes. Mr. Woods. What had her father said? *Jenny's father might need you.* Jenny's father? That drunken, ravaged man? Did he need her? It seemed Mr. Woods' only need was his bottle.

Then Virginia felt guilt wash over her for such thoughts. She'd had a glimpse of a far different man than the blustering, profane man she had known in their small town. She had seen a grieving father. A broken spirit. Sobbing uncontrollably over a beloved daughter in grave danger.

Virginia had never seen that side of Mr. Woods before. She wondered if Jenny ever had. Mr. Woods did need someone through the difficult hours ahead, she decided. But Virginia was unsure if she was equal to the task.

She looked directly into the eyes of the young minister who stood before her, and she felt a deep thankfulness for his presence, his understanding.

Whatever would she have done without him? Her father had been so right to secure some help in this strange city.

She nodded again. She would try to get some rest.

———

A soft rap on the door awakened Virginia. She pulled herself up to a sitting position, struggling to remember where she was and why. Swiftly it came back to her. She passed a hand over her hair to smooth the tangles and called, "Yes?"

Mrs. Black answered, "Tommy is here, my dear. He has Mr. Woods with him."

Virginia quickly stood to her feet. "I'll be right down."

It did not take Virginia long to pass a comb through her hair and repin it. Her face looked flushed from sleeping, and her dress, which she foolishly had not removed, was wrinkled. She had not expected to be able to sleep. She looked down at her skirt now, impatiently trying to smooth it with her hands.

From the lower floor of the house, voices drifted up to

greet her. She made her way down the stairs toward the sound and found Pastor Black and Mr. Woods seated in two chairs pulled up beside the fireplace. Though no fire burned, the room seemed to carry a warmth all its own.

Virginia could not believe the difference in Jenny's father. Though his face had high color and his nose still bore a shine, his eyes looked quite clear, his posture erect. The young pastor had done a good job of keeping the man sober.

"Good afternoon," Virginia greeted them both, and the two gentlemen, as one, rose to their feet.

"Were you able to rest?" the pastor asked.

Virginia admitted, with a bit of embarrassment, that she was, then turned her eyes to Mr. Woods. He still studied her, as though he could not believe she was really there.

"Have you been to see Jenny yet?" Virginia asked.

"No." He shook his head, his eyes misting. Virginia hoped she had not asked the wrong question. She did not want him to lose control again.

"We thought it best to go over together," Pastor Black put it.

"Yes," agreed Jenny's father with a nod of his head, then added with a plea in his voice, "If you don't mind."

"Of course not." Virginia was still in awe of the changed demeanor of the man. The big man turned to the pastor. "Virginia is my Jenny's best friend."

"So I understand," nodded the younger man.

"She's been a good influence on my girl. Even takes her to church."

Virginia was astonished. Mr. Woods had never even hinted at any appreciation for the fact she had coaxed Jenny into attending church on occasion.

The younger man just nodded.

"Tea is ready," Mrs. Black announced from the door. "Do you want it served in here, or in the dining parlor?"

"Why don't we just have it in the coziness of the kitchen, Mother?" suggested the young man easily. She looked about to object but closed her mouth.

"We're in rather a hurry to get back to the hospital," he added as they made their way toward the kitchen.

Mr. Woods nodded, his face very serious. Virginia wondered if he was the least bit interested in tea.

CHAPTER 14

$\mathcal{V}$irginia braced herself once again as the little group moved down the hallway and toward Jenny's closed door. They had been granted permission to enter by Dr. Moore, who seemed tremendously relieved to see Mr. Woods in a sober state.

Virginia was concerned that Jenny's father would take one look at his daughter and head back to the bottle.

The situation had not changed. A nurse moved about, changing tubes and checking the IV drip. She gave a curt nod when they entered, finished what she was doing, and stepped away from the bed.

Mr. Woods moved forward slowly. He was almost to the bedside before Virginia realized that he had her in tow, his strong grip hurting her arm.

Understanding his need, she did not attempt to pull her arm free. She waited silently while he studied every part of the scene before him—the limp form, the bandages, the medical equipment—then took Jenny's pale hand, much as she herself had done earlier.

His eyes filled with tears but he did not speak. Virginia wondered if father and daughter had been on strained terms for so long that he had forgotten how to commune with his little girl.

He bent over the bed and raised the unresisting hand to his face, rubbing it back and forth against his newly shaven cheek. Then he put the hand back down with touching gentleness, patted it, and turned to go. Virginia knew that for the present his father-heart was too overcome with emotion to stay any longer.

———

They agreed that Mr. Woods would be picked up again the next day for the visit to the hospital. Virginia knew that the pastor had a morning sermon to deliver, so it would be after the noon meal before they would be making the connection. She fretted that this gave Mr. Woods far too much time to nurse his grief with another bottle.

She rode to the church with Pastor Black and his mother. It was not a large congregation that gathered—rather the size of Virginia's own group back home. But they were friendly as they welcomed her to the morning service, though Virginia did notice many curious eyes.

"We wish to welcome Miss Simpson, who is with us this morning," the minister said from the pulpit by way of introduction, "though we deeply regret the circumstances for her visiting our city at this time. It was one of Miss Simpson's close friends who was involved in the motor accident of university students this past week. I want to urge you to remember Jenny Woods and her father, who is also here in our city, in your prayers throughout the week. I'm sure Miss Simpson would appreciate your prayers, as well." He went on to other announcements. Virginia could feel many eyes upon her with new warmth, a new understanding in their faces.

Virginia soon put aside her concerns a few minutes into the sermon. Pastor Black's sermon for the morning was taken from a psalm. Virginia had not caught the reference when it had been given, but he had not spoken many sentences until her attention was completely captured. "We often feel we are all alone when going through adversity," he reminded the audience. "We are not. God has promised to be there with us. He does not make promises lightly, nor does He disregard them once they have been made.

"How do you think Joseph felt, trudging through the heat of the desert, his colorful coat gone, his hands tied, feet shackled, as he was forced to accompany the Midianites who had purchased him from his evil brothers?

"How do you think Daniel felt as rough hands picked him up and suspended him momentarily over the mouth of the pit, from which came the muffled roar of hungry lions?

"Or the three young Israelite men as brutish soldiers forced their hands to their sides and bound them securely, a wall of angry flames awaiting them only a few feet away?

"What about Paul the apostle? Ridiculed and beaten. Driven from town to town or chained in dank, rat-infested dungeons? Did he—did they—remind themselves of God's sure promises? Or did they simply give up and give in?"

Of course they didn't, Virginia's own heart responded, and in the moments ahead the pastor took them through the pages of Scripture to remind them of how each of the individuals had responded to their plight.

Virginia felt strengthened and encouraged as she followed Mrs. Black from the pew. She wished that Jenny's father had been able—and willing—to hear the Sunday sermon.

———

The following days seemed to blend into one long tiring routine. Much to Virginia's surprise, Jenny's father stayed sober. Virginia often smelled liquor on his breath and knew that he had been imbibing, but he did not seem to overindulge to the point of losing control.

Each day Pastor Black and Virginia stopped at the hotel to pick up Mr. Woods, then proceeded to the hospital. Knowing that the pastor's days were filled with his own responsibilities, Virginia had insisted that he drop them off and call for them later. After a short argument he agreed.

It seemed to Virginia that nearly as much of their day was spent pacing the hall, or walking city streets to find a small diner, as it was sitting beside the unconscious Jenny. Each time they returned to the stark hospital room, they pleaded with Jenny to open her eyes, but there seemed to be nothing they could do to coax a response from the critically injured girl.

On the third day Virginia borrowed a copy of *The Pilgrim's Progress* from Mrs. Black and began to read aloud as they sat by Jenny's bed. She read for an hour in the morning and another hour in the afternoon, hoping that the sound of her voice would assure Jenny, even in her unconscious state, that she was not alone.

She watched for the flicker of an eyelid or the twitch of a hand, but she saw nothing. Jenny seemed totally unaware of their presence. And certainly the waning form was not listening to the tale of Pilgrim's journey. Still Virginia continued to read. She was on the fifth chapter before she noticed that Mr. Woods was listening. It both surprised and pleased her. From then on she read the story with clearer enunciation and a prayerful new purpose.

———

The week was drawing to a close with no visible change in Jenny's condition. Virginia was troubled and anxious. In two short days her return ticket required that she board the train for home. She had been given one week away from the post office. She did not think she could ask her new employer for more.

On their way to a nearby diner that had quickly become their favorite place for a sandwich, Virginia brought up the subject with Mr. Woods. "My ticket is for Saturday's train."

At first she thought he had not heard her, then she saw his nod.

"I would like to stay longer, but I really think I need to get back to work," she continued. Again a brief nod of acknowledgment.

"I feel so indebted to the Blacks. They have been very kind. I don't know how I would have managed without them. And he so busy with his church duties and all."

Virginia felt, more than saw, the man's head swivel to stare at her.

"What did you say?" he asked bluntly.

Virginia groped to remember what he might have missed. "They've been so kind," she ventured.

"No—that other."

"He's so busy?"

"With . . . ?" prompted Mr. Woods.

"His church," said Virginia simply.

"His church?"

Virginia looked at Mr. Woods. His jaw was working as though he were chewing through something tough and unpalatable.

He suddenly seemed to understand but still demanded verification. "Your young man's a *preacher*?"

Virginia felt her face going pale. "You didn't know?" Her step faltered.

"How was I to know? No one told me." He sounded angry as he stormed ahead toward their destination.

They entered the doors of the diner and selected their usual table. Virginia noted that the man still looked sullen.

She heard him curse beneath his breath and say something about being tricked and that he shouldn't have been such a complete fool.

It was too much for Virginia. She put her menu down on the table and slowly rose to her feet.

"Mr. Woods," she began, looking directly into his reddened eyes. "I have no idea what is troubling you or why the fact that Mr. Black is a minister should upset you, but the Blacks have been nothing but kind. Without Pastor Black you could very well *still* be waiting to see your daughter.

"If you can't appreciate the goodness of folks like him at a time like this, then I don't think I wish to remain in your company."

Virginia picked up her handbag. "And he's not my young man," she announced further. "I hadn't even met him until I arrived here." With the final words she fled the diner.

She had taken only a few steps, her eyes flowing with unbidden tears, when deep remorse overtook her. What in the world had she done now? She had longed to help the man. To see Jenny's father come to know God as his own Savior and friend. And now, in a moment of undisciplined rebuttal, she had completely destroyed that hope. Completely. She was so ashamed.

How am I ever to explain this to the Blacks? she mourned as she drew out her handkerchief and wiped the tears from her face.

Virginia desperately longed to be back in her own home—in her own room—where she could throw herself on her own bed and weep. Instead, she resolutely turned her footsteps back toward the hospital. She had only a short time to be with Jenny. She had to make it count. She could do without a sandwich. She would go back to the hospital room and read another chapter—or more—to her friend.

———

"Have I missed much?"

The voice made Virginia jump. She had not heard anyone enter the room. Mr. Woods stood there, dangling the black hat from one hand to the other. Virginia's cheeks burned with embarrassment.

"Here," he said a bit roughly. "Brought you a sandwich."

Now Virginia felt truly chastised. "I'm . . . I'm so sorry," she stammered. "Really, I'm sorry. I had no right . . ."

But he gruffly shoved the sandwich into her hands. It was clear to Virginia that he was awkward about apologies. It was also clear that he had no intention of pursuing the subject further. He turned their thoughts to the girl on the bed with, "Has she stirred?"

Virginia guessed that he knew the answer. She accepted it as simply a diversion and took up the conversation. "No. She still hasn't stirred."

"Maybe tomorrow," the man said as he pulled another chair up beside Virginia's. "Maybe tomorrow."

They were silent while Virginia ate the sandwich, then rolled up its wrapper to discard in the nearby wastebasket. *Now what?* she wondered.

Mr. Woods leaned over and picked up the book she had been reading. "Do you mind rereading the part I missed?"

Virginia did not mind.

———

Virginia's good-bye to Jenny was one of the most difficult she had ever said. As she walked away for the last time before catching her train, she wasn't sure if she would ever see her friend again. And if she did—if Jenny survived this awful accident—what would her condition be? Would she be able once again to take up where she had left off—or would Jenny's life be meaningless?

"I'll see you, Jenny," Virginia had told the still form through tears. "I will be praying for you every day." She corrected her comment. "Several times a day. Promise."

Mr. Woods, who had stood quietly by while Virginia said her good-byes, made no comment, but as Virginia turned to him he looked wretchedly uncomfortable.

"I . . . I hope there is improvement soon," she managed.

He nodded.

"You'll let me know if there's a change?"

He nodded again.

"I must go. Pastor Black is waiting to drive me to the train."

Jenny's father looked down at *The Pilgrim's Progress* he held in his hand. He had asked the Blacks if he could keep it long enough to complete the story for Jenny. Now it would be he who read the chapters morning and afternoon.

"Guess I'm somewhere in that dungeon right now," he muttered.

Virginia frowned. Pilgrim had already moved from the Dungeon of Despair. "No," she explained, "I've marked the page. We're—"

"Not Pilgrim. Me."

Virginia's heart constricted as she understood his admission. "You can move on, too, Mr. Woods," she said softly. "Honest."

He looked at her with such complete misery in his face that Virginia nearly reached out to give him a hug. But she wasn't sure how the man would respond. Instead she said, "Pastor Black will be available, I know. He'd be happy if you'd call him for anything."

The big man just nodded again. Virginia was relieved to hear no mumbled profanity. She turned and walked from the room without looking back.

———

Even though the train trip home seemed to take forever, Virginia was sure she would never be able to eat all the lunch Mrs. Black had packed for her.

They have been so kind—the Blacks, Virginia thought silently as she stared at the passing landscape. She could hardly wait to tell her folks about them. Certainly her father had chosen wisely. Or had it really been God who had done the choosing? Virginia thought maybe they had worked together on it.

Virginia kicked off her shoes and stretched her legs. She had hated to leave Jenny, but she would be so glad to get home. At the same time she knew she would be plied with questions, not just from her family but from town folks. She wondered how many times in the next days she would need to stop her mail sorting to answer another well-meant inquiry.

Well, she had very little to tell. At least very little that was good news. Jenny's condition had not seemed to change, in spite of the many prayers offered on her behalf.

Virginia felt very tired. Visiting with Jenny throughout the long week had been harder work than nursing Clara. At least with Clara there had been the hope that one day the situation would change. But would it ever change for Jenny? And if it did, would it be for the better? Jenny was not ready for eternity.

———

"They were so helpful. They did everything possible for me—and for Mr. Woods. Mrs. Black invited him for tea or supper several times, and Pastor Black drove us back and forth to the hospital each day. I felt so . . . so guilty, knowing how busy he already was."

They were sitting around the kitchen table, Virginia sharing with her family her experiences. Already she had told them that Jenny was still in her unconscious state. Now she filled in some of the details about her trip to Almsburg.

"I must write the Blacks a note," her mother responded.

"Perhaps we could make a contribution to their church," her father added.

"It's a small church—for the city," Virginia told them. "About the size of ours. But I'm sure it will grow quickly. He has only been there for a short time. But he loves the people— you can tell. And they love him. He's a good preacher, too. I felt challenged and encouraged after his message on Sunday."

"What's his wife like?" asked Francine.

"His wife? He doesn't have a wife."

Francine frowned. "Then who's this Mrs. Black you've been talking about?"

"Oh—his mother. No, Pastor Black is young. Very young. He just graduated from seminary. When his father passed away last year, his mother came to live with him. She was going to sell her little house in a nearby town, but he discouraged it. Said she might want to go back after she'd had some time to adjust. She's glad now. Thinks she might do that. She's missing her friends."

"Wait a minute," said Francine when Virginia stopped to take a breath. "Back up. You say he's young?"

"Yes."

"How young?"

Virginia looked at her younger sister, puzzled. "He's quite young," she replied. "Early twenties—somewhere. I don't know. I didn't ask him."

"Is he handsome?"

Virginia was annoyed. "Handsome? Why? I don't know. I suppose. I didn't bother to think about it."

She gave her sister a look that reflected her impatience. "Look, *you* might call him handsome, I suppose. And he might be young, but he's not young enough for you."

"I wasn't thinking about me," said Francine with a smirk.

"Jenny? She's not even conscious."

"I wasn't thinking of Jenny, either," said the coy Francine.

Virginia frowned, and then Francine's inference struck her. "Don't be ridiculous," she said with a disapproving look at her younger sibling. Such a foolish notion was the furthest thing from her mind. She had no intention of ever giving her heart to another. Jamison was still heavy on her mind. But she could feel her cheeks getting warm.

———

When the phone call came the following Wednesday, Virginia expected to hear Clara's voice, or perhaps even young Anthony's. But it was a man's deep voice that returned her greeting.

"Virginia? Jenny's pa here. She's waking. She's waking!"

Virginia's heart leaped and she could only stand, clasping the telephone earpiece for support.

"Hello. Are you there?"

"Yes. Yes," she managed. "I'm here."

"She's waking. Oh, she's not fully awake yet, but twice today she stirred a bit and her eyelids fluttered. The doctor thinks she's rousing from the coma." Mr. Woods' voice was full of awe.

Virginia was crying, but she finally was able to say, "That's wonderful, Mr. Woods. Wonderful."

"I'll keep you informed." The man sounded too choked up himself to say more.

"Here," she heard Mr. Woods say, and soon another voice sounded over the wires.

"Miss Simpson? This is Pastor Black. Dr. Moore is encouraged. Jenny does seem to be regaining consciousness. She is still in and out, but there is some response. It's an answer to prayer."

"Yes" was all Virginia could manage to whisper. But if she

hung up now, she would be upset for letting so many questions go unanswered.

"Does . . . does Dr. Moore say how long it might take?" she said through her tears.

"For full consciousness? No. He has no idea."

"Has she . . . said anything?"

"Not yet."

"How is her father holding up?"

"Doing well. Quite well. He's staying with us now. Took over our guest room."

Virginia could not believe her ears. Mr. Woods—staying in the home of a *pastor*? This was an answer to prayer as astounding as his daughter's recovery.

"We'll keep in touch," the voice on the other end of the line was saying.

"Thank you" was all Virginia could say.

A click, followed by a low hum, was the only sound as Virginia sat for a long time with the telephone in her hand.

CHAPTER 15

Now and then another phone call provided another report from someone regarding Jenny. Slowly, ever so slowly, during the weeks following Virginia's return home, she was wakening from her long sleep. Then the day came when she spoke her first word. "Papa."

Pastor Black told Virginia that Mr. Woods spent hours and hours at the bedside, massaging unused limbs, coaxing his daughter to swallow, showing her picture books, and naming each of the items to see if she could still remember. He read to her and eventually asked her if she could read to him.

Mr. Woods was more than elated when Jenny read the first halting words from the page, and his voice told Virginia more than his words did when he called to tell her the latest good news.

But it was going to be a long, difficult journey, the doctor soberly reminded all of those watching her progress with such interest and hope.

Mr. Woods made a quick trip home, accompanied by a tall, slender man with long, straggly, sandy hair, faded eyes, a handlebar mustache, and a constant cigar. "Mr. Aintree will be putting out the weekly paper for me until I get back" was

Mr. Woods' introduction of the new man. "No use letting the presses sit idle."

In spite of his rather unkempt appearance, folks were willing to give Mr. Aintree a fair chance for the sake of Mr. Woods. Sales of the weekly paper climbed to an all-time high, even though most folks eventually concluded that he was prone to a good deal of stretching the truth in order to put interest into local news. He tried to stir up issues, attempting to make Mac Dreeves' barking dog an entire neighborhood dispute and Mrs. Parker's bent toward gossip a public uproar. After his first few issues of the weekly, the folks waved aside anything that was reported—or even insinuated—as an outsider's misinterpretation. Virginia wondered if Mr. Aintree would catch on to the fact that he was mostly ignored as a source of news.

When Mr. Woods made his second trip back home, he dropped by the post office. Virginia did not catch any whiff of liquor.

"Jenny is able to sit up now," he informed her. "Not for long, and not without some support, but she's coming along."

Virginia was overjoyed. "When will she be able to come home again?"

"Soon, I hope. The doctor says if she continues to improve, she might be able to manage the train ride late spring."

Such a long ways off, but Virginia did not express the thought aloud.

"How is she doing?" Virginia knew that Mr. Woods would understand that her question involved more than simply how Jenny was progressing with her injuries.

"She's . . . she's pretty down most days. She knows that the two friends who were with her at the time of the accident are both up and about—going on with life. She doesn't understand why she should be the one to still be bedridden. I think—" He paused a moment, then continued, "I think she feels that someone, somewhere, has it in for Jenny Woods."

Virginia felt heartsick. *Strange*, she thought to herself, *those who deny the existence of God are just as intent on blaming Him when things go wrong in their lives.*

She turned her eyes back to Mr. Woods. "And you?"

His gaze dropped to the scuffed toes of his black boots. When he looked up again his eyes were thoughtful. "I guess I might agree—some," he said. "But I don't see it quite like Jenny."

He swallowed and seemed to struggle to express what he was thinking. When he turned back to Virginia his eyes were openly honest. "I haven't been the man I should have been. Jenny never really had much of a chance. Living with that young parson has opened my eyes to a lot of things. I take the blame for Jenny's troubles. I s'pose this . . . this accident is the only way that . . . something could have gotten my full attention. You would've thought I would've been smart enough to sit up and take notice after her . . . her other scrape. The one in the crick when you girls were young."

Virginia made no comment.

"But it doesn't seem right somehow that Jenny has to take the knocks. I'm still having a hard time trying to work that through," he admitted frankly.

Virginia nodded. It didn't seem fair. But maybe there was something they hadn't realized yet. She would have to hang on and trust the Lord to continue what He was doing in all this.

———

It was early June before Jenny could come home. Virginia was there to meet her train. She had tried to prepare herself for the worst, but even so, she was totally shocked by the sight of the girl who disembarked.

A thin, wasted Jenny was carried from the railcar and deposited in a wheelchair that sat waiting for her. Her hair had grown back to at least a covering over her head, but it certainly was not the burnished crown she had formerly taken such pride in.

Her eyes looked big and haunted in her white, thin face, and her arms were so skinny and frail that Virginia almost feared to touch them lest they snap.

Jenny did manage an uncertain smile, giving Virginia hope. Perhaps her mind and her memory had been restored.

"Papa said you'd be here," she said huskily. Her voice held none of its old buoyancy.

Virginia leaned over to place a kiss on the sallow cheek, hoping that Jenny would not misunderstand her tears. "It's good to have you home," she murmured.

"Well, I could say it's good to be home. But I'm not sure yet," Jenny replied.

Virginia determined then and there that she would do all in her power to make Jenny glad to be back.

But the days that followed were not easy for either of them. Virginia spent every spare moment with Jenny, attempting every way she knew to bring some spark back into the girl's eyes. Jenny fussed and complained and refused to take interest in anything about her. Enough of her memory had returned to make her grieve for her days at the university and the many friends she had left behind. Virginia wondered just how many of those friends had supported Jenny through the days following her accident. Virginia had certainly seen none of them in the week she had been there. But she wisely made no reference to that fact.

And then one day the tension in the sickroom turned to out-and-out war. Virginia had come over early on a Saturday morning, bringing with her Jenny's favorite sponge cake. Jenny had reacted with disdain rather than gratitude.

"Cake? Is a cake supposed to take the place of my arms and legs?"

Virginia bit her tongue.

"Honestly, Virginia, you are so . . . so downright . . . moronic." Jenny swore to further express her disgust. "Anyone who can stand there in front of a . . . a total invalid and offer a"—more expletives—"cake in place of life has no mind and no feelings."

Virginia's hands trembled.

"Get it out of here. You get out of here," Jenny screamed. "If it wasn't for your hateful, vindictive God, I wouldn't be sitting here in this chair." Another outpouring of horrid words.

Virginia held her breath. It was one thing for Jenny to turn her rage on a lifelong friend, but it was quite another for her to actually curse God. Suddenly she could remain silent no longer.

"Stop it!" Virginia shouted at Jenny, slamming the plate with the cake onto the side table. "You stop it. You will condemn yourself to . . . to—" But Virginia could not even say the word.

Jenny laughed. A cruel, hateful laugh. Then she stopped as suddenly as she had begun, her face contorted with rage. "Condemn myself? I'm already condemned. You think anything could be worse than this? I can't walk. I can't dance. I can't even *move*." She hurled the words at Virginia.

"You can breathe," Virginia flung back, stepping close to shout right in Jenny's face. "You can breathe. And you can think. Why aren't you thankful for that? Things could be far worse, you know. You could be dead. You could be brain-damaged. You could be a lot of things—worse than you are.

"You don't want the cake? Fine. I'll take the cake. But I'm not coming back until you decide to start trying and stop whining. I didn't put you in that wheelchair. And it was not a vindictive God who put you there, either. You made the choices, Jenny. If it hadn't been for a merciful God, you wouldn't even be here. Think about that, why don't you?" Virginia paused a moment, then finished with, "Why don't you stop feeling sorry for yourself and blaming others, and start working on getting out of that wheelchair? Or don't you have what it takes to do that?"

She snatched up the cake and stormed from the house.

Virginia was back again in the afternoon, remorseful and repentant. Jenny pretended not to be glad to see her, but Virginia saw the relieved look in Jenny's green eyes when she said, "I'm sorry." Jenny just waved a hand in a dismissive gesture.

No reference was made to the former outburst. They went on, a bit awkwardly at first, as though it had not happened. But over the days that followed, the relationship between the two gradually changed. Virginia did not attempt to see Jenny as often as she had at first, and when she did come, she did not come with offerings in her hand, nor cute little anecdotes to try to cheer the patient up. She laid aside those approaches. If Jenny was to get better, it would have to be her own doing. No one else could do it for her.

———

Clara's second son arrived with no complications. Anthony was beside himself at having a baby brother and coaxed and pleaded to hold the small bundle even when the baby was sound asleep.

They named him Jeffrey Luke. Jeffrey was his father's second name, and Luke was for his great-uncle who had given him such a good start in the world.

Clara had never looked better and declared she had never felt better, either. The mystery of her first troubled pregnancy remained, but everyone hoped that it was totally a thing of the past.

For the first few weeks, Virginia went over when she could just to give Clara a hand with the washing and heavier chores.

Francine pitched in, too. She was old enough and skilled enough to carry her share of the load.

Before they knew it, fall was again upon them. Virginia did not even think about going off to college. She had her job at the post office and was quite happy with it. She refused to think ahead to consider that she would be sorting mail and stamping envelopes for the rest of her life. But if she took it one day at a time, it was quite manageable.

Off and on, one or another of the local young men from the church invited her out to an event or expressed interest in beginning a relationship, but Virginia warded off all approaches. She had no intention of ever giving her heart again. She would never be able to love as she had loved Jamison.

———

The Christmas Day service fell on a Sunday. Virginia prepared for church with more than usual care and interest. It was not just another Sunday, with a later than usual dinner to follow. Christmas was always a special time, with thankful thoughts rekindled by the celebration over the coming to earth of a long-ago baby. And after the worship time, both personally and with the congregation, Virginia looked forward to the family being together. Especially the fact that Clara and Troy, with Anthony and Jeffrey, would be joining them. Virginia, a doting aunt, enjoyed her young nephews immensely.

Rodney and Danny had arrived home, as well, for the Christmas break, bringing added pleasure for all of them. And Rodney had excitedly met the train the night before to welcome Grace back to town. This time Virginia quietly observed that there was now much more to their relationship than friendship. She wondered if the Christmas season would bring an announcement.

Virginia had hoped that Mr. Woods and Jenny would join them for the service, but Jenny had pled a cold, and Mr. Woods said he would stay at home with her since it was Christmas Day. Mr. Woods had been attending services with some regularity since his return from the city. The congregation warmly welcomed him, but Jenny had resolutely refused to join him. Virginia continued to pray daily for Jenny.

With her thoughts on many things, Virginia walked with her family into the familiar church and hung her warm coat on a hook in the front hall. Smoothing the skirt of her new jade green suit and adjusting her hat, she followed Francine into the sanctuary.

She wondered absentmindedly what the pastor would find to say about Christmas that would be new. It had all been said so many times before. It must be difficult to be a minister, expected to find a new approach to a very old message. Even one as dramatic and significant as the one the angels had brought to earth so many years before.

Virginia slid into the bench beside Francine, and her eyes traveled over the rows of pews. There were the Ansons, the Carols, the Greens, and the Curtises in their usual places. Suddenly Virginia's breath caught in her throat. There sat Jamison. Her heart began to pound. She had not heard that he was home.

Virginia was totally unprepared for the strange feelings that passed through her. She had thought that with the passing months she had quite gotten over Jamison. At least she had hoped so. It had been over two years, and here she was with thumping pulse and wet palms at the mere sight of him across the aisle. She went from elation to heartache, from excitement to despair. She had no business responding in such a fashion. She shouldn't have responded at all. But she was caught so totally off guard, she excused herself. Why hadn't she been prepared? Why hadn't someone alerted her?

Virginia could not have reported what the pastor's morning sermon had contained. She stood when bidden to stand, bowed when invited to bow, sang when the rest of the congregation sang, but her mind would not cooperate. All she thought of was Jamison. The ache in her heart that had gradually lessened over the past months was rubbed raw and open again. Virginia longed to leave.

It did not help when the minister gave a special welcome to those who were back with them for Christmas. Rodney and Danny were named along with several other college young people, but Jamison Curtis was the name that stood out for Virginia, verifying that she was not imagining. Jamison was truly in their home church, sharing the morning service.

Once or twice she felt Jamison look her way. How was one to act under such circumstances? she asked herself. Controlled and uncaring? Kind and forgiving? She certainly had no intention of letting Jamison know how much his presence disturbed her, or that his very appearance set her heart to racing all over again.

When the service ended, she was of mixed feelings. She wanted to get up and rush from the sanctuary. At the same time she feared that he might. She longed to speak to him, but she feared that he might speak to her. What would she do? Could she keep her composure if he should say hello? Would he even wish to greet her? That thought brought more pain.

"Hello, Virginia."

Her heart stopped. Her face flushed. It was all that she could do to raise her eyes.

"Hello," she managed.

"How're things?"

She swallowed, a spark of anger mixing with the pain. How did he think she was? Hadn't he . . . ?

"Fine," she replied and even managed a small smile.

"Good."

"And with you?"

It was so awkward. Virginia felt as though the eyes of the

total congregation were upon them, watching to see just how they responded to each other. She forced her smile wider.

"Fine," he answered in turn. "College is going great."

"Good."

"We didn't win the championship this year, though."

"That's too bad."

It was all so forced, so artificial.

"How is Jenny? My folks told me about her accident."

For the first time Virginia's eyes expressed her true feelings. "She's not doing well," she said honestly with concern.

"I'm sorry to hear that. Tell her I said hello."

Virginia's head came up. "Why don't you call on her?"

"I leave later tonight."

"Oh."

So he was going away again—so quickly. Her throat tightened again.

"Merry Christmas." His voice sounded a little husky.

She was able to produce another smile. "Merry Christmas," she returned, hoping that it sounded sincere. The truth was, she wished to go home and cry.

———

Virginia could not nurse her broken heart for long. As soon as they got home from church, family members began to arrive. Anthony greeted Virginia with one of his childish hugs and a wrinkled gift extended in his small hand. "I made it for you," he informed her.

Virginia admired the scribbles he had put on the sheet of paper. "Oh, thank you," she exclaimed. "It's lovely. Tell me about it."

"That's a flower and this is its pot and this is a bunny rabbit sitting beside it with a white tail and a blue jacket."

Anthony had developed a love for the story of Peter Rabbit. Virginia assumed that the "blue jacket" was the one Peter wore in the pictures of the book. However, try as she might, Virginia could find none of the things the child listed in the picture he thrust her way. And there certainly was no blue in the crayon markings scrawled across the page.

"I will put it on my wall," Virginia promised seriously.

"Jeffy didn't make a picture," Anthony went on to excuse his baby brother. "He's too little to hold the crayon, an' he might eat it."

"Maybe next year," Virginia assured him.

From then on it was delightful chaos. It was the Simpsons' turn to have Clark and Marty join them for Christmas. By the time everyone had gathered, the long dining room table was crowded with happy faces. Eleven family members and their special guest, Grace, joined hands for the Christmas prayer, while one baby boy slept nearby in the much-used wooden cradle.

The merry laughter and good-natured teasing, served up with ample helpings of turkey, stuffing, and pumpkin pie, were enough to make one forget a broken heart.

Almost.

———

They gathered in the front parlor to sing carols and sip hot cider. Gifts had already been exchanged. The atmosphere was one of thankfulness and good cheer. Anthony, who had played himself out with the activities of the day, had fallen asleep in Virginia's arms and did not even stir as each new carol was enthusiastically begun.

"This has all been wonderful," Clark said after many songs had been sung together. He reached for his cane to assist himself in rising from his chair. "But Grandma and I better get us off home while the moon is still high."

A chuckle ran around the group. Grandpa Clark was always coming up with a new reason for taking himself off home.

Marty smiled, as well, but stood to her feet, also. "He's right," she exclaimed. "We aren't as good at stayin' up as we once were."

"We sure are gittin' better 'bout sleepin' in come mornin', though," Clark added, bringing another laugh.

"Guess we should be," Marty followed up the comment. "We sure been gettin' good practice at it of late."

They all enjoyed the laughter. Clark took a step forward, his wooden leg needing a bit of coaxing to get it to begin moving properly.

"Just a minute, everyone," spoke up Rodney, his face beginning to flush a deep red. "Before you all go, I have an announcement." He reached down and took Grace's hand, pulling her up beside him, slipping his other arm easily about her slender waist. "Grace has honored me by promising to become my wife," Rodney said in a rush, all shyness gone and in its place excitement and joy. He beamed as he looked from his family to the young woman at his side. Cheers went up. Congratulations followed. Belinda went quickly to Grace's side and gave her a motherly kiss on the cheek. The entire room erupted in well-wishing. Even young Anthony sat up in Virginia's arms, rubbed his sleepy eyes, and began grinning, though he had absolutely no idea what his family was celebrating.

It was hard to get everyone disentangled so that they could go off home. But at length it did happen. Rodney and the radiant Grace were left the privilege of the parlor, while others retreated to the kitchen to take care of the remaining cleaning up from the day of festivity.

"Wasn't this the most . . . most glorious Christmas ever?" said Francine, almost swooning with enthusiasm.

Belinda smiled. "It was very special. Starting with that wonderful sermon this morning. The meaning of Christmas just . . . just—well, it warmed my heart all over again to see it in that light. So many new thoughts—such reason for joy."

"And Rodney and Grace's engagement. Oh, I think I'd like to be engaged at Christmas. It would be so special," gushed Francine. "I can't think of a better time. Can you, Virginia?"

Virginia shrugged off the question. But Francine was not finished swooning—or making Virginia miserable.

"I'm so happy for Rodney. Aren't you, Virginia?"

"Of course." The words were curt, clipped.

She *was* happy for Rodney and Grace. Of course she was. But it could have come on a better day. It did not help to be so vividly reminded of just how much she had lost.

CHAPTER 16

"I'm taking Jenny on back to the hospital for assessment," Mr. Woods informed Virginia.

She looked up from the letters she was stamping. She realized he had walked over to the post office specifically to tell her this news. His office boy had already picked up the day's mail. She had heard no information from Jenny directly about another trip to the city hospital.

"I've been in touch with Dr. Moore," Mr. Woods explained. "He says there is little he can advise over the phone. He had hoped by now Jenny would have improved to a greater extent."

Virginia had hoped so, as well. Jenny's physical progress seemed to have been at a standstill for several weeks.

"Did he say if . . . ?" Virginia hesitated, not quite sure how to phrase the question.

"He wasn't willing to say anything at all over the phone. He wants to see her," Mr. Woods responded.

"But are there any . . . possibilities?"

"Well, he did say that there may be some surgery that could help. Or therapy. He won't know for sure until he sees her."

Virginia nodded, feeling guilty for the many times she had been impatient with Jenny for "not trying."

"I'll not be staying with Tom Black this time," the man told her. "I didn't want to put him out. Besides, he lost his good cook." Mr. Woods smiled, but at Virginia's concerned look, he hurried to say, "His mother moved back to her hometown. Tom thinks she may even have a special interest—a widower in her local church."

Virginia smiled in return, relieved that Mrs. Black was all right.

"Anyway, I'll stay at that little hotel he found for me before and take the streetcar back and forth to the hospital. That way the pastor can carry on with his own duties at the church. I have made arrangements to meet with him, though. Sort through some—some things I still don't understand."

Virginia looked at him in surprise.

"He's a good man," Mr. Woods said candidly. "He practices what he preaches. I figure a man could do a lot worse than to tie in with something like that."

Virginia's heart leaped. In all the years that she had been praying for Jenny, she had never expected God might work in the heart of her father first.

"I'll be praying," she promised the man now, finding it hard to fight tears.

"Thanks. I knew you would." He swallowed and licked his lips, as though having a hard time controlling his own emotions.

"I don't suppose there is any way . . . that you'd be at all interested in coming on down with us for . . . for a few days? I'd be paying your way and all."

Virginia could not hide her surprise. "I would like to, Mr. Woods—I dearly would—if I could be of any assistance. But I don't think I could ask Mr. Manson for any more time off.

It's a busy time of the year for us now—garden seed orders coming in and all."

He nodded. "Sure. I understand."

"But I . . . I do thank you."

He laughed. "Thank me? I wasn't offering you a favor, Virginia. I was asking you to do us one." His merriment faded. "Truth is, I don't know how to . . . to reach my girl. For many years, I know I left her on her own. I can't expect things to be much different now. But—well—she won't talk to me, won't tell me how she feels deep inside. I just can't touch her. She just locks me out."

"She has locked me out, too, Mr. Woods," Virginia said regretfully. "Oh, we talk—some—and we go through the motions of friendship. But it's not like it used to be. Jenny has shut herself away. I've about given up. All I can do is be there. And pray.

"I think I've finally realized that I cannot be Jenny's salvation," Virginia continued carefully, looking into Mr. Woods' face to see if he understood. "Only God can bring about the miracle, the rebirth. It is my job to love her, to pray for her, and to leave the rest to Him. I no longer push and prod—and grieve. It only causes stubbornness on her part and frustration on mine."

Mr. Woods nodded. He looked so concerned that Virginia's heart ached for him. But when he spoke, his words again surprised her.

"I guess I've put this whole load on you for far too many years. I've not been in the place where I could pray for my girl myself. Well, that's got to change. I can't go back and change the past, but I can change the future. The sooner I have that talk with the preacher, the better. I've known for some time that I need forgiveness—living the way I did with all that bitterness and anger that spewed out every time I opened my mouth. But I need to accept my responsibility as a father, too. I can't do that for Jenny if I keep on fighting God."

The tears refused to be contained any longer and rolled down Virginia's cheeks. She rubbed them quickly away with the tips of her fingers. The big man before her looked uneasy at his own confession. Virginia supposed it had been a long time since he had opened up so completely to anyone.

"When will you leave?" she asked in an effort to put him at ease.

"Tomorrow."

"For how long?"

"I've no idea. It will depend on the findings of the doctor."

"Of course."

He shuffled his feet and rubbed a hand across his unshaven cheek. Virginia knew he worked through the night on the paper. He very likely had not yet been home to take his breakfast.

"Is there any . . . message . . . you'd like to send?"

Virginia's brow wrinkled in confusion. To whom would she be sending a message? She didn't know anyone in the city. Except for Pastor and Mrs. Black, and Mr. Woods had said that Mrs. Black had left. So it was . . .

Oh. The young preacher. But what message would she have for him?

She smiled. "Just tell Pastor Black that I said hello and trust all is going well with him and his church," she responded lightly.

Mr. Woods gave her a grin and a nod before he turned to go.

———

Virginia had to readjust her thinking and daily routine with Jenny gone again. Instead of having to make time to go visit the girl, Virginia had to find other things to do to fill her spare time. With a sigh, she took up the handwork she had laid aside. For many months it had been nothing but a painful reminder that she had no need to be filling a hope chest with linens and laces. Now she began to have other thoughts.

There is no reason for Papa and Mama to be endlessly supporting an old-maid daughter, she thought to herself. *I'll keep my eyes open for a small place of my own. Even a spinster lady on her own has need for towels and pillowcases.*

Virginia once again began to embroider and stitch, carefully laying each completed project in her former "hope chest."

Francine, in her forthright manner, wanted to know what she was doing, and if she "had an eye on somebody." But Virginia refused to let the younger girl's comments disturb her.

She was finally over Jamison. Well, no—not totally. She wondered deep in her heart if she ever would really forget Jamison. But she could now think of him without such pain in her heart. The experience of his Christmas visit home had somehow managed to cut the cord that had bound her to him.

Perhaps it had been the shock. But more than likely it was the fact that he could approach her, could speak to her with civility, as an old friend, could turn and walk away as though she were no more, no less, than the other members of the local congregation. In those few moments, Virginia had clearly realized the fact that there would never be a reconciliation. It was too late. Maybe she wouldn't even want one. She sensed that Jamison was right. In some way she could not discern, only sense, everything was different now. He was not the Jamison she had loved when he was a boy.

And she had changed, too. How much or in what ways, she had not yet sorted through. But they both had become different people as young adults.

When her heart had finally recovered from this fresh wound, Virginia felt ready to lay all thoughts of love aside and go on with life. A life far different from the one she had romantically planned such a few short years before.

Now it was to be a life filled with her own activities and goals. It included God, as it always had, her church, family, and friends. It included her own little mission of reaching out to help in any way she could. It included self-sufficiency and responsibility—both to those she loved and to the employer in the job with which she was blessed.

Oh, it wasn't a magnificent career, Virginia realized. But it was one that put her in contact with many people daily. In spite of the fact that she had no higher education, it was work that supplied an adequate income so she would not need to be dependent on others. It even brought her a measure of satisfaction.

All in all, Virginia felt quite settled. Each month she was tucking away money in the fund that would one day buy her own house, and each week she added something more to her little chest of household items. There was no use grieving over what might have been.

———

Virginia was sorting the morning mail just in on the train. She hummed softly to herself as she went through the small pile of letters, almost automatically stuffing them into the proper boxes. Another letter for the Booths from their son in college. A letter to Mrs. Parker from her sister in the East. One for Mrs. Dunworthy from her elderly mother. *My, her handwriting is getting shaky*, she noticed.

Virginia stopped. The next letter in the pile bore her own name. And the handwriting was Jamison's. With trembling fingers Virginia tucked the letter into her pocket, anxious for the noon break to discover the reason for the correspondence. *Whatever it is*, she reminded herself sternly, *it is over between us.*

In spite of her resolve, Virginia found it difficult to concentrate. Why would Jamison be writing her? Had something happened?

There had not been a letter to his parents for several days. Surely if something was wrong he would have written to them first—or, certainly, as well as to her.

At last the clock on the wall granted Virginia her noon break. She strained to hear the footsteps of Mr. Manson as he came to relieve her. He was thirty-four seconds late, and it seemed an eternity to Virginia.

With one hand clinging to the letter in her pocket, Virginia hurriedly left the post office and crossed to a lone bench in the little square. Thankful that no one else was about, she quickly tore open the envelope. She had no idea what the message might be and how it might affect her emotions.

———

Dear Virginia,

Undoubtedly you will be surprised to receive a letter from me after all the months of not corresponding. You may even feel it strange that I would share my news with you, but I do hope you will understand that it is because of my deep respect for you as a person and friend.

It was good to see you at Christmas. I had dreaded the first time that I would face you and had put off coming home for that reason. I need not have feared. You were just as kind, just as personable, as ever. I so much admire you.

I have missed being able to share my heart with such a wonderful 'kindred spirit.' We were always able to talk frankly and openly about our thoughts and feelings. I will always cherish that. It got me through some tough times, especially when I came to college.

Things have changed, I know, but I do hope that our friendship might continue. You have every right to be angry, but I pray that is not the case.

The real purpose of this letter is because I wanted you to know that I believe God has brought someone new into my life. She came at just the right time. I was so low and so confused I hardly knew who I was or what I believed anymore. Then God sent Rachel. She is so strong and steady in her faith, and God used her to show me the way back to solid ground. I know you would love her. The two of you share so many common traits. Things I so greatly admire.

A little about her. Her father is a preacher with a growing church on the extreme west end of the city. She is the oldest child of a family of five, and because her folks have always been so busy with the mission church, she grew up quickly and assumed major responsibilities at an early age. I can't believe how mature she is in both attitude and action. I can hardly wait for the two of you to become acquainted.

We have made no definite plans as yet because I still have these classes to get out of the way. It was very difficult for me to backtrack and go for the accounting degree. I have had to earn money for my schooling, as well, so it has greatly slowed down the process.

I am still playing football. Coach says that he thinks I can make a professional team if I put my mind to it. Rachel assures me that she will back me if I decide to try. But at least now I have solid training to fall back on if it doesn't work.

I do pray that you can accept this letter in the spirit in which it was written—as a friend to a friend. You will never know the number of times I grieved over hurting you. That was never my intention. I am so relieved to see that the wounds have healed.

May God bless you always and bring only good things into your life.

> With deep devotion,
> Your friend Jamison.

Virginia sat, fingering the letter, and waited for the tears. They did not come. Jamison was telling her of a new love, and she could not cry. Instead, she felt strangely—what? Released. Healed. Restored. She had lost a first love, but she had regained a friend. A dear friend. She was uniquely blessed.

Rachel, her thoughts went on, *I don't know you, but thank you. Thank you for getting him back on track. Thank you for helping him to find faith in God—faith in himself again. He is a special person. I wish you every happiness with Jamison. He's a wonderful man. You are blessed, too.*

Slowly Virginia folded the letter and returned it to the envelope. That night she would write a reply. She was sure that she would not be able to express all the things that she was feeling, but she would try.

Suddenly, and without warning, the tears began to fall. But they were tears of thankfulness for the complete healing and the renewed joy that the letter had brought to her soul.

———

"Mama. I'm a bit worried." Virginia's words brought Belinda's head around from the pot she was stirring. "There is no smoke coming from Mr. Adamson's chimney," she explained hurriedly. "I went up and knocked on his door, but there was no answer. Is he away, do you know?"

"Not that I'm aware of," Belinda answered, concern on her face. "He has no place to go, as far as I know. No close family. Are you sure he didn't just miss your knock? He's getting quite hard of hearing."

"I knocked three times. And I called out. I didn't get any response at all."

"He might be dozing. That would account for the fire being allowed to—" But Belinda laid aside her spoon and started toward the back door. Virginia followed.

"Come to think of it, I didn't see him in the yard when I came home from the grocery store this morning," Belinda mused as they walked quickly together toward the little house.

"I didn't think much of it at the time. He spends more time indoors these days."

"His knees are getting so bad. I hold my breath when I see him walking about and trying to keep his garden."

"I know. He seems to be getting more and more tottery."

"I just hope he hasn't fallen."

"There certainly is not smoke from the chimney."

There was no response to Belinda's loud rapping on the front door.

"What should we do?" Virginia asked as fear gripped her.

"Mr. Adamson," her mother called out loudly, rapping again. "Mr. Adamson, are you there?"

Virginia clasped her hands in nervousness.

"We need to check," her mother said. "He might need help."

But the door, surprisingly, was locked.

"I didn't know he locked his door," Belinda murmured.

"He told me that it has a habit of coming open in the wind, so he keeps it locked. He always uses the back door. I'm sure it will be open."

At the rear of the house, a wheelbarrow stood under the willow tree, bearing pulled weeds and clipped grass.

"It looks like he was working here quite recently," Belinda noted hopefully.

Again she rapped and called, and with no response. Without hesitation she turned the knob, and the door opened.

Virginia was relieved to see there was no prone body on the kitchen floor. Used dishes sat on the table, a lone fly buzzing lazily over the contents.

"Mr. Adamson," Belinda called again. "Are you here?"

Still only silence.

They moved together from the kitchen. There was no sign of anyone in the parlor. On through to the little bedroom.

There was Mr. Adamson, tucked into bed, a peaceful look on his face.

"Oh, thank God. He's sleeping," Virginia whispered in relief. "I was so worried."

But her mother, the nurse, reached out an arm and drew Virginia close. "He's not sleeping, Virginia," she said softly. "He's gone."

Virginia looked at her mother with a puzzled frown. Understanding began to dawn, more because of her mother's face than because of her words.

"You mean . . . ?"

Belinda nodded.

"What happened?"

"In his sleep, I would suppose."

"But . . . ?"

It was hard for Virginia to accept. Their old neighbor. With his kindly nod and his arms of flowers. He had been taken from them. Silently. Alone.

She buried her face against her mother's shoulder and wept.

————

In a quiet ceremony, he was buried in the little cemetery on the hill. He had not been a great man who had accomplished great deeds, but he had been a good neighbor and a great friend. He had brought joy with his flowers and understanding with his willingness to listen. They would miss him.

Throughout the summer months, Virginia kept the weeds from his garden and picked fresh bouquets of flowers to carry up to his grave. It seemed like so little to offer the man who had given friendship and a word in season to a gangly, uncertain little girl at a time when she needed it the most.

CHAPTER 17

With Rodney's graduation in the spring, he and Grace were planning a late fall wedding. It meant excitement for the entire family. The Simpsons would travel by train to Grace's home city of Bremington and stay with her in her mansionlike home. "I insist," she told them. "That is the only reason I am keeping the house for as long as I am."

Already Rodney had a job with a pharmaceutical company in the growing city where they would live. It was a long way from his small-town roots and hard for the family to accept that he and Grace would not set up housekeeping nearby as Clara and Troy had.

But Rodney seemed so happy and excited by the prospects that they could do nothing but rejoice with him and wish them well.

He and Grace had decided to sell the large house that she had inherited and move into a less auspicious home in a newer neighborhood. But making those arrangements would take time, and they did not want to be rushed.

At first it had bothered Rodney that his new bride would be the one to provide the family home, but he explained to his family that Grace soon laid to rest any arguments that he presented.

"I didn't earn it, either," she had assured him. "Nor did my father, if it comes right down to it. It was passed on to him through my grandmother. She was the one who brought money to the family."

Grace shared more of her family history on one of her many visits. They all were gathered around the table after a Sunday dinner, including Clara's little family.

"My mother came from a lower income family. My father met and fell in love with her on one of his business excursions. She was working in the office of one of the companies he visited. He brought her home, and my grandmother was the first to give her approval. 'You'd be a fool, my boy, not to marry that girl,' she told him. 'And I have never set out to raise a fool.'

"My grandmother was a very outspoken woman. I'm not sure if the family was matriarchal, but if it was not, it was not for any fault on my grandmother's part. I learned all this from my mother's diaries that I discovered shortly after Aunt Sadie's passing.

"Every reference to Grandmother spoke of a wise woman— and she was fair. She didn't make snap judgments, and they were not based on bias. I guess that made her 'dictatorship' a little easier to bear." The lovely young woman smiled a bit ruefully.

"It wasn't that Grandfather was spineless," she said. "There were a number of times when he put his foot down. But he also respected Grandmother's judgment and invited her opinion on matters."

Clara pushed back from the table with a sleeping baby in her arms. "Oh, please, Grace, could you wait a minute while I put the boys down for naps? This is fascinating, and I don't want to miss a word."

They all laughed as she hurried out with the two boys in tow. They chatted quietly until Clara returned.

"Now, where was I?" Grace wondered. "Yes—my grandfather appreciated my grandmother's wisdom and wanted to know what she thought about various matters.

"My own father, an only son, grew up used to seeing a husband and wife work together in making decisions. Some in the business saw that as a weakness. He never did, and would have stood up to them regarding it. He took my mother with him on his trips as much as possible, and even at home they would discuss business deals and future investments.

"My mother did not have the same educational opportunities and experience, but she was astute—and she learned quickly. She was a much keener judge of character than my father, who saw everything and everybody as either black or white. Mother would say, 'Now let's just give him a chance, Benson. He may have learned from that mistake.' "

The group chuckled. They laughed harder when Drew put a playful arm around Belinda's shoulders and said, "Just like my dear wife allows me my mistakes—for learning purposes."

Grace's expression indicated her appreciation of the family repartee. When they had settled down, she continued her story.

"Mother was an only child, too, by the time she met my father. There had been two other children in the family, but they both died from childhood diseases. Anyway, my folks had not been married long when Mother lost both her parents over the same winter. There was only Aunt Sadie—my mother's aunt—left. She had been living in a teeny backstreet house by herself. I think that Mother felt dreadfully lonely after losing both of her folks in such short order, so she brought Aunt Sadie to live with us.

"At first I was afraid of her. She mostly sat in her room, looking stern and formidable. She would speak to me in this low voice, 'Come here, child.' I always went as bidden, because I was too afraid not to, I guess.

"Soon Mother was traveling with Father more, and I was left in the care of Aunt Sadie. I discovered that she was not one to be afraid of at all. In fact, I grew quite attached to her. What I loved most was that she could always be coaxed into reading me a story. I can still hear her rich voice, 'Once upon a time . . .' "

Grace laughed at her own imitation, and her audience laughed with her.

"Then," she said soberly, "on one of the trips my folks took there was a train derailment. That was the last I ever saw them. I was very young, and I don't remember them well. Just little bits and pieces here and there. Little snatches of what it was to be part of a family. Fortunately Aunt Sadie stayed on and took over.

"She would never spend a penny of the money that was left for my guardianship—not on herself. She had her own little income that she drew on. 'Nobody's gonna say that I cared for you to get what you got,' she told me every once in a while.

"But she was most particular about me. How I dressed. Where I went to school. My manners. 'Not going to have Carrie'—that was my mama—'feeling shame over her little girl,' she'd say.

"She never went out. Not even to church. She sat at home in her own room, her Bible on her knees. I think she was intimidated by the wealthy neighborhood and the big church down the street. She knew she wasn't a part of it, and she never wanted folks to think that she was pretending to be.

"But she sent me to the church. Every Sunday. Mr. Will drove me and Miss Emma accompanied me. Every Sunday. Me all dressed up in the latest fashion, feeling rather strange and like I was on display." Grace paused for a moment and looked down at her hands, no doubt remembering those rather awkward and lonely times.

"But the church was good for me," she said, lifting her head and smiling around at the group. "I took notes and took those new truths home every Sunday, and Aunt Sadie and I discussed them. It was at Aunt Sadie's knee that I asked for forgiveness of my sin.

"When she died, I was devastated. She had never permitted me to make friends in normal ways. I think she wasn't quite sure who my friends should be and didn't want to make any mistakes. 'God will show you who to partner with when the time comes,' she would tell me—any relationship to Aunt Sadie was a partnership.

"So I was quite lost when she was gone. For the first several months, I didn't know what to do or whom to talk to. Then one day Miss Emma, who was still with me, spoke frankly. Aunt Sadie would have said that she 'spoke out of turn,' but I'm so glad that she was brave enough, and cared enough, to break down those walls that Aunt Sadie had carefully constructed around me—between household help and homeowner.

" 'Miss,' she said to me. 'Seems that you have to get things back together one of these days, or you are going to be just sitting here like your aunt Sadie throughout your entire life. There's more to the world than this heap of stick and stone. I would suggest that you discover it.'

"At first her words upset me, but I did do some thinking about them. Soon I was praying about them. I had no idea where to start, so I got brave one day and asked Miss Emma. 'Why not talk to the parson?' she said. It sounded like a good idea, so I made an appointment to see the pastor of my church.

"He did give good advice. He urged me to consider getting training in some field. I imagine he was thinking more about getting me out and away from the house than anything.

I considered the possibilities and decided on nursing. He seemed surprised at that. He probably expected me to pursue something in the arts. My nursing took me to the university campus—" she stopped and smiled at Rodney, reaching for his hand—"where I met Rodney."

The look that passed between them made a little bitter-sweet catch in Virginia's heart.

"And I have discovered that God had it all planned—even before I had caught on to it," Grace finished.

It was a nice story, though certainly with its share of personal sorrow. Virginia felt even more regard for Rodney's wife-to-be. She hoped they would be very happy together and counted the days until they could all share in the upcoming wedding celebration.

———

Mr. Woods was making frequent train trips to visit Jenny. Once she had gotten back to the university city, she had pleaded with her father to let her stay. The doctors, though they searched with all the knowledge at their disposal, found no reason why Jenny should not be walking. The only thing they could suggest was further therapy.

Mr. Woods reluctantly left her and returned home, visiting as often as he could make the trip to see her.

Virginia was thrilled to learn that he had lived up to his promise to see Thomas Black, and the minister had led him through the Scriptures, and guided him through the sinner's prayer of repentance.

Even though his eyes held a new light and his face a new glow, Mr. Woods' expression turned sorrowful as he went on to report Jenny's response.

She was not the least pleased by the decision, the man had told Virginia. "Are you going soft?" she threw at him, then added sarcastically, "I liked you better when you were drunk."

Mr. Woods looked so shamefaced as he said it that Virginia wanted to put her arms around him in comfort. But she did not. He grieved over Jenny and her attitude, but he was determined not to give up on his only daughter.

Virginia, too, grieved. How could one who had been constantly prayed for over so many years be so distant from God? she wondered. But she was committed to keep right on praying.

———

Virginia had written back to Jamison, and they continued to exchange occasional letters. Little by little he introduced her, via the written page, to his Rachel. A few times Rachel added little postscripts at the bottom of Jamison's letter. Virginia always smiled. A few months earlier it would have seemed impossible that she would ever enjoy an exchange with Jamison's new love. Now it seemed quite natural—and even enjoyable.

"It won't be long now until Jamison is finished with his classes," Rachel wrote on one occasion. "Please pray for wisdom for us."

And Virginia did.

"I'm bringing Rachel home for the weekend," a hasty scrawl on the back of a postcard announced. "Can you meet us at the 5:45 on the 22nd?"

It was signed with the initials, J.C.

Virginia felt excitement—and also a case of nerves. But this time it was not the anxiety of seeing Jamison again. That was a thing of the past. But because she would be meeting Rachel for the first time. She truly wanted this young lady to like her. She could not easily have put into words why it was so important to her—she only knew that it was.

If pressed, she may have said she had this funny feeling

that Rachel might be critical of Jamison's past alliances. For her to make the discovery that he had chosen poorly in the past might reflect, in some way, on his character and good judgment. It was silly reasoning, but Virginia honestly wanted nothing to damage Rachel's perception of the friend from her youth.

Virginia took some time in selecting the dress she would wear to work that Friday. Very carefully she pinned her hair and chose the hat to complement it. There would be no time to come home and change before the train arrived.

"I just think this is so strange," observed Francine in her worldly wise manner when Virginia made her appearance in the kitchen. "I mean, what woman would go to the train to meet her former boyfriend's new girl?"

Belinda smiled as she shook her head at her younger daughter. "I think it's nice that Virginia is mature enough to be happy for Jamison."

"Well, I think . . . it's abnormal," insisted Francine. She was quite vocal about beginning to study the boys of her acquaintance with the thoughts of a possible suitor.

"She seems very nice from her notes," Virginia told her sister. Francine was doing little to put Virginia's nerves at ease.

"That's another thing—writing notes to—"

"Francine, would you get the cream from the pantry, please?" Belinda's assignment stopped Francine's verbal musings.

Francine went to obey, still muttering about the strangeness of the situation.

"You look nice." Belinda turned to smile at Virginia.

"Oh, I hope so. I mean, I know little about her. Well, I know quite a bit about her—her personality and all. But I've no idea how she will dress. She might be far more . . . more fashionable, like Grace. I'd feel just—"

"You look very nice," Belinda repeated. "Jamison knows you and the fact that you are not a fashion plate. Do you think he would invite you to the station to embarrass you?"

Virginia shook her head. But inwardly she knew that Jamison, being a fellow, might not be thinking ladies' fashion at all.

All day long Virginia fought to concentrate on the tasks at hand. When five-thirty arrived, she closed the door and tidied the small office, then reached for her hat. Carefully she fastened it with the long hatpin and smoothed the hair that curled about her face under its brim. *At least the hat is fairly new and quite becoming*, she thought with some satisfaction as she studied herself in the small wall mirror.

Locking the door behind her, she took a deep breath and started for the railroad station. She had five minutes before the train was due to arrive. She did hope it was on time.

In the distance she heard the train whistle. She increased her pace, wanting to have a moment to catch her breath and regain her composure before Jamison and Rachel descended the steps. She wished she had thought ahead to bring some small gift of welcome. Perhaps a few of the flowers from her mother's garden or a sweet from the soda shop. It was too late now. She should have thought of it sooner.

She was out of breath by the time she reached the platform. Already the train was coming into view just on the edge of town. Carefully she smoothed her skirts and checked her gloves. *Why am I so nervous?* she thought, laughing at herself. *It's not as if I'm a bride or something!*

The train rolled in beside her. She stood back until it came to a stop and the excess steam hissed out from between the wheels.

Soon people were descending the steps. One. Two. Mr. Welks. Another man she had never seen before in a dark pinstripe suit. Two ladies from an outlying farm whom she knew only distantly. Another stranger.

And then came Jamison, assisting a young woman whose arm was tucked firmly in his own. *Rachel*.

Virginia moved forward as Jamison and his friend moved toward her. Virginia's eyes swept over the softly pleated gray skirt, on up to the trim jacket, and on to the hesitant smile, the wide blue eyes, the brown curls beneath an attractive hat.

Virginia had the feeling that Rachel had given her the same quick appraisal. The mutual assessment concluded just as they stepped close enough for Jamison to turn from the one to the other. "Rachel—this is Virginia."

Virginia's searching eyes met Rachel's blue ones. There was a hint of question, quickly followed by a flicker of amusement. Virginia answered with a smile, and then they laughingly fell into each other's outstretched arms while a confused Jamison looked on. They were wearing identical hats.

———

Virginia could not have believed that she would like someone so completely and so quickly. It was easy for her to understand why Jamison had fallen for Rachel. She was warm and personable, and yet there was a sophistication and maturity about her that reminded Virginia of her own roots.

She is so much better suited to be Jamison's wife than I ever could have been, she admitted to herself. *She understands the city and its ways. I don't think I would ever feel totally at home there.*

Virginia finally felt that God's hand in their lives had kept her and Jamison from a terrible mistake. Jamison was going to find happiness with a girl better suited to the life and career he had chosen. She would have wanted to get him back to their old hometown—or would have chafed over having to leave it behind.

Virginia could smile now and accept what had been so difficult for her in the past.

The three spent long hours together, chatting and laughing, Jamison and Virginia sharing with Rachel tales of childhood adventures and anecdotes about their town. Never was there reference made to the days when the two had courted. Virginia was surprised to find out just how much of life and church and friends they had shared apart from the more recent years they had spent as a couple. It warmed her heart and gave her hope that the future could still hold a friendship for them.

When the two girls were alone, Rachel expressed her thoughts in a deeper, more transparent fashion.

"Jamison has told me so much about you. And, yes, he did tell me that you were . . . that you had plans when he went off to college. He also told me how deeply it hurt him when he . . . when he told you that he thought you should end the relationship.

"When I first met Jamison, he was really struggling. That group where he had been attending—I hesitate to call it a church—really had him confused. With their fancy arguments and cross-fire debates, they helped to destroy the faith of more young people than we'll ever know. Jamison held on. He really fought to continue with his beliefs. And a big part of the reason he was able to do so was you. He didn't want to let you down, Virginia. He told me that. His folks, his pastor, they were all important to him, but it was really his long talks with you in those growing-up years that held him steady.

"I want to thank you for that. Personally. Whether you knew it at the time or not, you had a great deal to do with shaping the life and character of the man I have come to love."

Virginia had tears in her eyes.

"He's going to try for a professional team," Rachel went on. "Whether he makes it or not, we won't know until he tries. He's a great quarterback, but going on with school—taking time for education rather than going directly to the sports world as his coach had advised—that might cost him. He's older now. I keep telling him that he's more mature, too. Wiser as a player. But it may have cost him. We know that.

"But if it is to be—or not—that's all in God's hands. He

will now have a career that he can pursue if football doesn't work out. We want God's will in this. We'd appreciate your continued prayers."

Virginia nodded. It would not be difficult to pray for Jamison and his lovely Rachel.

———

Mr. Adamson's little house had sat forlorn and empty all through the months of the summer. Virginia had supposed that it would always be so. It seemed that no one should take their beloved neighbor's place. Virginia could still feel his presence as she walked by in the morning when the sun was giving the first dewy kiss to the roses, or again at night when the fragrance of his carefully tended sweet peas wafted up the street to meet her returning steps.

So Virginia stopped in shock at a For Sale sign placed on the front lawn. She wanted to object, but she did not know where and to whom she would make such a protest.

"They are trying to sell Mr. Adamson's house" were her first words upon entering the kitchen where her mother worked on the evening meal.

"Yes, I know," Belinda answered. "Your father has the responsibility."

"Papa? But it's Mr. Adamson's house." It did sound pretty childish, even to her own ears. Her mother's head swiveled to look at her in surprise.

"You knew it would have to sell sooner or later," Belinda answered.

Virginia did not respond. She supposed it would. That seemed to be the way of things. But just the same, it would be very difficult to see a complete stranger in Mr. Adamson's garden.

CHAPTER 18

I don't know that Jenny will ever be back," Mr. Woods told Virginia as they stood on the steps after church.

"How is she?"

"Well, she's much improved from when you last saw her. But then, I guess she's finally found a reason."

Virginia's interest was piqued. She dared to hope that Jenny might finally be concerned about her spiritual well-being.

"A young therapist," explained Mr. Woods.

"A therapist?"

He nodded and continued. "He took over her treatment right after she went on back. She took quite a shine to him, and soon he seemed to return the feelings. They see each other regularly now, though on the sly. Doctors aren't to date their patients, you know."

Virginia didn't, but she was willing to accept his word for it.

"She has another five months of therapy. He has another eight before he's fully qualified. I've a notion that they might make some plans sometime in the future."

Virginia was not sure whether to be happy or disappointed.

"What is—what is he like?" she asked a bit tentatively, needing more information but not wanting to pry.

Mr. Woods didn't seem to mind. "Like Jenny, I'm afraid." He shook his head. "Likes to live high and fast. One of the night-life crowd."

Now Virginia did feel upset.

"Sure hasn't any interest in church at all," went on Mr. Woods. "Neither of 'em."

"I'm so sorry," whispered Virginia.

The man's shoulders sagged. "You reap what you sow, just like Scripture says. I resisted the church and all it stood for during the years that Jenny was growing up. I can't really expect her to turn to it now. I'd give my life to change that if I could."

Virginia felt so sorry for him. It didn't seem fair that he should have to carry this burden of Jenny's sins.

"And you think she'll stay there?"

"I'm sure she won't come back here. She always did think it a dead town."

"I know," admitted Virginia, "but I was hoping. . . ."

"I was, too."

"I'll write her again."

Even as Virginia spoke the words, she knew it would do little good. Jenny had not responded to her last three letters. Now, hearing of the young man in Jenny's life, Virginia was even more disappointed at her silence. Under normal circumstances, Jenny would have at least written to tell Virginia her good news. Did this mean that Jenny had completely crossed her off as a friend?

———

Rodney and Grace's wedding was a wonderful event for all of them. The trip to the city was exciting, the stay in Grace's beautiful home an experience they would never forget, and the wedding itself one that touched the hearts of all who attended.

It was a simple wedding, even by small-town standards. Only family members and close friends had been invited. The Bremington newspaper's society page had headlined it, *Million-aire's Orphan Daughter Weds Small-Town Boy In Simple Ceremony*. The columnist reported on the family fortune, the unusual young woman who now inherited all right to it, and the simple lifestyle she had chosen in place of taking her rightful spot in society. "A reverse of the Cinderella story," said the writer. "Heir claims that much of the family wealth will be set up in a trust fund to help educate worthy students in the fields of medicine and missions." The writer did not have to spell out the fact that he—or she—was in no way able to understand such unlikely reasoning.

Grace would not even read the article. "I have no idea where they researched their facts," she said with some disdain. "They certainly didn't get them from me."

However, Virginia knew that Grace and Rodney did intend to set up the trust fund. They had talked to her mother and father about it. Grace was particularly interested in sharing the plan when she learned that Belinda herself had turned her back on a fortune and put the funds to sheltering the elderly instead.

"Have you ever been sorry?" Grace had asked candidly.

"Never," said Belinda, not a shade of doubt in her voice or manner.

Though the wedding itself was small, Grace looked like a princess in her long, flowing white satin, the veil of lace trailing down the aisle behind her. Virginia and Danny, along with two of the bridal couple's friends from university, were the only attendants. Grace said she felt no need to fill the aisle with people who meant little to them just because society dictated that one should.

Following the ceremony, a small reception was held in a local hotel ballroom. This one did meet with all of Virginia's dreams of elegance. Huge chandeliers hung from overhead, sending splashes of soft mini-rainbows over the white linens that draped the tables. Bouquets of flowers, larger than any that Virginia had ever seen, graced each available cherry cabinet or marble mantel. The carpet on the floor was so luxurious that it felt like they were walking on the softest of newly mown lawn.

"Ooh," exclaimed Francine, "this is the way to live. How can she ever leave all this behind?"

Then the young Francine, who more often than not had her pretty head in some dream cloud, followed with, "Ooh, I wish she had a brother."

"I don't know what possible good that would do you," responded Danny in typical older brother style, dutifully doing his part to keep his younger sister's feet firmly on the ground.

Virginia caught Francine's disgusted scowl.

The truth was, Francine had developed into a very attractive young lady. Too attractive, Virginia often thought. She feared that the prettiness, plus all of the attention that it drew, would go to the young girl's head. She silently applauded Danny for setting the girl back on her heels again.

"She doesn't even have cousins," Francine moaned to Virginia when they were out of Danny's earshot.

"No, and she doesn't even have a fortune—at least she won't once the fund is properly set up."

Francine looked disappointed all over again.

"First Mama—and now Grace," she murmured in disgust. "Just think, we could have been living in a mansion all these years ourselves."

"Have you been unhappy?" quizzed Virginia.

Francine gave her a scathing look and did not answer. Instead, she said, "Is Papa going to set the fund up for her?"

"No," replied Virginia. "He has put them in touch with a lawyer here in Bremington. Someone he is sure they can trust."

"I still think they should have kept some of it."

"They will keep some of it. They are investing—"

"But the house—they should have kept that gorgeous house! Can you imagine giving up something like that?"

"A gorgeous house does not always bring happiness," Virginia replied. " 'Little is much, if love abides.' "

"Who said that?" demanded Francine.

"I don't know," shrugged Virginia. "Some wise soul."

"Daft, to my thinking," sniffed Francine.

Virginia smiled. She was sure that the young Francine would eventually get her priorities straight. She did hope, for the sake of all of them, that it didn't take too long.

———

"I think we've found a buyer for Mr. Adamson's house," Virginia's father announced at the supper table.

Virginia looked up, her heart constricting with sadness. She had been hoping that the house would not sell. She had even dared to hope that one day, with her saving of monthly wages, she might be able to offer a bid. Now her hopes were being dashed.

"Someone local?" Belinda wondered.

"No. In fact, they are coming from down south. They farmed down there, but the man passed away and the woman needs a place. Her daughter wants her in a town with a doctor. Understand she isn't in very good health."

"Another patient for Luke. He's worked nearly off his feet already."

"Or maybe it'll be another patient for Dr. Braden."

Belinda nodded.

"How boring," put in Francine, who must have been hoping for a much younger occupant with an interesting son or two.

"Anyway," went on her father, "they are to come up to take a look at it on Saturday. Understand that the daughter and her husband live somewhere out west and need to get the mother settled as quickly as possible so they can get back home. Sounds like a pretty good chance they'll take it."

Belinda smiled. "It will be good to have neighbors again."

"A neighbor," corrected her husband. "She'll be living alone."

"A neighbor then. You say she hasn't been well. Is she elderly?"

"Sounds like it. But I really don't know her age."

Virginia let her mind travel over the information. If an elderly, ailing woman moved in next door, the gardens would go unattended. She couldn't bear the thought of Mr. Adamson's flowers being neglected. *Oh dear*, she thought to herself. *This will solve nothing. I do hope they decide it doesn't suit.*

But Virginia said nothing.

She decided to make it another item for prayer. She would not be selfish. At least she would try hard not to be. Instead of praying for her own way regarding the little house, she would pray that God's will be done. She couldn't help but hope that God's will might be closely matched to her own.

———

When Saturday arrived, a car pulled up next door around noon, and Virginia's father put on his suit coat and went over to meet them as arranged. Virginia tried not to be obvious, but it was hard to see what was going on without going out into the yard. She pretended to be trimming her mother's favorite rosebush, though an unspoken rule was that no one was to touch it except Belinda herself.

It actually was too late in the fall to be doing much in the yard, and her father had already raked the autumn leaves. Virginia snipped at a stray twig here and there and stole a peek now and then. A pleasant-looking woman gently led an older lady toward the house while a rather tall man stood talking to her father, his broad back toward the Simpson yard.

The two ladies chatted amiably as they took the walk toward the house. The elder stopped often to admire one plant or another, even though the time of flowers was past and most of the leaves now lay in colored crazy-quilt fashion on the ground beneath the bushes.

"What is that? A lilac bush, do you think?" Virginia heard the older woman ask. "Oh, I do hope so. I love lilacs. I remember Mama had a lilac when I was a girl. It had the most beautiful lavender blossoms, and in the spring when it bloomed, you could smell it throughout the whole yard."

That one is pink, Virginia wanted to answer. *And its fragrance fills the whole block.*

"And is that a Hansa rose? They are lovely. Bloom all summer long."

On and on they went, exclaiming over Mr. Adamson's sleeping flowers.

"Oh, I don't think that I will be able to bear waiting for spring," the elderly woman enthused as her daughter coaxed her on down the walkway. Virginia noted that she walked with a distinct limp.

And who will be taking care of the flowers? Virginia wondered. *Surely they don't think that a garden cares for itself.*

They rounded the corner and passed out of earshot. Virginia turned her attention back to the man still speaking with her father.

"My wife used to live about forty miles southwest," she heard him say. "Hasn't been back much since she was a girl. Only to visit now and then. But it's been much dryer down there. Things sure don't grow like they do here. It's pretty here. Real pretty. Bet it looks real nice in the spring and summer."

Belinda's father agreed. "But not everyone in town has a garden like Mr. Adamson," he hastened to add. "The old gentleman spent all his time tending it."

Tell him, Papa. Virginia longed to cheer him on. *Let him know how much time a garden such as that requires.*

"My daughter has been caring for it since Mr. Adamson passed on," her father continued. "She has a real love for flowers, and she seems to have a knack with them, as well."

"Wonder if she would be interested in giving Mama a hand," asked the man. "I know that Mama will not be able to handle this on her own, but she would enjoy it so much that I'd love to see her have the place."

Virginia's heart sank. It seemed they had every intention of buying it.

"We tried everything we knew to try to coax her on out west with us, but she refuses. Doesn't care that much for it. Both times we managed to talk her into a visit, the wind blew the whole time and it was so dry the dust was flying every which way. For us who live there, it becomes commonplace. We're so used to it we don't much notice it anymore. But Mama says that as much as she loves her family, she'd go stark-raving mad living in the wind all the time."

He laughed. A deep-throated, good-natured laugh. They turned to follow the women up the walk.

Virginia, her shears almost forgotten in her hands, got a good look at him then. He was taller than her father, tanned a deep bronze. Even though he was about her father's age, he looked tremendously fit. Like he could still outwork—or outrun—men half his age.

"What do you have for churches here in town?" he was asking. "It's very important to Mama to find a good church."

Virginia's father began to describe the town's denominations, ending with their own and stressing that the elderly woman would be more than welcome to join the family in worship. "We'd be happy to give her a ride whenever she needs it," he finished.

The other man looked pleased.

Virginia was feeling embarrassed about her pretense and finally gave up on the rosebush. She put the pruners back in the shed where they belonged and returned to the house to find her mother laying the table for tea.

"I told your father to bring them over for tea once they have seen the house," she explained.

Virginia flushed. She could have accomplished her purpose without hanging around the rosebush. She went to wash her soiled hands so she could help her mother.

The new folks had not been in the house for ten minutes before it was forgotten that they had so recently been complete strangers, and the group was visiting like old friends.

In answer to the Simpsons' family introductions, the newcomers shared about their own. "We have seven," the couple said in unison. They looked at each other and laughed.

"Actually," said the younger of the two women, who to Virginia's thinking was very attractive, "we started our marriage with three."

It sounded like an interesting story. Virginia hoped she would go on.

"There were three little children in the town who were orphans. We were not married then. I decided to take them on, and Gil kindly offered to help me with them."

The man laughed. " 'Course I already had my eye on her," he admitted, "but I hadn't been brave enough to tell her so. The kids just sort of made it easier for me—gave me an excuse."

"So we got married with three little ones to care for," the woman explained. "Moved out to Gil's ranch. Then another four came along. Their births made seven."

"Sounds like you were busy," said Belinda.

"We were, but they were good years. I'd do the same all over again."

"We only have the youngest two left at home now," the man took up the story. "The others have married and are off on their own. Three beautiful little grandchildren. They sure do make our day."

"We have two grandsons," interjected Belinda. "And I agree. They are delightful."

"The two who are still at home?" Drew prompted.

"One girl, Rebeccah—she's our youngest. She already has a beau, so I expect we'll have another wedding come next year. And Jonathan. He's been ranching with his father," answered the woman.

"My wife gave all our four Bible names," the man added, nodding to her with a supportive smile.

"My mother had given me a Bible name, and it was because of that I became interested in spiritual things," the woman explained, giving her mother a look filled with love. "I decided that if it meant that much to me, it might mean something to them someday, so they became Daniel, Mark, and Jonathan— then we added Rebeccah."

"What is your name?" Belinda asked with interest.

"Damaris."

"Damaris. I've never known anyone with that name before. It's beautiful. But, I admit," she went on, a slight frown creasing her forehead, "I don't recall her story."

The woman laughed softly. "There's not much of a story there. All it said in Acts seventeen, verse thirty-four, is that a woman named Damaris became a believer."

"Became a believer?" repeated Belinda. Then she added, "I guess that is the single most important thing that can be said of one."

"That's exactly what Mother Dover said to me when she

showed me the verse in the Bible." The woman's eyes grew soft with emotion.

"And you, Mrs. Withers?" asked Drew, turning attention to the elderly woman. "You've never lived in the West?"

Virginia had noted that the little woman was very quiet during the exchange. She guessed that her father had noticed it, too, and wished to include her in the conversation. The mother seemed almost shy—withdrawn, listening but not taking part in what was going on. So Virginia was surprised when she responded and expressed herself so freely.

"This is as far west as I care to get," answered the woman. "I came from the East. I met my husband back on the coast, where things were green and the ocean breakers put me to sleep every night..He had the wanderlust, and soon we were moving a little inland, then a little farther inland. And on he went, bit by bit, and I was getting farther and farther away from my family and friends.

"We ended up farming, but the land where we settled wasn't all that good. We had some real dry years. Didn't do too well on the farm. They were hard years—nearly crushed him. I wasn't sorry to sell it. I really don't know why anyone would want it. But it's been raining more the last few years, and they're talking irrigation now. Land might produce something after all. Anyway, I was offered a good price—to my thinking. I wasn't going to argue."

Virginia could not help but smile. The woman who seemed shy—even uncertain—barely lifted her head as she spoke, but she was articulate and feisty in her own quiet way. Maybe a neighbor wasn't such a bad idea after all. Virginia thought that, perhaps, Mr. Adamson would have approved of her.

CHAPTER 19

I really am worried about leaving Mama," Damaris Lewis said as she shared a cup of tea with Belinda and Virginia on the following Saturday afternoon. "She insists she'll be fine, but I've noticed that she can be a bit unsteady on her feet. She's not as strong as she claims that she is, and I'm afraid that little house and big yard will be way too much for her. I do wish she would have agreed to come live with us."

Virginia could hear the deep concern in the woman's voice. She wished there were some way she could be more help, but her job at the post office took most of her time. Right now the yard took little care, but soon there would be snow to shovel off their own walk. Shoveling snow was one thing that her father found very difficult to do with one arm.

And with the coming of spring, their yard would take a good deal of time and effort. Virginia would be able to help with the new neighbor's, but would she be able to do it all? She wasn't sure.

"I'll help all I can. . . ." she found herself saying hesitantly.

"You have all been so kind," said a thankful Damaris. "You don't know how much that means to us. And we are so happy that Mama has found a good church. Good neighbors and a good church—those are things we all have been praying for."

Belinda refreshed the teacups.

"We've decided that Gil will return home and I'll stay on for a couple of weeks to see how things go. I do want to be back home for Christmas, though. I hope that I'll be able to talk Mama into coming with me, at least for that long. I hate to think of her all alone for Christmas."

"I know how you must feel," responded Belinda. "If she . . . really doesn't want to do that, we'd be glad to have her join us. I know that it isn't the same as being with family, but at least she wouldn't be alone."

"That's very kind." Damaris stirred her tea for what seemed to be a long time to Virginia. When she looked up, her eyes were misty. "Mama has not had an easy life," she began haltingly. "I . . . I don't believe in running round—spilling my soul—or laying my burden on others. But I know you will respect Mama's privacy, and it may help if you know something about her past."

She hesitated again, then sighed deeply and went on. "She told you the other day that my papa had the wanderlust. Yes, he did. He was never too settled. But he also had a . . . a drinking problem even as a young man, I think. The . . . drinking . . . was a way to . . . I think to try to escape what he knew to be his responsibilities. But the worse things became—and they did get pretty bad—the more he needed to drink."

She absentmindedly stirred her tea round and round.

"He became abusive. It grew worse with the years. As a child growing up I was often a target of that abuse, but so was Mama. Eventually I ran away from home and went west with a wagon train moving out that way. One of the last ones that made the journey, I suppose. Soon locomotives were taking the people to where they wanted to go.

"Anyway, it was then that I—through a dear friend—found a

personal faith." She smiled. "I also found Gil—and a ready-made family."

Belinda answered with an understanding smile.

"But I always worried about Mama. I felt really guilty for leaving her behind."

"I can understand," said Belinda, her eyes shadowed as she thought about the woman's story.

"I longed to write to Mama—to let her know where I was and plead with her to join me. But I feared that a letter from me would just increase my father's rage. And I admit, I still had no love for my father. Nor any sympathy. I was very angry inside for what he had done to us over the years.

"It wasn't until I became a believer—no, it was even after that. For some while I still struggled. I finally learned that I had to let go of my bitterness and forgive my father. It wasn't easy, but God helped me. I was able to write a letter to them both, telling them—honestly—that I loved them.

"Mother said that Papa said nothing when he read the letter—just laid it aside. But he didn't head for town and another bottle as I had feared he might. Oh, he didn't stop drinking. And he didn't stop being abusive, either—at least not at first. But he softened somewhat, and he wasn't quite as heavy-handed.

"Several months after the letter arrived, he had a stroke. The doctor said he should have died, but he didn't. He was left paralysed on one side. Mama had the heavy burden of nursing him. Day after day she cared for him. I longed to go back, but I was expecting my second child at the time." She sighed and stared out the window before continuing.

"At first he was terribly difficult for Mama to handle as he went through an alcoholic's withdrawal, but when they had finally weathered that storm he settled down. She read to him by the hours. Books. Any books she could find. When she ran out of storybooks she started reading from the Bible. He didn't object as she had expected. Soon they were both engrossed. They spent whole weeks going through the Old Testament. Then the New.

"One day when she was reading he made motions to her. She couldn't understand them. She brought him a piece of paper, and with an unsteady hand he wrote, 'Let's do it.' She still didn't understand. She looked back at the page that she had just read to him. It was the story of Nicodemus coming to Jesus.

" 'You mean . . . be born again?' she asked Papa. He nodded. And so they did. Both of them—together—with Mama saying the prayer and Papa nodding his agreement. The baby and I arrived home just in time for me to say good-bye. He died the next day. I've always been so thankful that God allowed me the chance to tell him I loved him."

She stopped and lifted her hankie to dab at overflowing eyes.

"I think that one special week was the most wonderful time of all their years together.

"Of course, we had been praying—every day—but we had no idea God would need to lay Papa flat on his back to keep him from the liquor so that he would have a clear head to understand the Scriptures.

"Gil came for the funeral. I tried to talk Mama into leaving the farm and coming to live with us, but she wouldn't. Didn't want to leave the farm—leave Papa. I think that her joy—and her sorrow—were still much too fresh. She stayed on, letting a neighbor farm the land and pay her a stipend from the crop.

"Now she has finally agreed to sell the land to the neighbor. It's a big step, and I know it will not be easy for her. I still wish she had decided to come with us, but she said, 'No, not so far away. I am still close enough to make the trip back now and then. And close enough to be buried beside him.' Rather strange, isn't it? I think that she has quite forgotten all of the . . . the bad times and remembers only that one beautiful week they had together."

She stopped again to wipe away tears from her cheek. Virginia realized that she had a few tears of her own. She determined anew that she would do all she could to make things as easy as possible for their new neighbor.

———

"Jenny's married."

Mr. Woods had made a special trip to the post office to tell Virginia the news.

"The young therapist?" she asked. Jenny had not written her even about this.

He nodded.

"I didn't know," she stated quietly.

"It was a very private wedding from what I hear," Mr. Woods said. "I didn't know, either." Then added, "She's walking again, you know. In fact, she is making real good progress physically."

Virginia wondered what he meant.

He explained, "Spiritually, she seems to be getting further and further away from God."

Virginia tried to imagine how she could get much further away from Him.

"Grandma Davis says that sometimes the darkest part of morning is just before dawn," Virginia said softly. "God loves Jenny, and I'm not giving up on her."

He nodded. "I hope the dawn comes soon." He looked so weary. So old. "They are back to the fast life. Running with a fast crowd. Partying. Drinking a lot. That sort of thing."

Virginia did not know how to respond. What could she say?

———

"Aunt Gina, do you know why bees buzz?" young Anthony asked, his face screwed up in all seriousness.

Virginia shook her head, wondering where this conversation was heading.

"They have a little auto motor—right down here in their tummy."

Virginia frowned, then smiled. "Who told you that?"

"I fig'red it all out." He looked quite proud.

"Well, I'm not sure you figured it out correctly."

Now it was his turn to frown.

"The buzz is the sound their wings make as they move."

"Uh uh," he argued, shaking his head and causing a soft brown lock of hair to fall over his forehead. "I don't think so. Wings couldn't do that."

"Have you watched them? Did you see how quickly they move?"

"I can't see their wings when they're moving them fast. And when they sit, their wings don't move."

Virginia smiled. It was true. "Well, if you watch closely, you'll see a little blur."

He still looked doubtful. "They are sleeping now. In their hibe. Papa said so."

"Your papa's right. They are in their hibe—hive," she said with a warm hug.

"Like dead," he said, wriggling free of her embrace.

"Sort of like dead, I guess. But they are very much alive, and as soon as spring and the warm weather comes they'll be out again."

"Then I'll look," he informed Virginia, "but I don't think you'll be right."

"So how do you plan to see if you are right—if they have a little auto motor?"

He frowned as he thought about it. At last his face brightened. "Cut one open and let it pop out."

"That wouldn't be very nice for the poor bee."

He looked very intent. "Maybe I should just ask Uncle Danny. He knows all about bees and things."

"That's a better idea. Ask Uncle Danny."

A muffled sound came from the nearby bedroom. Anthony's head came up and his eyes shone. "Jeffy's awake. We better go get him."

Virginia was only too happy to comply.

———

Jamison and Rachel were married on the eve of December twenty-fourth in her home church with her father performing the ceremony. Virginia was invited and would have attended, but the distance made that trip unwise. Besides, she had promised that she would keep an eye on Damaris Lewis' mother. They had given up trying to persuade Mrs. Withers to travel out to the ranch in the West for Christmas. She would be spending the day with the Simpsons.

So Virginia sent her best wishes and a gift that she had selected and packaged with great care. She did genuinely hope they would be happy together. At last she had come to the place where she no longer nursed any feelings of regret and could agree with her grandmother, "God knows best. We can trust Him with our lives as well as our eternal souls. He does not take something from us without filling that spot with something just as good—and because it's from Him, even much better."

Virginia supposed that the peace she was enjoying was the "something better" in her own life. At first she found this difficult to believe, but when she stopped to think about it, she *was* happy. Settled and content. Should spinsterhood be in store, and she fully expected that it was, she would have no regrets. Her life with God, family, and friends was full and complete, leaving no room for sorrow or bitterness or might-have-beens.

———

Virginia thoroughly enjoyed her visits with Mrs. Withers. It was no hardship at all to fill her evening hours calling on the woman, sharing cups of tea or hot cocoa as they sat and chatted by the living room fireplace or at the kitchen table warmed by the big iron range. Virginia took treats of baking and small casseroles to be used for the next day's dinner and shared community news and stories of Mr. Adamson and his beautiful flowers.

"I can hardly wait for spring to come," the woman told her many times. "It will be so wonderful to watch them all bloom."

Virginia smiled. She was anticipating spring, as well. The only task she had found at all difficult was keeping Mrs. Withers' walkway clear of snow.

Mrs. Withers, over their evenings together, gradually shared more details of her life—of their difficult struggles on the farm and the heartbreaking work of her husband. She always ended with a shine in her eyes, repeating the story of the last week of their lives together and how he held her hand in his own weak, trembling one, and tried to thank her, without words, for her love and care.

Virginia never failed to have a lump in her throat. Never once did the woman refer to the difficult years of his drinking.

———

Virginia hurried up the walkway toward Mrs. Withers' house. She always delivered her mail in person whenever a letter came. It was awfully cold for February—more like a January day. Virginia's fingers were numb from the cold as she hurried around to the back door, anxious to be home herself and out of the wind.

"It's just me," she called as she knocked, opened the door, and thrust her head in. The warmth of the wood-burning stove and the smell of the evening meal cooking were most inviting, and Virginia was tempted to shut the door behind her and stay if her own family had not been expecting her. "I have your mail. I'll put it on the table."

From the adjoining room a quivery voice answered, "Thank you, dear."

"I'll see you after supper," Virginia called as she closed the door firmly behind her to shut out the cold.

She'll be excited when she sees a letter from her daughter, Virginia thought as she hustled off home.

Damaris wrote regularly, and Mrs. Withers was always thrilled to see those precious envelopes. Her old eyes would sparkle and her mouth work slightly as her shaky hands worked at opening it without any damage. Each letter was carefully added to the little stack in the metal box that she kept on a bedroom shelf.

Supper seemed to take longer than usual as Francine chattered on about all the events of her school day. Francine liked to share the details of her life, large and small. Often they seemed childish to Virginia, but she tried to listen with a measure of patience. She supposed they weren't much different from the small happenings that had seemed so monumental in her own life such a short time ago.

"And Andy said, 'Really, Josie, you've only yourself to blame. You knew when the assignment was due. Why should you think that you are above everyone else?' And Josie, you know what a temper she has. She threw the book right at him. Andy ducked, and the book just about hit Mr. Randolph, who was going by in the hall. We almost had to stay after school—the whole lot of us—while he tried to sort out what had happened."

And on and on it went. Virginia chafed at the delay. She was anxious to wash up the dishes and get over to Mrs. Withers' before the woman retired. She went to bed very early.

"So how do you see it?" asked Drew. Virginia couldn't help but smile as she saw their lawyer father "prepare the case" for her unsuspecting sister.

"What do you mean?" from an innocent Francine.

"Who was at fault here?"

"Well, Andy was just sticking up for me. It wasn't his fault."

"And you?"

"It wasn't my fault that Josie's assignment was late."

"But you only have one book to share for research."

"Yes, but I did get it first."

"Could you have gotten it back sooner?"

Francine hesitated.

"You knew other members of the class needed it?"

Francine tipped her head.

"Did you know they would be penalized for a late assignment?"

Francine's reluctance to nod was very evident.

"It seems that it would have been considerate to finish with the book as quickly as possible to prevent that," her father continued.

"Josie did spend the entire weekend . . ."

Can't we just go? Virginia was getting fidgety. Let Mr. Randolph sort out this . . . this teenage dilemma.

At last they were excused, and Virginia hurried with the dishes.

"I'm going over to see Mrs. Withers," she called to those reading the evening paper in the parlor.

A rustling of paper and a "Fine. Wrap up. It's cold," followed her.

Mrs. Withers met her at the door. Virginia had the feeling the woman had been watching for her to come up the walk.

In her hand she waved her latest letter like a flag of triumph. Her eyes were shining, and her unsteady feet looked about to break into a dance.

"He's coming," she said, excitement making her voice more wavery than usual. "Damaris says so, right here. Next Thursday. Coming right here. And he's staying—just as long as I need him."

Virginia stopped, her hand still on the doorknob. What was making the woman so excited?

"He's coming," the lady repeated again.

"Who?" asked Virginia.

"Jonathan. My grandson. He's coming from the West to stay with me."

The elderly woman lowered her voice conspiratorially. "I've never told this to a single soul," she whispered. "One isn't to have special pets, you know, but out of the whole bunch of them, he's always been my favorite."

Virginia smiled and gave the small figure a hug. If she was so happy about this visit, Virginia would be, too.

CHAPTER 20

$\mathcal{M}$rs. Withers is just thrilled," Virginia informed her folks when she came in the door. "Her grandson is coming to stay with her," she added as she shrugged out of her coat.

"Her grandson?"

Virginia nodded.

"Which one?"

Virginia chuckled softly and shook her head knowingly. "Her favorite one. Though don't you tell a soul. Grandmothers aren't supposed to have favorites."

Belinda smiled.

"There is only one who isn't married," her father remembered. "Must be him."

"Oh yes. Damaris told us. He has been ranching with his father. What was his name again?" This from her mother.

"Jonathan," filled in Virginia. "Mrs. Withers called him Jonathan."

"Jonathan. That's it. So he's coming? That will be so nice for her. Will he be here by spring?"

"Next Thursday."

"Next Thursday? My, he made up his mind in a hurry."

"Or his mother made it up for him," put in Drew.

"Oh, I hope he doesn't feel . . . feel that he has to do this. I mean, it's not easy looking after the elderly and especially if . . ." Belinda did not finish her statement.

"How long will he stay?" Virginia's father wondered.

"Well, I didn't read the letter, but Mrs. Withers is counting on him staying as long as she needs him. Settling in with her."

Both of her parents looked surprised.

"That could be a good long time," Drew said doubtfully. "Mrs. Withers may look a little frail, but I think she's hardier than one would think. I don't suppose she's much beyond seventy."

"Seventy-three," said Virginia, who had been informed by the lady herself.

"So this Jonathan is planning on staying? His father doesn't need him on the ranch?"

Virginia hung up the coat she had been dangling since returning home. "The younger girl—I've forgotten her name—and her husband-to-be are to be married next month. He will work with Mr. Lewis, according to Mrs. Withers."

"And what will—Jonathan, is it?—do here? It doesn't seem that Mrs. Withers' yard will be a full-time job." Her father sounded a bit skeptical.

"He plans to find a job."

"A job? Not many ranches round about." Drew went back to his newspaper.

Virginia did not try to answer. It was neither here nor there to her if or how the young man chose to avail himself of whatever work there was. She was pleased for her friend Mrs. Withers, who was almost beside herself in her anticipation. Virginia hoped she would be able to sleep.

"Well, Mrs. Withers is nearly skipping around the kitchen," she said with a smile. "She can hardly wait for Thursday."

"How old is this Jonathan?" Francine suddenly called from

the kitchen where she was supposed to be studying at the table.

Drew looked up from the paper. "I don't think anyone ever said."

"Twenty-four," said Virginia. She could feel her cheeks warm. "Mrs. Withers said he is twenty-four."

"T-o-o-o old," they could hear Francine mutter.

Virginia and Belinda exchanged glances. *Francine is far too interested in boys* was the unspoken message.

———

It snowed lightly all afternoon. Virginia watched it lazily drifting down outside the post office windows and would have enjoyed its silent beauty had not her thoughts been on Mrs. Withers' walk.

I will need to shovel—again, she thought to herself. *Well, at least it isn't as cold as it has been. That will make the job a little easier.*

Following a busy day at work, she hurried home to change into clothes more suitable for shoveling. She called to her mother as she left her room, "I may be a little late for supper. Please go ahead without me. I want to clear Mrs. Withers' walk before it gets too dark."

"Fine, dear," she heard her mother's answer.

She was just getting started when she heard the creak of the gate. She looked over her shoulder in the gathering dusk to glimpse a figure walking toward her, a suitcase in each hand.

"Excuse me," he said. "I must be totally confused. I'm looking for Mrs. Withers. My directions got me here, but I must have made a mistake. Do you by chance—?"

"This is Mrs. Withers'," Virginia answered as she straightened and looked through the darkness. She could not see the face of the stranger, but he was tall.

He stepped closer. "Then, who are you?" he asked, placing

241

one of the heavy suitcases on the ground and lifting his hat from his head in one easy motion. "Excuse me, ma'am. I didn't mean to be rude. It's just that my grandmother . . ." He sounded flustered.

Grandmother? Virginia's thoughts whirled. *It's Thursday.* She had totally forgotten that this was the day the grandson—Jonathan—was to arrive.

Before Virginia could explain, there was a flurry of activity behind her, and Mrs. Withers came rushing down the walk. Virginia never would have guessed the elderly woman could move so quickly.

"Jonathan," she cried, her arms outstretched.

"Grandmother." The second suitcase was quickly discarded. He moved to meet her and picked her up right off the ground as he embraced her.

Virginia stood awkwardly to the side, feeling a bit like an intruder. *They've scattered snow all over the only part I'd managed to clean*, she mentally noted.

"You've met Virginia," the grandmother stated as the tall young man set her back down on her own two feet.

He reached down to pick up the Stetson that had fallen unnoticed during their exuberant meeting. He dusted the snow off against his knee with sharp little raps. "Can't say that I have" was his answer.

"This is Virginia. She is my—our—neighbor."

He nodded. "Pleased to meet you, ma'am."

"Virginia's not a ma'am. She's a miss," the grandmother said with a chuckle.

He returned his hat to its place, and he dipped his head slightly. "And why is Miss Virginia shoveling snow?" he queried. His voice was deep, but warm and interested.

"She always clears the snow," the grandmother replied.

The young man stepped closer to Virginia and removed the Stetson once more. "I sincerely thank you, miss, for looking out for Grandmother. But from now on it won't be necessary. I'll be manning the shovel."

She nodded slowly, feeling a mixture of relief and regret.

"If you'll excuse us, I'm going to get my grandmother in the house before she catches her death of cold." As he spoke he reached out and removed the shovel from Virginia's hands. "I assure you that I will clear the walk—just as soon as Grandmother is back inside. I do thank you for your assistance. You have been most kind. Mother spoke highly of Grandmother's good neighbors. I see she was not exaggerating. Now you'd best get back home, too, before—"

"Come in, Virginia," Mrs. Withers interjected. "Come on in. You really haven't had a proper introduction."

Virginia hung back.

"Can't you come in?"

"I . . . I really must get home for supper. Mother will be waiting."

"Of course. Well . . . you come on over just as soon as you're done."

"I . . . I don't think so tonight, Mrs. Withers. You and your grandson will have a lot of catching up to do."

"Nonsense. We have months to catch up. Come on over and get acquainted."

"Tomorrow, perhaps. You need some time. . . ."

The young man was gently guiding the woman toward the house. Virginia knew he was concerned with her being outside without proper wrap.

"I'll see you tomorrow, Mrs. Withers," she called after them, feeling that some kind of promise would make the woman more compliant.

As Virginia trudged toward home, she felt unsettled. It was nice to be relieved of the responsibility of walk clearing, but she was going to miss the quiet evenings with the older woman, sipping tea and hearing stories from her past.

She briefly wished that the grandson had not come but quickly put the thought out of her mind as being selfish.

———

Virginia did not rush with the supper dishes the following evening. She wished she had not promised Mrs. Withers that she would pay a visit. She would now truly feel like an intruder. The elderly woman really did not require her company anymore.

Virginia was reluctantly removing her apron, still uncertain about what she should do, when there was a knock on their kitchen door. Francine, who had been doing the dish-drying chore, crossed the room to open it.

Virginia looked over to see the younger girl standing stock still, her hand still holding the door open, her mouth slightly open as she stared at the young man standing on the porch.

"Good evening," he said, "I'm looking for Miss—Virginia."

Francine's eyes switched from the young man to her sister and back again.

"Good evening." He spoke over Francine's head. "My apologies for barging in like this. But Grandmother would give me no rest—nor would she rest—until I came to see if you were planning to come over as you indicated."

Virginia now could see the young man clearly. He was even taller than she had thought, broad shouldered and muscular, yet lithe in movement as he stepped past the dumbstruck Francine and entered the kitchen as he spoke.

His hair was a shade of brown Virginia had never seen before. She would not have known the proper word to describe it. Maybe glints of amber? His jawline was neither square nor sharply angular. In all, it was a pleasant face—not handsome in the fashion that made Francine swoon—but appealing. But it was his eyes that drew Virginia's attention. They were of a shade of blue Francine would later dramatically describe as "amethyst." Virginia finished hanging the apron. "I . . . I was just on my way," she managed.

"Good." And he smiled. The pleasant face lit up from an inner light. He was—actually—rather handsome.

"I'll get my coat." She also picked up a plate of cookies.

They walked over together. Virginia noticed that the walkway was totally cleared of snow. *A person who keeps promises,* she noted.

"Grandmother has been talking of your visit all day," he informed her. "She says you are the best company she has ever had."

"I don't think she is much used to company," Virginia responded with a bit of a laugh.

He chuckled with her. "If I didn't know better, I'd maybe feel a little jealous," he said.

They laughed again.

The evening passed pleasantly. Virginia found Jonathan to be easy to visit with, and as they drank hot cocoa and munched on the cookies Virginia had brought, they sensed an easy camaraderie.

When it was time for Virginia to go, he reached for his Stetson. "I'll walk you home."

"There's no need. I just live across the fence," she said lightly. "I've been making this little journey every evening—"

"I'd like to," he said. Virginia did not argue further.

"You haven't heard of any jobs around, have you?" he asked as they walked the short distance.

Virginia took a moment to ponder but came up empty.

"I don't suppose there's much need for workers here. Well, I won't get too anxious. But I've no intention of sitting about. I'll find something, if I have to invent it." He laughed good-naturedly. "Well, there certainly are things to do around the house. I've spotted several items that could use some fixing. That will keep me busy for a while. And Grandmother says the pastor was asking for volunteers to do some repairs at the church. I'll check into that. Then we'll see what comes. Just thought you might have heard something—being in the post office and all."

"If I do, I will certainly let you know," Virginia promised.

"I'd appreciate it."

He left Virginia at her door with a "Good night" and a tip of his hat as she entered the kitchen. As soon as she stepped through the door, Francine began hounding her with questions and comments.

"I can't believe it. Where did he come from? Right next door. He's so . . . so manly . . . and so mannered. And those amethyst eyes. They—I could just drown in them."

"Francine," Virginia said with some impatience, "you read far too much—literature that is not literature."

"Tell me," went on Francine, ignoring her comment. "What is he like?"

"A gentleman," replied Virginia curtly.

"Oh, I could see that in a moment. One can just tell."

"He came here to look after his grandmother," Virginia reminded her.

"That is so . . . so *precious*," Francine cooed. "What man— his age—would do a thing like that?"

"He happens to think—" began Virginia, but then stopped. Francine had made an astute observation. What young man his age *would* do a thing like that?

Very few, she concluded. Very few.

Perhaps there is a reason that Jonathan is his grandmother's favorite, she noted. *He must be rather special.* But she gave no hint of her thoughts to her sister.

Francine was still expressing her opinion. "His smile. Have you ever seen a smile like that? So . . . so manly, so—"

"So mannered," quipped Virginia meaningfully.

Francine seemed not to notice. "And he isn't old at all," she concluded.

———

Over the weeks that followed, Virginia did continue to visit the house next door. She soon did not feel she was imposing. Her welcome was warm and genuine from both occupants.

Day by day she noted little improvements one after another taking place in the small house.

"I had no idea you were such a skilled carpenter," Virginia observed one evening as the grandmother proudly showed off the newly restored hall closet.

He smiled his easy smile. "Well, 'carpenter' might be putting a rather officious title to what I do. But Pa brought us all up knowing how to hold a hammer. I took to it a little more than the other boys. I like the feel of making things look better than they did."

"It shows," mused Virginia.

"And see that spot up there on the ceiling where it had leaked in? He fixed that up, too," Mrs. Withers proudly pointed out.

Virginia smiled her approval.

"Well, it's time to hang up the hammer for tonight," he joked as he laid an imaginary hammer aside. "Grandmother made some gingerbread today. We've been waiting for you to come so we can test it."

"I'll make the cocoa, or do you want tea tonight?" Virginia asked, moving toward the kitchen cupboard. "Oh, this cupboard door swings more freely," she observed, swinging the door back and forth.

"Jonathan fixed that, too."

"It's much better. It used to protest."

"Just needed a new hinge," the young man explained.

Virginia made tea, and they gathered in the front parlor by

the fireplace. The gingerbread was delicious, and Mrs. Withers seemed to enjoy the compliments.

"It's rather nice to cook when you have something to cook with—and someone to cook for," she observed. But she made no further reference to the many years when her cupboard was almost bare, or to the years she had been alone since losing her husband.

When it was time for Virginia to leave, Jonathan reached for his hat. It was a routine now. Virginia did not even attempt to protest.

"I still haven't heard of any work," she said as they walked out together into the starry night.

"Thanks for keeping an ear to the ground. Things are going pretty well. I've finished up Grandmother's house, but the minister has a couple of weeks' work for me. By then it'll be nearing March. Calving time if I was back home."

Virginia could hear wistfulness in his voice. "You're missing it, aren't you?"

He didn't try to brush it aside or deny it. "Yes, I guess I am. Always enjoyed working with the animals."

"And you can't do it here? No, I don't suppose. We've no ranches in the area."

"No, but there's plenty of good farmland. I've thought about that. But I don't think I'd bother raising cattle. I think I'd try my hand at horses. Got me a couple real good ones back at the ranch. One young stallion that's a beauty. Pa's got some nice little fillies. I think he'd sell me a few."

He hesitated a moment and then went on. "I haven't been quite ready to talk to anyone about this, but—well—I've looked at a couple of farms in the area. One looks like it would make a good horse farm. Good corrals, nice-sized barn. Lots of good grazing land and a creek that runs through the lower pasture. Kind of makes my heart beat just a bit faster even thinking about it."

For some reason she could not have explained, it made Virginia's heart beat just a little faster, as well.

"Could you—would it be possible?" she asked him, holding her breath as she waited for the answer.

"I think so," he said slowly. "I've been saving money. I'd sell off my cows. Pa might want them, or one of the boys. And if not, they'd do well on the market. Prices are pretty good right now, and they're from good stock."

It was exciting to share his dreams, even though those dreams were only in the talking stage.

They had stopped walking. He was leaning his elbow on top of the corner post of the fence. Virginia stood facing him, forgetting the chill of the night, thinking only of the hope and anticipation in his voice. Without realizing it, the short trips from the Withers' home to the Simpsons' had begun taking longer and longer.

"Is it a fair price—for the land, I mean?"

He nodded. "I've checked it out. Seems reasonable."

Then he went on, "But there's no house on it. Burned down last fall. That's why they want to sell. The woman is tired of being on the farm. Wants to get back to a town somewhere. The man had resisted, until the house burned. He had to move her into town then."

"You mean the Connery place?"

"That's it."

"I remember their fire. They were fortunate that no one got hurt. It burned very quickly, from what I've heard."

"That's what she says. He thinks he might have put it out—might have saved it—had he been there."

Virginia nodded, then picked up the excitement again. "It does have a nice lane. I have always admired all the trees around the place."

"You have? You do know it then?"

"I've driven by many times."

"Well, with some fixing—more corrals—I think it would make a real good horse farm."

"What would you do for a house?"

"I'll still need to stay with Grandmother. I'd live on here and drive back and forth for a while. It would give me lots of time to get things started—maybe even time to build the house myself."

"It sounds wonderful." She gave him a smile that the moon overhead illuminated. She heard his intake of breath.

"Well, I'd better get in. Your grandmother will think you got lost," she teased.

He smiled then. "I've a notion that Grandmother has a fairly good idea where I am—and why," he returned.

Virginia felt a small fluttery sensation somewhere in her chest. She was not sure what it meant—or if she welcomed it.

CHAPTER 21

Virginia, do you hear me?" Francine looked quite put out. "You are sitting there with that faraway look in your eyes, not listening to a word I've said."

"I'm sorry," admitted Virginia with a flush to her cheeks. "I was . . . I was just thinking of Mrs. Withers."

"Mrs. Withers?"

"Her . . . her flowers."

Francine gave Virginia a look that said she was doubtful but uncharacteristically let it pass.

The truth was, Virginia had been thinking of Mrs. Withers' flowers—in a way. Jonathan had recently told her that in recent exchanges of letters with his father, the older man had quite agreed with Jonathan's interest in buying a farm in the area. Jonathan had even made an offer to the Connerys and had every reason to think that it would be accepted.

Through the early weeks of spring, Virginia had watched as the snowdrifts gradually gave way, revealing beds of potential blooms. There was much work to be done, and the two young people had tackled it together, raking up leaves to reveal early daffodils and pulling aside last season's growth to let the crocuses lift up shy heads. So—yes—she was thinking of flowers.

Now the garden was almost all exposed, although there were many plants that would be blooming later into the spring and into the summer and fall. Virginia, as she mused about the garden, also thought about the possibility of the rose off-shoots being transplanted by the gate that led to the garden at Jonathan's new farm. Or a cluster of forget-me-nots by the swing, or the pale blue violets at the side of the path that led to the creek.

She flushed now as Francine's frank question exposed her thinking—not aloud, but to herself. She had not been aware where her unguarded thoughts had been leading her.

"You were saying?" she asked her sister, determined to bring her thoughts in check.

"I said that Danny wrote today. Mother has his letter. He has a job for the summer and won't be home again."

Francine sounded disappointed—and bored.

"Well, a job is good," Virginia offered, trying to cheer up her sister.

"I guess." But Francine's shoulders still drooped.

"What about Jonathan? Has he found a job yet?" Francine had finally given up on trying to get the young man's attention. Another reason she now felt bored.

Virginia shook her head. The news of Jonathan's intention to buy the local farm was not yet public. She couldn't be the one to disclose it, but she did not wish to actually mislead her sister either. "Not exactly," she answered. "He has some . . . some possibilities."

Francine nodded. "I hope they work for him. He seems like a . . . real nice fellow. Don't you think?"

Virginia said nothing. She was seeing the pink rosebush out by the gate again.

"Don't you think so?" The question was so direct that Virginia could not avoid it.

"I—he's nice. He is very good to his grandmother."

"That wasn't what I meant, and you know it." Francine's well-shaped eyebrow lifted along with the hint of a smirk. "You've been spending an awful lot of time together."

Virginia tried to be casual. "There is a lot to do in Mrs. Withers' yard."

"Pooh," said Francine. "I've seen your moony eyes."

"Moony eyes?"

"You have feelings for him, and you know it, Virginia. You may as well admit it."

Virginia was about to admit nothing. Not even to herself. The truth was she felt all mixed up. She had loved Jamison. Had been heartbroken and angry when the relationship ended. Gradually she had accepted that he was not to be part of her life. She had even, with God's help, come to the place where she could forgive him. Even be happy for him and for his Rachel. And she had constructed, in her own thinking, a life for herself that included no one but her family, her beloved nephews. Perhaps a complacent cat or a tail-wagging dog. She had been happy thinking about that future—that little home of her own.

And then had come Jonathan, and that little dream didn't seem so perfect anymore. It did not even seem desirable.

But Virginia really did not know if her recent plans could—or would—change. Jonathan was her neighbor's grandson. He had come with the distinct plan to care for his elderly grandmother. True, they had spent many evenings entertaining her together. Many hours working in her garden. Many evenings chatting before saying good-night. But there was no reason to believe that there was any more to it than that.

For all she knew, he might have a girl back home. They had never talked about it. How would she know?

Virginia felt edgy, fearful, whenever she thought about the future. She did not want to be hurt again. Not ever. She wasn't sure that she could live through such pain. Slowly and carefully she constructed a protective shield, withdrawing into a little shell of pretended indifference.

———

"Have you time for a little walk?" asked Jonathan.

The evening was mild and still early. The birds were still singing, and the summer sun had not yet nestled into the green of the distant trees. She nodded. There was no reason for her to hurry home. "Gram seems to go to bed earlier each night," he commented as they turned their steps toward the outskirts of the town. "I think working in the garden really tires her out. Yet she won't give it up. I've stopped trying to fight it."

"Guess the most important thing is for her to be happy— just as long as she doesn't overdo."

They walked on in silence for some minutes, then Jonathan spoke.

"I've been a little worried lately. Have I . . . have I done something to offend you?"

Virginia's head swung around. *Of course not*, she wanted to quickly respond, but she couldn't say the words. She had hoped that he wouldn't sense it—her cautious backing away. She did not want to read into this relationship more than what was there. She did not want to leave herself open to more disappointment. More pain. The truth was, over the months that she had known him, she was discovering a unique and special person. She found herself drawn to him. Looking forward to the moments that she knew she would be with him. Making silly excuses to extend those times. Watching out the window in the hopes of catching a glimpse of him. And yet always carefully drawing herself back emotionally.

She knew he was waiting for her answer. She swallowed and forced out some words. "No, you've done nothing—wrong."

"You're sure?"

"I'm sure." She tried a smile.

"Good," he said with relief.

His face relaxed into one of his delightful smiles. It made her heart thump.

"I've got good news. I haven't even told Gram yet."

They had stopped beneath a large spruce tree. He leaned over and swept aside some small twigs with the brim of his Stetson, then nodded for Virginia to sit down. She did. He lowered himself beside her and rested the hat on one knee.

"I'm going home."

The news hit Virginia like a bolt. What? Going home? He had said he had good news.

She looked at him, her face blanched, her eyes puzzled. Was it true? But what about his grandmother? Had he finally talked her into going with him?

"I . . . I don't understand," she managed.

"I'm going home."

"When?"

"Just as soon as I can get my ticket. Grandmother's yard is in pretty good shape right now, and if you don't mind popping in on her in the evenings . . ."

Of course she didn't, but it seemed unfair of him to put the responsibility off on her.

She shook her head to clear it. "I still don't understand. I thought that you wanted the farm—here."

His eyes took on a shine. "I got the farm. The deal went through. I got it." He seemed tremendously excited.

It didn't make a bit of sense. "So . . . if you got the farm, why are you going?" Did she really want to ask the question? Did she really want to hear the answer? Her heart thumped harder.

"Pa sold off my cattle. Bought some himself and sold the rest. He says I can pick out the best ten fillies he's got. With my own stock, that will make a pretty nice starting line. I'm going home to get them."

Relief washed all through Virginia. "You're coming back?" she said weakly.

He reached for his hat and twisted it round in his hands. He seemed suddenly nervous. Thoughtful. He looked over at her, his gaze holding hers.

"I'm coming back." His words held promise. Silence for one long, anxious moment. Virginia felt her heart race as she wondered if—

He lifted his eyes, which seemed to be eager, yet pleading. "I . . . I had rather hoped that . . . that when I do, you'd allow me the privilege of calling—more officially, you know."

Virginia's breath caught in her throat. He had asked to call. To court her. He would be back. Soon, her heart hoped.

She looked at him and gave him an encouraging smile as her racing heart responded with joy-filled leaps.

"I'd like that," she said simply, but her eyes told him she could hardly wait.